WHISPER
Book 1 The Voice Trilogy
Noelle Bodhaine

Published by
Naughty Nellies Pervy Press
ISBN-13: 978:0692208151
ISBN-10: 0692208151

WHISPER

Table of Contents

Prologue

Two weeks ago, my heart was broken, broken by the man who helped to piece it back together. I served it up on a silver platter, free for the taking. But that is the end and this is the beginning. I should have known better. I did know better. He had his secrets and I had mine. It was just a fling, a momentary affair that went on too long.

My life was in desperate need of reworking. Something had to change. I needed to reinvent myself, to do something spontaneous and prove to myself that I still had 'it', whatever 'it' was. Four years of struggle and heartache had left me feeling older than my 24 years. I was in desperate need of an escape when Olivia called and offered me just that, a wedding, in Miami, her wedding, new people, new town, celebrating new beginnings; a perfect elixir for this unreachable itch. Between caring for my aging and forgetful grandmother and working full time, I had little time for myself or friends, if I had any left. Most of them went away to college and never came back, rightfully. I landed on a different path and have been afraid to change course ever since.

Nineteen years old and returning home for Christmas from my first semester away at college, I was homesick. My parents were so proud of me, as was I. I had made it to the University of

Washington, my first school pick. First semester went off without a hitch and I found myself falling into a good rhythm. I crushed my finals, packed up my suitcase and headed to the airport. The weather in Washington was less than ideal. Snow really sends that State into a tizzy. But being from Colorado it was no big thing to me, I was used to the snow and cold temperatures, after all it was December. I just really wanted to get home. The winter storm covered the entire western half of the US. The snow wasn't very heavy in Washington, but the temperatures were frigid, so everything was covered with a blanket of invisible ice. We sat on the tarmac for two hours, just waiting to hear if we would even take off. When they finally de-iced the plane and gave the green light I was ecstatic if not a little nervous. I'm pretty sure ours was among the last planes to go in or out of Denver International Airport, as the airport closed soon after dusk, stranding hundreds of travelers that had not yet made it out. The wind was too fierce and temperatures were too low, but I was so happy and relieved to be home. Even though I had gone to Washington with my best friend, Olivia, I still felt a little lonely and longed for my family. She was enthusiastically swept up in the camaraderie and excitement of rushing a sorority, which was something I had no interest in. It was only natural that we drift a bit, but all in all we were having a

2

great time, college was everything we had hoped.

We were so close to home, painfully close, crawling along at a snail's pace on the ice slicked highway. I could see the Christmas lights on our house from where we were, a bright white star that my father had always perched atop of our garage. Lost in thoughts of all the delicious treats my mother had waiting for me, I turned my head to ask a question and everything slowed to a crawl. It was as if the world was turned on its side. The strained screaming of rubber fighting ice and the stillness of the snow collided in a torrent. I watched the truck slide across the ice and fishtail, tires slipping and struggling against the slide. The truck narrowly avoided two other cars in his lane before losing control. He came crashing across the wide median, blowing loose snow and ice in his wake. Skidding tires echoed in the stillness of the storm and echo still in my dreams. The ice screamed under the abuse of rubber and a ton of steel. New snow crunched under cold tires, offering no resistance.

My life did not pass before my eyes in that moment. There was nothing but my mother's horrified face. My father reached over to her, to cover her with his arm, but nothing was going to save us from what was coming. She reached out for my father, a silent scream passing her lips. No sound, just terror. Her cry would have stopped my heart if it wasn't trying to escape from my chest.

3

The truck slammed into the driver's side, crushing the car. The sound of twisting metal filled the heavy winter air. We were pushed violently from the road, skidding off the shoulder. Heaven became hell, up was down. The sheer inertia of the truck pushed us for one hundred yards, gliding easily over the freshly fallen snow. Smoke poured from the wheels of the truck as it rolled over us and then everything stopped, my heart, my breath, my life. Everything was crushed under the weight of that truck. I briefly remember the world being upside down, my hair a curtain in front of my face, my body hanging by my seatbelt, and the noxious smell of burning rubber and crushed steel. There was no sound. My mother was silent. My father was silent. The next thing I knew, I woke up in a hospital, two days after Christmas, alone. Empty, broken, battered and lost.

I could not bring myself to go back to school. The only person I had left was a broken-hearted Grandmother, her mind half gone. I moved in with her, enrolled in a state university, got a job at the local paper and buried my head, watching from the sidelines as Olivia lived and did all the things we had planned to do together. When she headed to Cambridge last year for a year abroad reality crept over me. My life had come to a stand-still, while the rest of the world continued to turn. I stood still for years, willing the world to return to the way it had once been, but that was never going to happen. And

4

now I am faced with a best friend who has moved on, who has continued to live while I merely exist. We have always been close, like sisters, but now she's starting a new life. She went off and traveled the world, like we had planned to do together. She came back from Cambridge with a fancy degree, a haughty new world view, and a fiancé to match.

4 years later I have become a whisper in the background, quiet and inconsequential. I have a small, half empty apartment, a fractured heart and battered body, a Grandmother mired in the early stages of dementia who hardly knows me and a rotating cast of hospice nurses who tend to her care.

Miami was calling my name. Miami changed everything. Escaping my past had never been an option until Olivia's wedding. I needed to forget, to get lost, and be swept away in the romance and magic of a wedding. I didn't count on him. I didn't count on how I would react to him. A man, a series of soul racking orgasms and a young woman who listened only to the cries of her wanton body, it was magic. And it was bound to end in disaster, but still it hurt more than I ever could have imagined.

Chapter 1

Stepping off of the plane in Miami, wafting coconut oil and salt water tickles my nose and the thick air wraps its welcoming arms around me. I am warm to the core of my body, warm and dry. A welcome change from what was beginning to feel like a never ending Colorado winter. The weather has been so cold, I swear my bones were beginning to rattle when I walked.

Olivia is getting married to Matthew a successful real estate developer. Just her luck, he is wildly successful, comes from an important family and travels the world. Poor girl. It seems the only drawback, so far, is the future mother-in-law that she can't seem to crack. I know nothing of what she is about to enter into. Neither of us grew up with much money, but we always had what we needed. To even try and comprehend the kind of wealth she is marrying into is mind boggling. I say 'no, thank you' to the responsibility and pressure she is taking on. I like my low key life.

My eyes scan the terminal for Olivia. Everyone is so tan…..and thin. All around me women are strutting and swishing like they are in a secret fashion show, swaying their hips side to side as they walk down an invisible cat walk. Men pretend not to notice under their dark shades, leering sideways. Languages float about like a Latin symphony, people greeting one another, or saying goodbye. And then I hear her, over every other sound in the terminal.

"Sophie!" I look to my left to see the crowd part just as a wash of blonde hair launches at me, embracing me like a sister. We hug each other for a moment and swing in one another's arms like we did when we were little. I hold her back from me so I can get a good look. It has been a long time since we have been face to face. Our lives have gone off in such different directions, sometimes I fear I will lose her for good.

Now she is getting married and looking forward to a wonderful life, so adult, and refined. She looks amazing! I cannot believe this is the same girl. Her hair is long and blonde, her tan flawless and she is glowing with that sickening look of love. She is head to toe class in a sleeveless ivory silk top and crisp gray slacks. Her ears are weighed down by sparkling diamond studs, and a matching single diamond sits at the base of her throat.

"You look amazing, you Bitch!" She punches me square in the arm, deadening the muscle, stinging just like it used to.

"Me? Look at you, Soph, you are so cute!" Cute, that's me, the cute one. Even in my best jeans and cutest lacy tank I'm still painfully underdressed, under adorned, and generally unremarkable.

"Yeah, right, Liv. I am never going to fit in here. I cannot believe how beautiful every single person is. I am surprised they even let me off the plane." My head starts to swim as my pulse picks up and pearls of sweat rise on the nape of my neck. "Oh, my God, Olivia I am freaking out! You are getting married!" My palms are so wet that my bag begins to slip and I lose my grip. I let it drop to the ground and use the back of my hand to wipe away the gathering curls from my damp forehead. Olivia grabs both my hands and pulls me in close.

"We are going to go to that bar, right there," pointing just behind her to the Admirals Club. "We are going to have a cocktail, maybe two, we are going to calm down, catch up and everything is going to be fine. I am so glad you are here, I have missed you so much, Sophie!" She pulls me in for a hug and squeezes so tightly it is hard to hold on to any emotion other than relief when she finally releases me. That is an offer I cannot refuse and she knows that well.

Inside the Admirals Club deep overstuffed leather chairs arranged in small groups face a wall of windows that looks out onto the tarmac. A heavy mahogany bar anchors the large room, with a walk in humidor behind and a floor to ceiling wall of wine with a petite, divinely dressed waitress climbing an old fashioned rolling library ladder, allowing her access to the farthest bottles. The air is slightly scented by cigar smoke and breathy scotch, the faintest sounds of classical music floating over the hidden sound system. Everything in the room feels rich, with me being the obvious exception. The host greets Olivia, kissing her hand, and leads us to the farthest corner and a deep round booth. The banquette is sunken and looks out onto a private stone patio, above hangs a frighteningly large crystal chandelier.

"Sophie, sit down. What shall we drink?" Olivia pulls me back to the moment and into the sunken leather booth.

"I think champagne is appropriate, don't you?" I open the wine list intending to treat my best friend to a glass of champagne. My eyes pop and the hairs at the nape of my neck stand on end as I get a glimpse of the bottle prices and the fact that there is no "*bubbles by the glass*". Are we in an airport bar or the Ritz? I begin calculating in my head when the waiter appears with a silver bucket full of ice and a bottle of Moet. Oh My God! I choke on my own breath as he places the bucket into a stand and proceeds to present the bottle to Olivia.

"Courtesy of the gentleman in the corner," he gestures and our eyes follow him to an overstuffed chair against the farthest wall. There is a cluster of suits buzzing about, the man sitting amidst the chaos nods at Olivia and tips his glass of amber liquid.

"I'll be right back," she blurts at me and quickly slides from the booth heading towards the swarm of gray suits and cell chatter. I watch her cross the room, her beachy blonde hair swaying in time with her hips. She is like a force of nature; tall, thin and blonde. If yoga was an Olympic sport she would be a gold medalist. The whole swarm of suits watches her approach, but his eyes seem to be locked on me. I glance over my shoulder to make sure no one is standing behind me, nope, just me in this corner. His attention is focused. His intensity wafts from across the room like the smell of aged pipe smoke and well-worn leather. His face is chiseled and rugged with pale skin and full peach lips. His square jaw covered by the slightest hint of maybe one day's shadow. He furrows his brow and shakes me off just as Olivia approaches him. They exchange words as Olivia hugs him and points me out. She waves, expecting me to wave back? Awkwardly, I raise my hand and wave like a parade float princess. *Aargh! What is wrong with me?* Olivia giggles and leans in to whisper something in his ear. He is polite, smiling graciously, but hardly gets a word in the whole time she is talking to him. I pull my attention from his chiseled face, back to the glass of champagne in front of me and decide I may need a little liquid help to get through the next few days. I quickly toss back the champagne with my back to the rest of the room and refill my glass before Olivia returns.

"That," she pauses with her mouth turned up, "is Rhys, Matthew's best man. He said to send his regrets that he couldn't come over to meet you, but he is off to New York. He should be back by morning, and then you two can meet and get to know each other." Her sly wink puts me on alert, while she sips her champagne.

"I know what you are doing, Olivia. You cannot expect that man to be interested in me." The words fly out of my mouth before I can stop them and her jaw falters, slightly.

"Sophie! Why would you say that? You don't even know him."

"I can see him." He is striking and I watch his lips take in the last drops of his drink, the ice reluctantly pushed back with his tongue, sadly clinking to the bottom of his now empty glass. His long fingers casually wrap around the crystal glass, tapping a mindless rhythm as he listens to one of the suits chatter about something. He looks in our direction and catches me dead in his sights. I watch him put the glass down, his eyes locked on me. His fingers caress the rim of the glass, around and around in slow circles, his fingertip slides across the fine crystal while he watches me. With every turn of his fingers a knot tightens deep in my belly. A small crooked grin raises the corner of his knowing mouth before we are torn from the moment by another of his suits handing him a cell. He turns his back to me and I snap back to the table, back to Olivia. "No worries, Sophie. I promise not to interfere. Rhys is a distraction guy, not someone you want to get involved with." She winks and raises her glass. "He is a short term kind of guy; you are a long term kind of girl." What was that? Olivia is a master at backhanded talk and compliments laced with acid, but I let it go, washing it down with a sip of champagne. "I am so glad you are here."

"Thank you, Olivia. I have missed you and I am so excited to be here!" And down the hatch goes my second glass of bubbles. I look over to see Olivia finishing her glass in one gulp, as well, and I'm comforted again by our familiar ways. "That was so nice of him to send us such a nice bottle, we have to finish it, right?!" I whisper, a Cheshire grin slowly spreading across my face. I haven't been on the ground for an hour and already my head is swimming.

"Of course!" Olivia proclaims with another toast. "Then we will head back to the hotel. I have dinner with Matthew and his parents tonight. Will you be alright to entertain yourself? I know the girls want to meet you. Kylie and Melissa, remember?"

"Yes, I remember and I will be fine. I will most likely have to sleep off this champagne!" A champagne fueled giggle pops out. I love being back with my girl. There is such comfort in friends that you have known your entire life.

***

Once at the hotel, I get checked in and Olivia and I head up to my room. The hotel is beautiful, light marble floors and walls accented by dark wood and heavy furniture. Elaborate blown glass chandeliers hang throughout the lobby. Tall palms and other tropical foliage are fed by the sunlight that filters through the glass walls and ceiling of the inner lobby. The elevator is glass and looks into the lobby from one side and out onto the white private sand beach from the other. Everywhere I look I am overwhelmed by beautiful things and beautiful people. When we arrive on the sixteenth floor, we turn down the hall and find my room. The furnishings are light and airy, as you would expect in Miami. The entire back wall of the room is windows hung with gauzy curtains blowing in the warm salt air. The room overlooks the private beach. A terrace, three floors down, has a bar and chaises with private cabanas and an infinity pool. I turn to Olivia completely speechless. I have never been anywhere like this.

"I know, it's amazing and it is only going to get better! These next few days are going to blow your mind so just take it in and enjoy, ok? You deserve this trip, Sophie, and I want you to enjoy every minute." She hugs me tightly and turns to go. "You will be surprised at how fast you get used to all of this," she says, waving her hand about the room. "I have to go get ready for dinner. If it's not too late when we get back I'll call you."

"Sure." I try to sound reassuring. "I'll be fine, go. I am just happy to be here and I am so happy for you, and a little wiped out."

"I am so happy you are here, too, I love you! Wish me luck!" And with that she was out the door.

***

"Rhys, I am so glad I caught you." She breezes through my closed office door like an unwelcome draft, a heady cocktail of Chanel No. 5 and stale cigarette smoke. Just her presence in this office sets my body on high alert. To think of all the memories, all the surfaces we have fucked on. She is everywhere. I need to redecorate.

"You didn't, Nadja. I am out the door, I am on a plane. I am in Miami." I grab my duffle, slip my phone into my pocket and walk past her to the elevators. I was called away from the wedding festivities once already for this bullshit. I will not miss another minute of Matthew and Olivia's celebration. Not for Nadja, not for her father, but I know her too well to think she will let it go. And as predicted when the elevator comes, she slides in next to me, thinking she has me trapped, no doubt. She needs some new tricks.

"Rhys, please." Her faded Russian purr rattles

14

down my spine like nails on a chalk board. "You know that this company is everything to my father. You cannot let this happen. Help him. Help him and I will do whatever you want." She sidles up to me, her breath sickly sweet, an attempt to cover the smell of cigarettes and vodka, no doubt. I put my hands in my pockets and stare forward, determined not to give her an inch. "Please, for me?" Running her fingers down the lapel of my jacket, her eyes glow with an unearned triumph. I hate her ego, I hate that look. Batting her hands away, I push her into the corner and loom over her slight, stick like figure.

"You stay there," I demand, glaring at her. She lowers her eyes, as she should. Straightening herself, she presses her hands against the cool, stainless steel walls of the elevator and waits. I back against the opposite wall and drop my bag. Scratching at the stubble along my jaw rouses the blood in my fingertips, it's coarse and soft. Not my usual look, but I need a change. She raises her head, looking me dead in the eye, defiant little wench, watching me with those piercing blue eyes, and an inscrutable expression on her face. Narrowing her eyes at me, she rakes over my new scruffy face, wrinkling her turned up nose at the tight, dark, two day stubble that covers my jaw.

"You need to shave." Her disgust is palpable, that alone makes me want to keep it.

"No, I don't think I will. Now, I just spent the last three hours in meetings with Viktor and his investors. I am doing what I can to help him, within reason. I cannot take on a sinking ship, it is not good business. I am waiting for the final financials to come back. Once they do, we will have a better picture of what needs to be done. In the meantime, I am on my way to Miami. I will not be taking calls or working. I am a ghost for the next four days. I do not want to see you until I have to, do you understand?"

"What is in Miami, why go so early?" Her attempt to disarm me with her coy questions only fuels my frustration.

"You know very well that Matthew is getting married."

"Oh yes, to that all American white bread girl. I don't know how she managed to tame him. Do you need a date?" I watch her dull eyes dance and wonder about her motives. "Are you looking for white bread, too, Rhys? To be tamed? I can do that. Is that what you think will make you happy? These American girls that stand by their man, someone to follow you around like a devotee? Is that what you're hoping for? Maybe you'll find one of white bread's Middle American friends. They are sure to be dazzled by all that you can offer, all that you have. Not to mention the things you can do." She stalks slowly towards me. "Things we taught each

16

other, remember?" Her hands are raised in surrender, but she is pressing in, ever the aggressor. I meet her in the middle of the elevator, clutching her arms. My hands wind easily around her small, bony wrists, her blood surges, pulsing against my grip.

"Don't!" I growl, dropping her arms to her sides. "Do you want my attention, Nadja?"

"Yes," she breathes, pressing into me, arching her back. She is so predictable, so needy. Like dangling a carrot in front of a trotting mare, she chases what she wants, blinded to anything else.

"Then you shall have it. *If* you can follow my instructions, can you do as you are told?" A slight curve to her pouty mouth tells me she is game. "I don't want to see you until Thursday. Do you understand?" She lowers her eyes and nods. "Nadja?"

"Yes, I understand," her voice is soft, her body curled into itself, passively waiting for further instructions.

"Good." I gather my duffel and make a beeline from the elevator, onto the curb and into the waiting Town Car, leaving Nadja in the dust. She infuriates me, her defiance, and her aggression. She is so manipulative, using her body to get whatever she wants. All of her lies, her utter betrayal. She made a fool of me. I was sure that I was her white knight, destined to save her from herself. But, I wouldn't save her now if she was drowning in front of me. She has become so wicked and twisted, taking pleasure in other people's pain in the extreme. She is predatory, but you would never suspect from the outside. Her beauty masks the vicious animal inside. The more fame and attention she gets, the more horrible she becomes. And now she has created this façade, this mask she wears. Always appearing to be on her best behavior, when behind it all, rages an out of control, sex crazed, selfish, sociopath.

I rest my eyes and try to distract myself as we wind through rush hour traffic in Manhattan. Shit, I may as well take a nap, or do some work. Or maybe consider my pick for the weekend. Lord knows there will be a gaggle of willing ladies down in Miami this weekend for the festivities. Any one of them could help to distract me and occupy my time. Problem is, I have been with a good number of them already, and I don't like to double dip. As for the others, as I go over the catalog in my head my thoughts wander around to Sophie. Is that her name, Sophie? I'm not entirely sure. It is far too easy to tune Olivia out when she drones on. And, man does she drone on about this girl, Sophie, dropping none too subtle hints about me meeting Sophie ever since she invited her down to Miami. *You are going to love Sophie. Sophie is so great!* I don't know what could be so great about a small town girl who graduated from a state school and works for a local paper. I would be willing to bet that she has never even left the country. What on earth am I going to have in common with this girl? Does it even matter?

The way Olivia described her I was expecting some pudgy Pollyanna, but she is beautiful, what I could see of her. Olivia definitely undersold her there. It was a fleeting glance as they walked into the lounge. Her short, dark hair bounced around her face as she laughed, her giggle is what caught my attention, but it was her curves that kept me fixed. Round hips and a narrow waist. It was clear from looking at her that she wasn't the kind to starve herself or fret over a meal, the word buxom comes to mind. If it wasn't for that round little ass of hers, I doubt she would be able to balance the weight of those beautiful, no doubt natural breasts. What the hell? Snap out of it, man. It hasn't been that long. Besides, this girl is not the kind of girl I am used to. Women have been willing to do almost anything for my affections and attention for as long as I can remember. I have been surrounded by bright shiny objects my entire life, most of which I could have at a moment's notice. But I have a feeling that this girl may not be so easy. The way she looked at me in the lounge and so easily shook me off. No, I should set my sights elsewhere, on a more seasoned target perhaps. I wouldn't want to do anything to upset the balance, or God forbid piss off Olivia. I run through the catalog of others as we pull onto the tarmac and the plane is loaded. I switch off my business cell with a satisfying finality and slip it into the outer pocket of my duffel, with no intention of switching it back on until Sunday. From now until then it is all about Matthew and Olivia, no business, just pleasure. And I will find my pleasure.

Chapter 2

I wipe the sleep from my eyes in a darkened room, confused by my stark surroundings; my head fuzzy from the afternoon welcome wagon. Stretching out on the bed I realize I still have my boots on. I sit up to unzip them, but my head protests. The Moet is beating me. I run the zipper down from my knee and pull my feet from their prison. Rising from the bed, I turn on the bedside lamps, illuminating a note that has been slipped under my door.

"Hi, Sophie! The girls are going to be in the hotel bar tonight. Please come down and have a drink with us, we cannot wait to meet you! Kisses xx"

Oh geez, I exhale a deep breath and I am resigned. I will take a shower, go down and meet "The Bridesmaids" and immerse myself in Olivia's new world.

The shower does the trick, washing away the sins of the afternoon. My muscles are loose and my skin is soft and fragrant from the designer hotel soaps. Wiping the steam away from the wall size mirror, I step back and take a good look at myself.

Same as always, short and soft, but perfectly round in all the right places. I wink at myself in the mirror, caress my skin and cup my breasts, all natural and proud. Repeat, repeat, repeat. The exercise is futile as my eyes search for flaws by habit. I know that this is when I should step away from the mirror, but I don't. I watch myself comb thru my damp hair, curls already springing to life. I dry my hair quickly and decide to set it, having a glass of wine from the well- stocked mini bar while I wait for the rollers to heat up.

Rummaging through my suitcase I find my favorite new sundress. It is pale green linen with hand-embroidering along the deep neckline with a full skirt and goes perfectly with my braided sandals. I splurged and bought all new clothes for this trip, light dresses replace my winter uniform of heavy sweaters and jeans. Cloaked in new threads, anxious to take in Miami, I swipe on some blush and ChapStick, and gulp down the rest of my wine. Pause in front of the weathered, floor length mirror that hangs from the back of the door, flip my head over, run my fingers through my new bob and I am out the door. When I decided to cut it, I said I wanted that 'just fucked look.' I can feel that my request was fulfilled as my hair swirls around me, bouncing about my crown as I walk down the hall. I feel confident and like a million bucks!

My mood takes a nose dive as the elevator

doors open on the ground floor, revealing my worst nightmare. A swirl of sequins, satin and labels surrounds me like an all engulfing storm. A unifying squeal brings them all to heel and a breathtaking blonde grabs my arm, pulling me in for a hug. My head is pressed into her buoyant bosom, as she is far taller than I am, even without those sky high pumps.

"You *must* be Sophie!" She looks to me for confirmation, but I am speechless, taking in the sea of unnatural perfection that surrounds me. I have walked into a magazine spread, or a reality show. I look back at her offering an unsure smile.

"I am Kylie and these are the girls. We aren't *all* bridesmaids." She waves her hands above the girls as if to remind some of them of their exclusion. "I am the maid of honor, Melissa is a bridesmaid, and then there's you." Her smile is forced, inspecting my clothing. My dress is far too loose and shoes far too flat. I can see her take the inventory in her head. "Let's go in and get a table and then we can all get to know each other." She locks her arm with mine and walks me to the bar. The other women look at one another with disdain, but quickly fall into line behind us.

The bar is quiet and posh with dark walls covered with brocade and wood. The bar reaches to the ceiling and is surrounded by a large gilt mirror. All eyes are on our party as we walk in. Kylie motions to the Maitre'd and leads us to the corner where a large booth has been roped off and marked for the wedding party. The dance floor has yet to entice a crowd, creating a relative runway for the women to sashay their way across the room, clearly reveling in the attention that they must be so accustomed to. I prefer to fly under the radar. The whole scene makes me anxious.

We all scoot into the adjoining booths and Kylie leads the introductions. There are sorority sisters, schoolmates and friends from yoga, I will never remember them all, if any. And then there is Melissa, who seems a little too eager to party. Her mocha skin and dark hair set her apart, but her dress is too short, her breast a little too big and she is very loud. She sneers at Kylie as she leads the conversation. There is a tension between them that feels almost comfortable, lived in. Thankfully, Kylie calls for a bottle of champagne. Drawing my attention away from Melissa, I welcome the beautiful flutes full of the golden bubbly elixir as the waitress places them on the table. Taking a deep breath, I swallow the lump in my throat and stand up with a glass in my hand, offering a toast.

After all of the introductions, toasting and drinking, I am warm and comfortable, but rapidly fading. The travel and champagne are catching up to me and I am spent, a haze sets in over my eyes making them heavy, sleepy. Listening to the conversations around me about places I have never been, designers I have never heard of, a prickly heat climbs up the back of my neck. I need fresh air. I slide out of the empty half of the booth, as the majority of the ladies have taken their party to the dance floor. They hoot and holler, dancing in a circle. I take my glass with me and raise it to Kylie in salute as she gyrates on the crowded floor with some frat boy looking Adonis.

I duck out of the lobby, through the revolving doors and into the fresh sea air. A deep draught of the thick night air relieves my rising heat and helps to clear my mind. Slipping off my sandals, I walk around the side of the building to a small patio that overlooks the private beach. There are chaise lounges, tables and chairs with striped umbrellas that have all been tied down for the night. I walk to a table at the farthest edge of the patio and drop my shoes. My body is heavy and I slump into the low slung chair with a sigh. My hands are drawn to my warm, moist skin. Wiping the dew from my neck and chest, I gently stroke my skin and revel in the gentle caress of the ocean breeze, contemplating the last time I was caressed, the last time my skin was on fire from someone else's touch. My heart tightens, strangling the breath from my lungs. It has been too long. Gentle waves lap at the darkened beach, the moon shining off the water's rolling surface. The air is different here, heavier, headier.

25

With a deep exhale I turn and am caught by a bright orange ember, slowly growing then fading. A swirling plume of gray smoke calls my attention and I squint in the direction of the smoke, trying to get a look at who I have disturbed. A man in a white linen shirt, cuffs unbuttoned and rolled to the elbow with dark pants, one foot slung over his knee, barefoot. Nice feet. He takes another puff from his cigar and leans forward into the light revealing a straight nose, full lips and dark hair, a faint shadow of which covers his chiseled jaw. He rises from his chair and makes his way towards me, the light from a dozen torches dancing across his form as he moves. He is tall, lean and lithe like a stalking predator. Coming to a stop a few steps away from me he sits, but says nothing. *Rhys.*

From this close he is disarmingly handsome, striking cheek bones frame his dark eyes, hooded by heavy brows. His tongue runs slowly along his bottom lip before he raises the stub of his cigar to his waiting mouth. Slowly he pulls a deep hit and releases it in a long controlled exhale, deep and satisfying. I catch myself mimicking his actions, exhaling with him. He groans softly and sits up, turning his dark eyes on me.

"Sophie?" The question holds contempt, and I swear he rakes me over for flaws. I can't help but squirm in my chair, hot under his smoldering glare. Even in the dark his eyes sparkle.

26

"I am," I return trying to smile. "You must be Rhys." I can't tear my eyes from his full mouth and the thick cigar he continues to puff on. He releases another slim tower of smoke with a smirk and a chuckle.

"Yes, I must be." He is arrogant and smug, and oh, so sexy. My heart flutters like a hummingbird. I'm thankful for the darkness that shrouds us both, imagining my body's telling betrayal. It conspires against me, releasing a torrential rush of blood through my heated veins, a flush I can feel down to my toes.

I quickly stand and take a few steps towards the edge of the patio, trying to shake off the wanton feelings that creep in my wine addled mind. He watches me with amusement, a slight crooked smile pulling at the corner of his mouth. The breath catches in my throat, and I shrink inside. The wine, the heat and this man's energy are conspiring against me. I cock my head to the side and run my hand roughly through my hair, shaking my head, whipping the curls about. Taking a deep breath, I step forward into his light, and our eyes connect. His gaze is blazing, his eyes dark and mysterious. The crooked grin has slipped from his stone cold face, leaving him unreadable. He snubs out his cigar in the stone basin next to his chair and rises from his seat. His strong arms pull at the fabric of his shirt as he stands and hovers above me, the air

27

between us thick with unexplained tension. He towers above my slight 5'3 frame. Screwing his eyes shut, he pulls his hands roughly through his hair, releasing a deep sigh. When he turns his eyes back on me, his face is screwed tightly in a cold stare.

"I should go to my room," I whisper while looking down at my feet, trying to dispel the heavy feeling in the air. "It's getting late."

"I will walk you up," he says with a sigh.

"You don't have to do that, I'm sure I can find it just fine." The words slide out like silky venom, and I immediately regret my tone. Looking up at him, my eyes full of remorse, he just smiles with half his mouth and winks.

"I'm sure you can, too." He gently places his palm against the small of my back and my heart breaks into a dead sprint from the electricity in his touch. The contact is subtle, but his pulse radiates through my lower body. Such a small gesture, but a gesture just the same, the gesture of a man, a gentleman. He leads me around to the front of the hotel and through the lobby. Just as we come to a stop in front of the elevators an unholy shriek cuts through the air. I swing around to see Melissa, skipping towards us, arms flung sloppily open, her designer bandage dress struggling to contain her.

"Rhys! There you are, come have a drink with us." She is face to face with him, due to her sky high heels and throws her arms around his neck. Rhys backs away and grasps both her arms by the wrist, releasing her grip, returning her hands to her side. She scoffs at him and ignores his intentions, winding her hands around his waist instead, begging again for his company in the hotel bar. He prudishly rests his hand upon her exposed shoulder and looks down his nose at her with barely hidden contempt.

"Not tonight, Melissa. I am going to walk Sophie up and turn in." He smiles briefly at her fallen face, and then removes her hands from around his waist. She looks towards me with sharpened daggers in her eyes and lets out an undisguised huff. Turning to Rhys with a look of utter disdain she grins before leaning in and whispering, all too loudly in his ear.

"I see what you are doing Rhys, preying on the newbie. Just be gentle, I don't think she can handle you." She looks at me and winks. "You know where to find me if you need something a bit *stronger*." She turns on her heel and sashays away, swinging her hips like Matahari.

Confused by the whole interlude, I turn to Rhys as he rakes his hair with his long fingers and shakes his head with a sigh. He turns his eyes on me, they are dark and full of something I cannot define. We step into an empty elevator and the doors close, trapping the stifling tension.

"Ex?" I ask with a grin, anything to cut the

tension. Being around this man when he is silent is unnerving, dangerous.

"Not exactly," he replies under his breath, keeping his eyes focused forward.

"Do women usually throw themselves at you like that?" I ask with a giggle, intending a joke to lighten his mood. He turns his dark eyes on me, the corner of his mouth twitches and his eyes narrow. He exhales, blowing away the tension. His features soften, his eyes slightly warmer, and a crooked grin arises on his chiseled face.

"I am a very… popular man." His pause is pregnant with innuendo and ego. He arches an eyebrow at me and traps his lower lip with his teeth, stifling a rude comment no doubt. I can't help but laugh at his response, looking at him with disbelief, his arrogance a new extreme for me. I shake my head, crossing my arms in disgust.

"You are amazing."

"I have been told." A wide, lascivious grin breaks across his lips, his eyes alight with playfulness. How quickly his demeanor changed. Before I can retort, the doors open and an older couple joins us in the confines of the glass elevator. I move to the opposite corner of Rhys and keep my eyes straight ahead. I won't let him see me rattled, his arrogance burrowed under my skin, threatening to turn me inside out. From the corner of my eye I see him grinning that crooked grin, a look of triumph all over his smug face. A low groan rolls from my throat as the doors open and I can thankfully exit the space I'm sharing with this megalomaniac. I turn as the doors are closing and with my sweetest grin wish Rhys pleasant dreams. The doors close and my shoulders drop as I release the breath I didn't know I was holding. His presence is maddening, oppressive and exhilarating. All at once I am glad to be away from him, and ache to be back in the elevator, alone with him. Olivia has him nailed, a distraction indeed.

When I get back into my room I quickly change, wash my face and slip into bed. The elevator ride is playing on a continuous loop in my head. His smug grin, those full lips, I toss and turn trying to find comfort. Never has a man affected me so quickly, or deeply. The thought irritates me. I kick off the blankets and writhe in the warm Miami air. My skin is sticky and soft, and my internal temperature is off the charts. Rhys provokes a serious physical response that I cannot deny. I wish I could for the sake of all the women I assume he has victimized with his shrewd charm and massive ego. I close my eyes and try to focus on sleep, bringing happy thoughts of the upcoming days into the forefront of my mind, wanting to focus on anything but Rhys. I finally find comfort with my legs wrapped around a long silky pillow, the pressure and friction offering slight relief. I am so exhausted I feel sleep take me.

Chapter 3

Wrapping his hands around my ankles, he slowly pulls me towards the foot of the bed. I sit up to see him kneeling at my feet, his eyes full of carnal lust, his lips wet and swollen. His eyes are beseeching, begging for permission. I reach down and push the linen shirt off his broad shoulders, running my fingernails up the back of his neck through his coarse hair. He closes his eyes and releases a deep moan, leaning his head into my waiting hands. Urgency clouds his vision as our eyes meet and lock in an erotic knot. He reaches for the hem of my top and pulls it over my head, my breasts fall free and into his waiting hands. He strokes and squeezes my inflamed flesh, his finger and thumb twisting and pulling at my little pink nipples, making them pointed and hard. He leans in and takes one breast into his mouth, rolling my hard nub around with his long tongue. He nips at me with his teeth and looks to me for my reaction. He pulls my nipple between his teeth, never breaking eye contact, and then begins to knead and pull at my flesh with his other hand. Slowly he pushes me back onto the bed and sinks back to his knees, his hot breath tickling the inside of my already warm thigh. He pulls my ass to the end of the bed and dips his head between my splayed limbs, taking a deep breath of my scent. "Mm mm," he hums and pulls

*my panties to the side revealing my swollen folds.
He slowly blows on my sensitive skin and I writhe
and shift my hips. "Don't move," he demands in a
husky whisper. He stills me with his strong hands,
wrapping one arm around my leg, resting my thigh
on his shoulder, he strums my clit with his thumb
and watches my face. His gaze is so intense,
watching him take so much pleasure in touching me
is surreal and I have to turn away. I close my eyes
and let every movement wash over me.*

*He continues to strum my clit as he dips a
finger between my eager lips. "Oh, you are so wet,
Sophie." My name drips off his tongue like syrup.
He slips two fingers in and begins to pump, slowly
building a rhythm while he presses on my clit with
his thumb. The knots in my body tighten in
response. My hips sway of their own accord and I
press against his hand, begging for more, raising
my hips off the bed, lifting myself into his palm,
wantonly waving my pussy in his face. I feel an
orgasm building as he puts more pressure on that
bundle of frantic nerves, he slowly pushes his
middle finger between my folds and massages me,
making slow methodical circles. His hands continue
their ministrations and my head is swirling in a
torrent of heat and pleasure. An explosion is
building more intense than anything I have ever felt,
my body is no longer my own, moving on its own
accord, responding to every move he makes. He*

lowers his head and gently begins to kiss and tease
me with his mouth, licking and nibbling my most
sensitive spot. Around and around his tongue swirls
as his fingers push me higher. He blows onto my
hot, wet flesh and then plunges his tongue inside of
me, pushing and sucking the nectar he has coaxed.
Into a million pieces my world shatters, my body
humming and pulsing, waves rippling through me.
Blood pounds in my ears as my body convulses in
his hands, slowly he lets me down, pulling his
fingers from my sex he looks at me with dark eyes,
licks his lips and sucks my juice from his fingertips.
I am shocked and gasp in response, as a wicked,
crooked grin spreads across Rhys' triumphant face.

The air in the room is too warm and bright, the
morning sun assaulting my face. I try to screw my
eyes more tightly shut and block out the light when
I am startled by a knock at the door. I shoot up from
my half sleep and realize that the sheets are damp
below me. Trying to shake the fog from my head
and from the dream that felt so real, my body is still
pulsating. One brief meeting and this arrogant man
has invaded my dreams and done things to me I
desperately need. Another knock at the door and I
bound off the bed without a thought, pulling the
heavy door open, expecting Olivia, instead coming
face to face with dream boy. His eyes take in my
state of dress and he examines my form, a devious

grin rising on his beautiful, crooked mouth.

"Rise and shine, Sophie. Good dreams, I hope."
With a wink, he invites himself in sweeping past
me. I choke on his sentiment, the effects of my
dream spread all over my body. He can't possibly
know! I barely stifle the groan that accompanies my
transparency. He is in a crisp white shirt with
sleeves casually rolled up his strong forearms and
khaki linen pants that hug his perfectly taut bum
and hang just right. Closing the door behind him
and striding into the middle of the room, he slyly
examines his new surroundings. Turning to me he
raises a paper bag in the air. "I brought bagels and
yogurt for the lady." He smirks and sets the bag on
the rumpled bed.

Still feeling half asleep, confusion clouds my
mind and I excuse myself to the bathroom to splash
cold water on my face and cover my exposed
bottom. I turn to the mirror to find my hair still full,
slept in and tousled, my face clear and bright thanks
to my meager makeup routine. I wipe the sleep from
my eyes and splash cool water on my cheeks, gently
pinching to get a fresh blush. I brush my teeth and
pull on a pair of yoga pants from my luggage.

Rhys is casually lounging on the bed, his legs
stretched out, shoes kicked off, and head resting in
his hand propped on his elbow. He pops a piece of
bagel into his mouth and tips his head at me. This is
a different creature than the man I shared an

elevator with last night. He is light, jovial even. His face is young and bright, that crooked grin pulling at me somewhere deep and dark.

"Is that what you look like when you first wake up?" He smirks as he slowly chews. MMmmm A low groan escapes his throat. "Nice," he whispers and takes another piece of bagel to his lips.

"Are you always such an ass?" I ask leaping onto the bed, taking him by surprise. His mood is markedly different from last night. Casual and relaxed. I take the bagel from him and tear a piece for myself before thrusting it back into his hand. He sits up and casually folds his legs, tucking his feet under his knees. Leaning back against the padded headboard, he crosses his hands into his lap and smiles. His smile is disarming.

"That is subjective, I suppose," he offers, contemplating the question, his eyes warm but tentative. "No one has ever called me 'an ass', not to my face anyhow. Certainly not a woman I have just met." Taking the last bite of bagel he shrugs to himself in thought, bemused. His arrogant, crooked smile returns to full wattage, and I scoff at his reaction, taking a piece of blueberry bagel into my mouth, hoping food will help me to bite my tongue. His charisma fills every space in the room, leaving me flushed and charged, but my tongue feels sharp. I start moving about the room, opening curtains and tidying up, anything to avoid his immense gravitational pull. Watching him casually recline on my bed, this spoiled, beautiful man, his jovial playful mood a stark contrast from our first meeting.

Clearly he is accustomed to getting precisely what he wants at all times, and expects nothing less. I'm reminded of the scene at the elevators and Melissa's bile-filled offer. He must have women wherever he goes. I imagine models and spoiled trust-funders hanging on his every word, giving in to his every whim. I feel a deep blush crawling up my body, contemplating those whims. I wonder if any woman has ever made him work for it or do they just fall into bed with him. I see how the latter would be the case. He would be very hard to resist.

Our eyes meet and he halts me in my tracks, his eyes like steel traps. I feel like he has caught me, he knows what I was thinking, he can see it all over my body. A moment stretches between us, the air filled with something heavy, something explosive. I watch him swallow, his Adam's apple slowly rolling down his throat, the corner of his mouth curling into a scorching grin. I melt onto the cool wood floor, mesmerized. My hand floats up to my throat, my heart fluttering like a trapped animal. I am trapped, hopelessly drowning in his pale green eyes, my ragged breath echoing in my head.

"Knock knock, Rise and Shine…." A familiar voice and a knock at the door release me from

Rhys' hypnotic spell. Saved by the Bride! Olivia and Matthew.

"Hi, sweetie! We thought we could all go to breakfast." Pushing into the room, she takes in the sight of Rhys in my rumpled bed and swirls around in a tornado of blonde hair and sheer shock. Her eyes are wide like grapefruits, her mouth gaping, but fighting back an auspicious grin. Matthew, on the other hand, seems unfazed. He kicks his shoes off and takes a spot next to Rhys on the bed, helping himself to a bagel. The boys launch into a conversation about golf and tee times. Olivia pulls me into the bathroom.

"What. The hell. Is he doing here?" she begs, her eyes bright with curiosity. "Naughty!" She laughs as she swats at my arm and turns to herself in the mirror. Fluffing her long blonde mane, she eyes me shrewdly, before launching into a lecture on the pitfalls of endless one night stands and Rhys' propensity towards just that. I balance myself on the edge of the tub, listening to her drone on, my mind wandering to the beautiful man on my bed. What is he doing here, with me this morning? Why didn't he take Melissa up on her offer last night? Is he trying to add my name to his roster? Do I want that? I smile wickedly to myself, because I know a part of me does, but I have learned the hard way not to be so reckless with my heart and body. My eyes meet with Olivia's. She is standing in front of me with her hands on her hips, a question having just passed over her lips. "Well?"

"What Liv? I didn't hear you."

"Where is your mind, back in bed with Rhys? What happened last night, tell me everything!" Her excitement barely contained. She takes a seat next to me and braces herself for illicit details, giddy with anticipation.

"I hate to disappoint, but he just brought bagels."

"What?" She shakes her head, like the scenario is an impossibility. "Really, bagels and nothing else?"

"Don't you think I would tell you? Really, just bagels. Besides, I'm starting to get the picture that I am not his type, so…." I leave the comment hanging, and get up, shuffling things about the counter. "So, what is the plan for today?" My casual attempt at changing the subject.

"Oh, no. You are not getting off that easy." She says, joining me at the sink, admiring her reflection.

"I have never known Rhys to ….be so friendly, especially when he's not, you know, making a girl squeal first." The comment takes my breath away. I turn to her and a smile raises on my face that strains at my cheeks.

"You are so bad! Listen, I am not trying to get mixed up with any of Matthew's rich playboy friends. The cliché single desperate bridesmaid is not me." Trying not to let her comment play over in my mind, *make you squeal*, I splash my face with cool water and grab a fluffy hand towel. When I look up Olivia is watching me, skepticism all over her face.

"Seriously, what do you think of him?" She retakes her seat on the tub and waits.

"I don't know Liv, he is intense, arrogant and, according to you, a distraction that I don't need."

"I know, but how awesome would it be if you two got together? We could travel and double date! Oh, I would love that." She is carried away by her far-fetched fantasy of a jet-set foursome. "Just be careful. I have seen girls lose their minds over him. Seriously, he is a force, but, if you can get past it, he really is such a great guy. I have told him all about you. He has a hard shell and he doesn't trust people, but it just takes some warming up. It seems he is warming up to you just fine. He is the greatest friend. We are having our wedding at his family's winter house and he has gifted us his father's yacht for our honeymoon!"

A Yacht?! Holy hell.

"Wow, that is really generous." I can't help but feel totally intimidated. Yet, I am distracted with wonder at what ridiculous things she told him about me.

"He and Matthew are like brothers, they grew up together, went to the same boarding schools.

41

They would do anything for each other."

"Well, I think it's pretty clear that he is…that I am…. We exist in different spheres. I wouldn't even know what to do with him. He is too good looking, too intense, way too rich and far too conceited." I shake off the conversation, not wanting to think about all the reasons why a man like that wouldn't look twice at a girl like me.

"I wouldn't be so sure," she offers coming up behind me, tousling my slept in curls. "He brought you bagels," she teases me. "Don't sell yourself short. You are different. You are generous and sweet, idealistic to a fault and real. I talk about you all the time. He is going to love you, just be yourself, he won't stand a chance." She hugs me, saunters out of the bathroom and into Matthew's waiting arms.

***

Brunch, shopping, dress fittings and tastings. The day is scheduled to the minute, the wedding chaos officially beginning. The men golf while we have our fittings and final tastings for the reception. The wedding party meets for lunch after which time the sexes go their separate way for the respective Bachelor and Bachelorette parties. The chatter is becoming static, I am an outsider here. The others in the wedding party are familiar and have shared experiences and memories. They all have a history, having grown up and traveled in the same posh circles. I have only Olivia, but I am glad to see her surrounded by so much support. She is going to need it. Taking another sip of sparkling water, I hear Rhys' name drift across the table. My eyes meet with Melissa's. She is sharing her conjecture of Rhys' evening activities while her expression oozes contempt and jealousy. The others pick up on her gossip and he quickly becomes the subject of the tables' idle chatter; who he was last pictured with on Page Six, or the gossip rags. His name volleys across the table like a ball, back and forth they giggle and wonder at his most recent carnal activities. Gossip and conjecture is all I am hearing, so I turn to Olivia for respite. She reads me like a book and pulls me into a conversation about home.

My life has been nothing but change and upheaval for so many years. I have become numb to the daily mess of it all. Being here with Olivia is supposed to serve as a distraction, but it is always looming in the back of my mind. I have no one left. Just as Olivia is embarking on this amazing journey with a new husband and extended family, I am alone. Color me green, because I am envious.

***

Olivia is surrounded by two scantily clad police

officers and a gaggle of squealing women. Her face flaming with embarrassment and amusement, I catch her eye and motion that I'm going to step out. The room is too hot, smells of sex, leather and expensive perfume, crowded with overheated women. I walk through the double doors into the foyer of the suite that sits atop our hotel and go into the kitchen for a glass of water. The water is cool and crisp, taming my wild thirst, coating my throat. I am a buzz from the day's activities and decide to take a walk. I stumble to the door on the tragically high heels that Liv wanted me to wear and decide to leave them behind. I prefer bare feet, my feet don't like to be trapped, and I am more comfortable being that much closer to the ground, thank you. I walk out into the hall and wait for the elevator.

I sway to the tune stuck in my head as the elevator glides toward the ground floor. The doors open to none other than every woman's favorite topic of conversation this evening, Rhys, in all of his arrogant, electric perfection. He is headed out the side door towards the patio where we first spoke. He doesn't see me as I follow him outside, my bare feet not betraying a sound. I silently pad behind him until he stops at the end of the patio, he swirls his drink in the heavy crystal glass and takes a sip. He looks lost in thought and totally unaware of my prying eyes. I watch the muscles in his back move under his crisp shirt as he takes another drink, his back straight with a perfect ass to anchor a pair of powerful legs. He is all business. His crisp white shirt, sleeves rolled over sculpted forearms, his hair is rumpled and his collar loose. I feel myself heating from within, the sight of him mingles with the gossip of the day and I remind myself to keep it together.

"Do you always linger in the dark?" Rhys turns and locks me in his sights. Fuck! I didn't think this through! He closes the distance between us in two long strides and comes to a stop inches away from my face. He bends down coming eye to eye with me and takes a deep breath. A low groan rumbles in the back of his throat. He closes his eyes for a moment and pulls back, standing straight, looking down upon me like the imposing man that he is. "Why aren't you upstairs?"

"Strippers are not really my thing." I have never enjoyed the thought of some strange man waving his junk in my face, call me a prude but, no. "What are you doing here?" volleying his question.

"Something that had to be taken care of."

"What's her name?" I ask coyly, peeking out from under my lashes. I feel the rush of blood all over my body, releasing my inner flirt. She is bad when she wants to be.

"Her name is work," he returns flatly. Oh, excuse me, Mr. Grump. He can be so cold, his mood flips on a dime. His face is stern and offers nothing. Feeling the need to divert his attention and douse my rising temperature I reach for his crystal glass.

"What are we drinking?" I ask bringing the glass to my lips in the place where he had been drinking from, the smell of scotch filling my nostrils. He holds his hand up in warning, but before he can I take a long greedy sip and lick my lips, returning the glass with a grin. It is a taste and smell I am familiar with, my father having been a scotch drinker.

"Dalwhinney," he says, shaking his head in disbelief, then looks at me with an admiring smile in his eyes. He really is beautiful when he smiles, but the naughty girl inside me is intrigued by his cold side. The sweet scotch spreads through me, warming my blood and loosening my tongue. It's clear that this man lives to intimidate and takes great pleasure in it, but I can be disarming when I choose to be. What better place or time than right here and right now. With liquid courage flowing through my veins and his scent swirling in my head, I surrender to my curiosity. There has been too much talk about him going around today for me to not find out some truths about Rhys.

"There was quite a bit of talk about you this afternoon." My eyes hardly hiding the smile I am trying to stifle, yet once again I seem to have hit upon another locked lip topic. He looks from the side of his eye at me.

"Really? And was there a consensus, I hope?" Forcing a half grin to keep his mood light, but the question holds no humor. Turning to me he takes a step forward, and waits for my unprepared answer.

"You have quite the reputation." I search his face for a reaction but he offers none. "It seems you are a ride not to be missed." A slight twitch in his eye betrays the proud grin he is trying to suppress. "So why haven't you tried with me?" WHAT!!! I want to pull the question back and swallow it, erase it from the face of the earth, but it's too late. He turns his smoldering gaze on me and I almost combust. He closes the gap, leaving only a sliver of air between us, not touching any part of me, yet I can feel him all over.

"Is that what you want?" His voice laced with promise, his eyes search mine, waiting for my answer.

"No," I hiss without thinking. His face falls slightly, but he recovers just as quickly. "No, I was just.. wondering, why....I'm sorry that was stupid." I shrink from him, ice filling my veins where once hot blood had flowed. My inner flirt kicking herself, wishing we both could be swallowed up and disappear.

"Well, now I surely won't. Now, you will have to beg, Little Sophie" He puts his hands in the air in surrender and steps back, triumph and mirth reflected in his face. He smiles at me with that most sexy crooked smile and bows his head. Little Sophie? Those two words start a fire in me and I am compelled to challenge him. I resolve to win this battle and step up to him. He balks for but a moment before he gains his footing and puffs his rock hard chest. I take a deep draught of his scent, being careful not to touch him. He smells of scotch, cigar smoke and salt water, it is intoxicating. I raise my index finger and hook it into his shirt just above the top button, being careful not to touch his warm, radiant flesh.

"I think it will be you that will be begging, Mr. Ego," the words slither from my tongue, wrapping around him, teasing.

"I thought that was not what you wanted," he whispers, leaning in closer, the smell of musk and salt water flowing through me.

"Hmmm, I think you like to play games, Rhys. But, I am a woman, I can change my mind." A gentle flick of my finger and I pop the top button revealing more of his chiseled chest, peppered with dark hair, the skin glistening from the warm, sticky sea air. A sharp intake of breath and he closes his eyes, stretching the moment, torturing me with silence. His eyes are like liquid pools when he turns their full power on me. His lips part and his tongue emerges to swipe at his bottom lip before he leans in and gently kisses me on the corner of my waiting

48

mouth. I want explosions and sparks, but the kiss is painfully chaste, prompting an empty ache deep in my core. Leaving me wanting. I want him to kiss me like he means it, like he can't think of anything else. Instead, he is kissing me like a silly school girl. My heart is sinking, my head flooding with self-doubt and loathing. The gentle contact is torturous. His hands are firmly at his sides, our bodies separated now by the deepest chasm, inches become miles. The silence is unbearable, like an empty cave, my misguided words echoing off the walls in my head. I want to run and hide, but my legs are anchored to the spot, afraid that if I take a step I may sink to the ground from embarrassment and rejection.

"Rhys! There you are." Matthew comes around the corner, followed by four other slightly wavering forms, the rest of the bachelor party. I am instantly relieved to be interrupted, just waiting for the men to get closer and engage Rhys so I can run. The moment feels like an eternity as I watch them approach. Rhys' eyes never leave my face, I can feel him burning me up, but I refuse to meet his gaze. I cannot bear the thought of looking him in the face, the man who apparently makes it his business to bang most women that he comes into contact has denied me. Humiliation has replaced any warmth that he provoked, the blood rushing from my head into my toes, leaving me flushed and dizzy. Rhys releases me from his sights to nod at Matthew and I seize the moment. I turn away from him and making a break for the side entrance. Turning on my bare heel I go for the door when Rhys' strong grasp pulls me around, his hand covering my upper arm with more force than necessary. I look down at his hand, then to his waiting face.

"Sophie," he whispers, his heavy brows creased, a slight twitch raising the corner of his tight mouth.

"No," is all I can manage as I pull my arm from his grasp and retreat from this battle he has waged on my body and mind. Hearing the door click behind me, I release a deep breath, dropping my shoulders from their defensive position. I want to get to my room as quickly as possible and move towards the bank of elevators. I try not to look behind me as I wait, wanting Rhys to leave me alone, but also wishing he would come after me. When I get to my room it is stuffy and dark. All of the windows have been closed up all day and the air is heavy and stagnant. I open the gauzy curtains and pull open every window along the back wall welcoming the cool sea breeze. I change into my coolest night dress and lie down on the bed, watching the curtains dance in the breeze, the lights from outside painting moving shadows on the walls.

I can't keep my mind off Rhys, his crooked

smile dancing in my head, mocking me. Rejecting me. He has infiltrated every recess of my body and mind, creating a raging war of overstimulation and delicious confusion, tying me up in a sensual knot. Every fiber of my being twisted and wanting, a touch or a breath could push me over. I am teetering on the brink of insanity, his presence the cause and the only cure. No man has ever taunted me so thoroughly, creating such an intense awareness of the emptiness in my loins, illuminating a chasm that aches. Aches to be filled, over and over, filled to the bone. I am drawn to him without explanation. If you don't take into consideration his imposing form, stunning face and the intense 'fuck me' glare he throws around. He embodies all the things I hate about cocky men, and have avoided my entire sexual life. Guys like that just take what they want, believe they deserve the world, and discard you when they get bored. They are superficial and arrogant and only see women who are impossibly perfect. I imagine that I am the antithesis of all he looks for. Undereducated, under traveled, underfunded and over fed. The thought repeats in my mind, like a taunting echo. I close my eyes and take in a deep cleansing breath of the fresh air that slides over my body from the open windows. I am unable to quiet the incessant chatter cluttering my head. And the heat, the heat is inside of me, making me so aware of my body. Attempting to banish

Rhys to the farthest recesses of my mind I sit up in the dark and search for the television remote.

Chapter 4

"*….In the World.*" I vaguely register Jeremy Clarkson's voice declaring the worst car in the world, eyes closed, breathing deep and even, on the edge of sleepy oblivion when I am roused by a soft rap on the door.

"Room Service." With a blanket wrapped around my shoulders, I pull the door open, a protest already passing my lips.

"I'm sorry, but I didn't…" Before I can get the words out Rhys peers around the corner and dismisses the room service waiter.

"I'll take it from here, chap." Pushing past the dumbstruck waiter, he rolls the silver cart into the room, turning and slipping the young man a tip before closing the door, turning his attention to me. "I thought perhaps a midnight snack," revealing an array of snacks from underneath the shiny silver serving dome. Plump, ripe figs, green globe grapes and Chevre accompanied by a sliced baguette and shaved prosciutto. My stomach growls at the sight. Realizing I haven't eaten since brunch, I momentarily forget to question what he is doing in my room, yet again. I pick at the grapes mindlessly watching him move about the cart, he is fidgeting. Is he nervous? What on earth for?

"What are you doing here, Rhys?" quizzing as I nibble on grapes, pushing the sleepiness back.

53

"We should talk." His tone is pensive and unsure. God, I hate those words, we should talk. Nothing good ever comes from that phrase, I hate those words.

"OK." I am unsure of his motives, but intrigued and a little hungry come to think of it. He moves into the room, scanning his surroundings, looking anywhere but in my eyes.

"You're a good girl, Sophie." Was that a question? It sounded like a declaration. Whatever it is, I am immediately defensive.

"You don't know me." With only five little words this man has got my back up.

"I know enough to know that I don't want to hurt you." He moves to sit at the edge of the bed. "And if this happens... Us. You will get hurt. I don't do relationships." I stand above him, arms crossed, trying to hide the growing anger in my eyes.

"Wow! Does your ego know no bounds? We have known each other for a minute, and you think I want to be in a relationship with you? You don't know anything about me, Rhys. You have made assumptions about me, but you are very wrong."

"Fine," he says. "Are you a good girl, Sophie?" His wide eyes wait. My mind rages and I open my mouth to respond with a bite, but quickly snap it shut.

"I. What is wrong with that? Why does it sound

54

like an insult? What does it even mean?" I am exasperated. Why would being good be a bad thing? He stands, resting his hands on my shoulders, sending a spark across my skin, looking down on me with soft, pity filled eyes.

"It means you are good and sweet. You are Olivia's friend and I hope you will be mine." I push away from him and cross the room. I need distance, moving into the corner, closer to the open windows and fresh air, air that is not riddled with his scent.

"So, now you want to be my friend?" Frustration at his judgment boils over and I lose control of my tongue, while Olivia's words echo in my head, *'Be careful, he is a force.'* "I see what you do Rhys. You like to keep women off balance. Well, you won't rattle me. Just because my bed post isn't whittled to a toothpick from all the notches doesn't mean I am a good girl! Just because I am not sexually hyperactive or walk around with my body on display, like your contemporaries doesn't mean I am not a grown woman. You have misjudged me and overestimated your effect, I might add." I move back into his orbit. "It is one thing that I have had to listen to these women talk about you like some prized stud while they leer at me, assuming already that I am your latest victim." I jab my finger into his chest, his hard, unyielding chest. "But it is another for you to stand before me and proclaim it for yourself. I have some dignity,

55

Rhys. And if you think I was just going to fall flat on my back for you, you really don't know anything about me." He throws his hands up and takes a step back, backing up against the bed.

"OK, I'm sorry. Let's start over. Can we start over, please?" He pleads. I take a deep breath and watch him fill his lungs with a deep breath. His face softens and the edge in his stance wavers. I don't want him to go, and I didn't want to come across so angry. I take a deep, cleansing breath and smile at him, taking a grape to fill my mouth and still my tongue.

"Fine, let's start over," I offer, taking a seat at the foot of the bed.

"Good. I brought snacks. I thought we could get to know one another, Sophie." His lips caress my name. His eyes are wide and hopeful. "Get friendly." His crooked smile wins the day, helping me to shake off the last ropes of frustration. Sure, it was a product of the scotch, sleepiness and his intoxicating proximity. His intentions were painfully clear in the way he kissed me outside, like a silly young girl with a crush, he gently dismissed me. Now that I know where we stand why should I not demystify and get *friendly* with this enigma? I look up at his waiting face, dark lashes framing emerald green eyes, freckles dusted across the bridge of his straight nose. There is warmth in his face that was not evident before now, his grin is eager, no intimidation in his manner. I offer a warm smile and climb to the head of the bed, pulling the comforter up over my legs, clearing space for Rhys and his meticulously arranged platter of nibbles. He offers me a glass of Perrier, kicks off his shoes and lowers himself onto the bed next to me, careful to sit on top of the comforter.

"Are you watching Top Gear?" His voice betrays surprise and awe.

"I forgot the TV was on, you can change it if you like, or turn it off."

"No, no it's good, leave it on." He tilts his head in curiosity and turns back to the TV. "They drive some beautiful cars." I watch him take a bite from a fig, his lips full and soft. The smallest action, so bewitching, and before I can regain myself and look away he catches me. Slowly, he rolls his tongue along his lower lip, reveling in the sticky drops of nectar from the fig then offers me the succulent fruit. All reason is shattered the moment he wrapped his lips around that damn fruit. Every cell in my body is pulsating, a fire rising in my abdomen. A dull hum fills my head and my pulse quickens, threatening any amount of control I convinced myself that I wielded. His long slender fingers hold the delicate fig, careful not to bruise or damage the tender flesh. I can't help but wonder if those fingers are always so careful and agile. The thought is rattling. I have to kick this man out of my

57

head. The fog clears from my eyes in time for me to see his crooked, triumphant grin. He knows what he does, there is no question about that. I have to shake him off and look away, denying his offer.

"Why did you leave the bachelor party?" I ask, a seemingly a safe topic to distract myself from his overtly sexual energy and the sting of his earlier rejection.

"It was about to get dirty." He is very matter of fact.

"I thought the dirty bits were the part men loved the most." I can't help but be playful. There is an energy between us that makes it almost impossible for me to hold my tongue, we have a verbal chemistry and my sharp tongue has been in desperate need of a counterpart.

"I prefer a…..higher caliber of entertainment." His eyes hold me in a death grip, refusing to let me go. Raising the remainder of the fig to his mouth, he slowly licks the soft pink center, his eyes never leaving mine, he pops it into his mouth with a low groan and a wicked smile.

"Like debutantes and socialites?"

"You twist my words. And you shouldn't place any value on idle chatter, Sophie, women are wicked and ruthless," he says flatly.

"I am a woman."

"I suppose there are exceptions to every rule," he offers warmly, the cynicism quickly melting from his face. "The women in these circles have too much time on their hands and too many fetishes and secrets to count." His elusive language tickles my ears, commanding my full attention.

"Fetishes and secrets, huh? That sounds eerily like the conversations that were floating around about you this afternoon." The words just sit there, I don't know what to expect.

"Fetishes? No, I am devoid of any kink you may assume, Sophie. I'm as vanilla as the next guy." I raise an eyebrow in total disbelief. "Perhaps *French vanilla* would be a better descriptor." He winks and sends a pulse through my belly. "But nonetheless, don't let them fool you. I possess certain talents, talents that make me a popular topic of conversation apparently. But I acquired those talents by paying attention, by listening and adapting." Humor flashes in his eyes while he watches me squirm. My mind is swimming in a cocktail of confusion, thoughts of heart pounding, sheet ripping, sweat drenched sex swirling in my empty head. I am suddenly gripped by frustration and anger at being played with.

"What is this?" My tongue is slightly sharper than I had intended, a scowl painted on my face. His eyes betray no emotion as he reads my face and then returns his attention to the platter of fruit.

"Well, these are figs and those are grapes..."

"Rhys, what is this? Is this how you make

friends?" I wave my hand between us, waiting for an answer but all he offers is that crooked half smile. "What are you doing here? Why are you taunting me? It seems beneath you." I can see the mirth in his eyes, turning up the wattage on his grin to full panty busting power. My god he really is sexy. That grin has a direct connection to my center, burning me up from the inside.

"Sophie." His lips curl around my name, a whisper of promise. The lines of his face change, harden, all joking gone. He sits up carefully and turns to face me, our knees touching through the comforter. He squares his shoulders with mine and traps me with his clear green eyes like a doe in headlights. "Sophie, you are Olivia's best and oldest friend. That makes you my friend, besides, she talks about you constantly. I feel like I do know you and can I just say that she did not do you justice." His face is soft now, expectant, waiting. "I just…like you." I release the breath I have been holding in frustration and my shoulders drop from relief. Sitting face to face with Rhys, the air is electric, his scent hanging like a spell, intoxicating and unmistakably male. His eyes are disarming and genuine with anticipation, but my tongue is twisted. His eyes are so deeply green, it is like being lost in a deep forest, he has wiped my mind clean.

"I am sorry that I cannot say the same about you. Olivia has never mentioned you." His face falls momentarily, realizing that I truly know nothing about him.

"Never?" He mulls the reality momentarily. "Perhaps that was for the best, I wouldn't want you to have the wrong impression."

"And what impression would that be?" My curiosity peaked. I know the impression I have gotten from others and it is one that I cannot soon forget.

"I think you had a taste today. Did you not say that I was a popular topic of conversation?" The arch of his eyebrow is sharp and knowing. "Never mind that. I rarely have the opportunity to make my own first impression. What a concept," he quips to himself, lost in the impossible idea of his anonymity. The carousel that is his revolving mood is exhausting. His mercurial nature ever changing and confusing, keeps a girl on her toes. With a renewed energy he bounds off the bed and goes to the mini bar.

"Let's toast to getting to know each other, Sophie and Rhys, fast friends." The emphasis falls on friends, as he pulls two crystal rocks glasses and a crystal decanter of amber liquor from the bar, adding ice cubes to the glasses from the silver bucket on the room service cart. Climbing back on the bed, he hands me a glass with a smile that makes him look so young and carefree. He pours one finger for me and then for himself before placing the crystal decanter on the bedside table. He raises his glass to me. "To Us, Sophie, new friends and first impressions." I don't take my eyes off of him as we toast, waiting for his mood to shift.

"Why is it so important to you that I didn't know who you are?"

"Clearly you do not read gossip columns. I grew up in a bubble. Everything was dictated by my father and his standing, our name. From a young age, I have been in the public eye, I have never been anonymous. People know about me and think that they know who I am. They see pictures of me and think they know me. People project who they want you to be and then are disappointed when you don't measure up. Women can smell the money from a mile away. They always want more. I learned from a young age how to give people what they want, without giving them a piece of me. It can be exhausting," he reveals himself without hesitation. "It is refreshing to meet someone who doesn't know me, or better yet, want something from me. I can truly be myself." Relief emanates from his body, he is visibly relaxed. He has removed his mask.

"So, the idle chatter and general excitement that you rouse in these women is what, unwarranted?"

"No, I am aware of my reputation. And I have earned it," he quips with a sly grin. "I am not opposed to the occasional casual encounter. I enjoy the company of women and have cultivated a very healthy set of skills. But, it has been a very long while since I have dated. I prefer to keep things light. One night, any more than that and people start to get the wrong idea. What they do once they have moved on is not my concern."

"So you collect virgins?"

"No, not virgins," he chokes. "But, I suppose you could call me a collector. I collect beautiful things, beautiful women." He taps his temple. "But, women are fickle. I give them what they expect from me, and not a drop more. I don't encourage emotion. Emotions are messy. I'm not in the business of investing emotion in others."

"So your life is one endless one night stand? That sounds sad." And lonely, I think to myself.

"I prefer to think of it as tidy. Let's change the subject," he begs, not meeting my eyes.

"OK. Who is your father?" I ask. The look of utter shock on his face is priceless. Either I am truly out of the loop or this man's sense of self-importance is bordering on delusional. He lets out a burst of laughter and shakes his head.

"My father is Michael Slate." He waits for the information to sink in. I search the recesses of my mind for that name.

"The shipping guy?" I question, less than eloquent. I vaguely recall recently skimming an article about the expansion of his holdings in

Europe. His net worth is practically immeasurable. He could support a small country. Shipyards on both coasts, International holdings and a family name that reaches back a century or more. How did I not make that connection?

"Shipping, among other things, yes." I turn my eyes on Rhys in question and forget to run my thoughts by the internal editor.

"Am I supposed to feel sorry for you because your daddy is a billionaire? You are barking up the wrong tree." I take a deep pull from my glass in an effort to stifle my biting tongue. Rhys laughs a deep belly laugh and the sound is musical.

"I like the way you talk to me, Sophie, you are honest, sharp." The look of admiration on his face is enough to melt my icy façade and I can't help but smile, wide and true.

"So tell me about your sad, rich childhood." Baiting him, I finish my drink and let the warmth spread through me like sunshine spreads across the horizon. Placing my glass on the table I fluff the pillows behind me and pull the blanket up, comfortable and ready to listen.

"There isn't much to tell. I spent a lot of time at boarding schools. That is where I met Matthew. My father comes from a large family so I spent quite a bit of time with them when I was younger. I have always done what was expected of me. Played rugby like my dad, went to St. Andrews like my dad and now I am in business with my dad. There was never much opportunity to stray from the prescribed course, if you know what I mean. I have always had to tow the line in my public life, be mindful of the family name. That is my life, in a nut shell."

"What about your mom?"

"They divorced when I was young," he snaps, downing the remainder of his scotch. "Enough about me, I would rather hear about you." The way he effortlessly turns the tables is maddening, he makes it impossible to get control of our interaction. He leads every time.

"I thought Olivia already covered me."

"That is knowledge by relay. I prefer my information to come directly from the source. What do you do, for work?"

"My degree is in education, but I write for our local newspaper. Usually the community column, you know, what's happening around town, new restaurants, events, stuff like that. Occasionally I get to write about more important things, but not often."

"Why don't you teach?" he asks, looking truly interested.

"I don't know really, it just didn't appeal to me. My good friend Mary is the editor of the paper. When this position came up, she mentioned it to me and I just couldn't pass it up. There is more freedom and flexibility with the paper. I can set my own hours and make my own assignments most of the time."

"What about your free time?" he probes. I cannot remember the last time someone was interested in my life. It's not really that interesting.

"I take care of my Grandmother, she has dementia. She is the only family I have, and that takes a lot of my time." It sounds so dull, and sad when I say it out loud. My life could be the life of a middle aged woman, just add a few dozen cats and the picture is complete. The thought puts a sour taste in my mouth, and I wish I had lied, made myself sound more interesting, anything other than my reality. "And I volunteer on the local school board, planning and helping to maintain kitchen gardens for the school lunch programs. You know, fresh food, nutritional pyramid, that sort of stuff." I feel myself begin to ramble, spewing information at him with fervor, dying to fill the silence, I cannot stop talking. Please stop me. I look up into his face to see a wide genuine smile that halts me in my tracks.

"Why are you looking at me like that?" He laughs off the question and shakes his head.

"I admire what you do. You are a good girl, Sophie." It sounds more like an accusation than a compliment.

"I am sure it is very dull compared to your jet set, high profile life. You must think my life sounds so boring, and ordinary." My fingers lace and twist in my lap, an uneasy feeling of inadequacy churns in my gut.

"Just the opposite," he offers. "Your life sounds quiet, nice. You have a good heart, Sophie. What are your plans?" He is eager and patient.

"Plans for what?" He pulls me from my increasingly evil inner thoughts.

"For the future, for your life." His brows knit together, his face stern, while I mull the question, stirring up so many reasons why I no longer make plans. Plans suggest control and life cannot be controlled.

"I don't really have a plan," I have been so stuck in the past, frozen in a moment. I wouldn't dare think of the future now, not when I know how easily it can be taken away. "I like my job. I take care of my grandma. That is my life, I'm fine with that."

"You miss your parents."

"What?" He has ripped the carefully tended bandage from my tender flesh with his obnoxious observation. What does he even know about my parents? His statement burns like a hot poker and puts me on high alert. I don't talk about them, and I don't want to rehash it here, now.

"Forgive me, Sophie. Olivia told me what happened. Is it okay to bring it up?" Pausing tentatively he swirls his finger around the ice in his glass, watching me, waiting for me to crack.

"No." My face is stone, a mask I learned to wear when people probed. I stare down into my lap, fingers wrung and twisting around one another, unsure of how much to share, unwilling to open old wounds. "Of course I miss them. When they died, everything that I had planned died with them. But you play the hand you are dealt and that is what I am doing." A mist falls over my eyes, but I push it back. He asks questions I don't want to answer. He has invited himself into the deepest recesses of my life, a small part of me wants to welcome him, but I cannot. "I don't like talking about them."

After an hour of gentle interrogation I cannot think of anything more that he could possibly want to know, that he hasn't already asked. And then the question that no one has ever asked.

"What do you dream about, Sophie? If you could have anything in the world, what would it be?" I splutter at the question and my head swims with the possibilities. This man sitting in front of me, wanting to know me, I cannot help but wonder why? What will he gain from probing my life, what is he hoping to find? I feel like I am in a job interview, the way he hangs on my answers, jotting down mental notes and silently filing away my replies. The whole conversation is completely one sided. He refuses to allow me to ask even the smallest of questions. "I want to know all about you, Sophie. I'm bored with myself. Now, when you close your eyes and dream what do you see?"

I cannot remember the last time I looked past my everyday life and considered the future. I have my head buried so far beneath the sand, I can hardly see two feet in front of me, much less into the future. But as I allow myself to consider the possibilities I know the answer could be infinite. However, at this moment I know if I closed my eyes, I would surely see Rhys and his wicked grin. The scotch and the hour are starting to weigh heavily on my eyes. I scoot my body down the bed and fluff the pillows under my head. Pulling the comforter up over my shoulders, I am cocooned in down and linen, comforters, buzzed, content. I launch into the stock answer as I can feel myself drifting into a shallow sleep.

"I would travel, all over the world. I want to touch things that have history and meaning. I want to experience the world, life. I want to walk across Ireland, explore castles and churches. I want a cottage with a big garden. I just want to be happy and loved."

"That sounds like a plan," he teases, my mind half asleep and drifting quickly away.

Chapter 5

Awash with sensation, hands all over my body, so many hands roaming and skimming over smooth, heated flesh, every fingertip leaving a burning a trail. A mouth, warm and moist, everywhere, overwhelming me, sucking, biting, teasing me. I wrap my arms around powerful shoulders, pulling them into me, closer, harder, now. Need builds deep in my belly, pooling in my groin like warm honey, blood rushing to my core, throbbing, pounding in my head. I am surrounded, enveloped by the need to fill myself with you, to be part of you. I am aching with need when a great void opens, threatening to swallow me up, and there is no one to pull me out, you have disappeared. I struggle against the darkness, reaching for you, but you are gone, and I am all alone. A breath tightens in my chest, my lungs struggle for air under the weight of my loneliness. There is so much space surrounding me, empty and dark. I'm being crushed by the absence of everything, disappearing into oblivion with nobody to pull me back. I struggle to wake myself, wanting to escape the dream that has me trapped, the empty space that threatens to swallow me.

Gasping for breath I shoot up in bed, frightened and reeling from my dark dream. I fight to regain my breath, to calm my pulse. The room is dark, but the television is still on, some midnight infomercial promising rapid weight loss. And Rhys, his dark solid form, next to me, sleeping, softly snoring, arm flung over his head. He looks so sweet, almost harmless. I watch him sleep for a minute, his chest rising and falling with every shallow breath, his lips slightly parted, thick eyelashes splayed across his cheeks. Yet even in his gentle sleep, he conveys power and control. I want to reach out and touch him, brush the hair off his forehead and trace the lines of his cheekbones, run my fingertips over the stubble of his beard, but I think better of it. I rise and shuffle to the bathroom.

Just being out of his direct vicinity affords me more clarity, he is like a drug, fast working and highly addictive. I quickly brush my teeth and rinse my face. I fill a tall glass of water for myself and one for Rhys, placing it on the bedside table next to him. I crawl back into bed, switch the television off and drift back to sleep, the dream of empty oblivion skirting the recesses of my mind.

***

When I wake I am too warm, twisted up in the comforter and blankets. My nape is damp from sweat and I kick off the covers, begging for a breeze of cool air to condition my overheated skin. I roll over to find the bed empty. Rhys is gone, but he left

71

a note.

Sophie,

I want to take you out today.

Please come to my suite

when you are ready.

Don't keep me waiting.

Rhys

A room key sits atop the note, Penthouse, of course. I decide that since he has left so unceremoniously, I will take my time getting ready. I will not give him the impression that I will come running whenever he calls. Even though blood is pounding in my head and I am giddy about the idea of spending the whole day with him. I feel like a young girl, just waiting for a glimpse of a crush. Friends, that is all he wants to be, but I can live with that. I want to be near him, it is all I can think about. And the promise of the day is too good.

After a leisurely shower, I dress in a pale pink linen dress, slip on my braided sandals, swipe on some blush, a little lip gloss and I am done. Looking at myself, reflected in the mirror I can't help but see an ordinary girl looking back at me, perfectly ordinary and nothing more. I have to shake the thought from my mind. I slip my phone into a hidden pocket, grab my purse and sunglasses. I slide an emergency twenty dollar bill into my bra, as I have always been coached to do, and head out the door to the elevators.

The doors slide open to a large, brightly lit foyer, windows on every side welcome the warm Florida sun, bathing the marble floors and soft plaster walls in golden light. There is a large heavy table with a massive gaudy arrangement of birds of paradise in a tall stone vase. There are two doors, Rhys' is just behind the flock of flowers. I knock and then insert the key, but before I do the door opens on a scene I did not expect.

Kylie, disheveled and sweaty, dressed in a tiny tank and tight yoga Capris. She is the epitome of health and beauty, and my stomach turns at the sight of her. Her long blond hair is swept up into a pony tail that she has wrapped around her fingers, playing mindlessly with the golden strands. Her face is bright and flushed, glowing maybe. I am frozen to the spot, shocked and confused. Kylie steps around me, leaving the door open behind her.

"Oh, hey, Sophie, Rhys is in the shower, you can go on in. See you tonight." She dashes into the waiting elevator, jogging in place while setting her iPod. I am left standing in the doorway, dumbstruck by what just happened.

Why did he spend the night in my room if he

73

had Kylie waiting for him? What sort of game is he playing? My fight or flight instinct begins to take hold and as always I lean towards flight. The internal struggle rages as I try to reason with my inner cynic. There has to be a reasonable explanation for why she was here. Or maybe the reasonable explanation would explain away why he was with me last night. The bile rising in my throat is the nudge I need. I spin on my heel to make a break for it when Rhys steps out of the master bathroom. Good Lord! He is wrapping a fluffy white towel around his well-defined waist when he catches me in his sights.

"Sophie." A crooked smile spreads across his face, erasing every thought in my mind. His hard body dripping still with rivulets of lucky water, his torso is dusted with dark hair, accentuating every plane of tight muscle, he steps through the French doors into the living area. His arms ripple and flex as he dries his hair, revealing a slight curl, and tosses the towel onto the chair. He could make David weep in jealousy. His body is tight and dripping with sex. My eyes travel down his form, unable to look away. Into a perfect V it all comes together, the most sexy side muscles that point to the sweet spot. I have never seen a man like this in the flesh.

Every cell in my body is reacting and responding to him. I look at his body and can't help but think that I would gladly drop to my knees and worship at his altar. His rock hard body is calling to me. A dark trail of hair teases, leading to the darkest of treasures. He ties me up in knots, and I can only silently beg. Beg to touch him, to run my fingers over his beautifully chiseled chest, followed by my tongue. Over every curve and muscle of his taut abs, I need to taste him and suddenly I am starving. I want his scent to flow through me. I need to be filled by him, to be his vessel, to fill me up until my head spins, and then do it again, and again. Snap out of it! His wicked eyes rake me over before he grins, arrogant and knowing.

"Do you need to sit?" He winks and pads over to the bar. His back almost as beautiful as his front, tight strapping muscles give and take as he walks, his heart shaped ass high and tight, strong legs perfectly tapered to well-manicured feet. He takes very good care of himself. It is evident in every pane of his body, every strand of hair on his head. He pours two glasses of orange juice from a glass carafe that sits next to a silver bucket with a bottle of champagne and a platter of fruit and croissants.

"I am glad you came." Handing me a glass of juice he takes a seat next to me on the sofa. He smells of citrus, soap and testosterone, it is a heady mixture in conjunction with his proximity and the tiny towel that barely covers his powerful thighs. "I thought it would be nice to go get a coffee and then take a drive." He places his hand on my knee light as a feather, but the contact is heavy and electric. His eyes grow wide, his soft lips part and I feel my pulse accelerate and my slack jaw falls open. We both snap to at the same moment and he pulls his hand away and stands, moving towards the bedroom. "I'll just be a few minutes, make yourself at home." He disappears through the French doors and into the master bath, closing the door behind him.

Still slightly a flutter from his gentle touch I rise and walk through the suite. The large living space is decorated in soft pastels, very Miami. Delicately upholstered couches flank both sides of the room, a heavy mahogany bar in the corner. Beyond the bar are two large frosted glass French doors leading to the bedroom that has to be twice the size of my entire hotel room. The large bed that anchors the room is unrumpled, made up, everything in its place. Clearly, it has not been slept in, or romped in for that matter. The thought makes me smile, bringing me back to Kylie in his doorway, wondering if he turned her away the way he had Melissa two nights earlier. If he had, she was in much better spirits about it.

The bed is large and inviting, like a cloud, piled with too many pillows in shades of mint and sea foam green, the comforter a crisp, bright white. The only other furniture in the room is a stark wooden chair, placed facing the bed and the bank of mirrors that are on the other side. It is a peculiar place for a chair, stuck in the middle of the room. I move around and take a seat. I find myself looking into the wall of mirrors, reflected back at me is the whole of the bed, myself and nothing else. My mind struggles to reason when I feel Rhys standing in the open doorway.

"Do you like to watch, Sophie?" He asks, stalking slowly towards me. He is dressed in crisp, lightweight honey-colored slacks and a light blue button-up shirt, sleeves rolled to the elbow, exposing the most amazing, roped forearms. I scramble out of the chair before he can get too close and stumble over an explanation as I edge out of the bedroom, back into the implied safety of the living area.

"Do *you*?" I manage to choke out. He follows me slowly, like a predator trying not to startle his prey.

"Very much." He grins and I think my panties catch fire. "It is an extraordinary thing to watch a woman lose herself. To witness and be party to a woman's utter undoing, it's an honor." I stand as still as a pillar of salt as he saunters towards me. "Don't be so bashful, Sophie," he commands as he reaches around me and grabs his wallet, a pair of tortoise shell sunglasses and a set of keys off of the table next to the door. "I watched you sleep."

"Oh, my God! For how long?"

"Just long enough. You snore." He declares matter of fact. His wicked smile twists at my embarrassment. My mouth is wide in shock and I am speechless, mortified. "You talk as well." A groan escapes my diaphragm before I can stifle it. "Very enlightening," he grins as he places his hand on the small of my back and leads me out to the elevators.

The elevator ride is silent and woven with tension. Even as people shuffle in and out on various floors I feel no one but him. His eyes are on me, watching my pulse rise and fall on the intensity of his gaze. It is like a game for him to see how quickly he can disarm me before strangers. It's a game he is very good at. When the car comes to rest on the ground floor I am grateful for the reprieve. Knowing that if I had to spend one more floor in that elevator with Rhys staring at me like that, I would be nothing more than a pile of smoldering ash. He bites his bottom lip, stifling a knowing smile as he grasps my hand and pulls me out through the lobby and into the warm Florida air. The fresh air renews my perspective and sharpens my tongue.

"I ran into Kylie." My tone more forceful than I had intended and he raises an eyebrow at me just as the valet pulls up, distracting him from my declaration. I look down on a sexy car. A sleek black Jaguar Eagle Speedster, low to the ground with beautiful, curved lines. Two bucket seats covered in supple café-colored leather, cross-stitched and trimmed. The dash is sleek and minimal. Rhys rounds the car as the valet twirls the keys wearing a bright grin.

"Nice car, Mr. Slate." He is young and looks at Rhys with reverence and admiration. His life full of beautiful women, fabulous hotels, hot cars and money to burn, yeah, it must be nice.

"Thanks, kid." He slaps him on the back as he slips him a tip, a bill he had folded into the palm of his other hand. Mr. Smooth. He winks and moves to open my door, exaggerating every movement to put on a show. I slide into the soft leather seat and put my oversized Audrey shades on, buckling my seatbelt. Now I have my mask on. I turn to Rhys as he buckles himself and adjusts the mirrors.

"Nice car, *Mr. Slate*." He chuckles as he pulls out of the circle and onto the driveway.

"I am glad you like it." The winding drive away from the hotel is lined with palms swaying in the gentle breeze. "Do you know what it is?" He quizzes me with a cryptic grin.

"It's a Jag. E-type." A wide smirk crawls across his lips.

"It's going to be a good day, Sophie." He drops his foot to the floor and opens up the engine. We drive in silence just soaking in the sun and enjoying the ocean air.

Quicker than I had expected, we are off the tranquil hotel grounds and deep in the heart of Miami. The city pulses and heaves with energy. Car horns and emergency sirens become the melody as we drive through what I assume is downtown. A quick left and a right turn and Rhys pulls to the curb in front of an old brick building. Under a grubby green awning several little old men stand drinking coffee. A few are huddled in the corner around a small table playing dominoes. I cannot believe that this is where the billionaire playboy has taken me for my first outing in Miami. I look to him in question. He rounds the car and opens my door, offering his hand to help me from the car.

"Trust me. This place is the best." Grasping my hand, he pushes the door closed behind me and turns toward the awning, leading me along the pavement until we are in front of the small hand written menu. He doesn't drop my hand, instead splaying his fingers between mine, locking them together. He folds his middle finger between our locked hands and begins to gently stroke my palm, back and forth. The smallest contact and movement so sensual it reverberates in my pelvis, clenching every muscle south of my waist. "How do you like your coffee?" his voice warm and easy, but his eyes are steamy.

"Strong and sweet."

"Cream?" he whispers with a wicked grin.

"No, thank you." He turns to the window and orders two café Cubanos and two pastelitos. I stand next to him, trying to absorb the sounds and smells of the city when I feel a tap on my shoulder. I turn around to see a grubby, disheveled kid, no older than fourteen maybe. He looks homeless, and hungry.

"You got any change, lady?" He thrusts his empty hands towards me. Rhys turns away from charming the elderly lady behind the counter and tugs me away from the boy. Pulling me behind him, he tells the kid to get lost. How can he be so cruel? I yank my hand from his and step around him. He tries to stop me, but I glare at him. He needs to get out of my way. The boys' hollow eyes watch me pull the emergency money out of my bra, and I press the bill into his stained, worn hands. His eyes are sad and weary as he snatches the bill and backs away.

"Good luck to you. And God bless you," I offer, watching him back into the shadows. I turn to find Rhys behind me, his intimidating glare firmly in place. He grips me by the elbow and twirls me away, towards an empty table.

"What are you doing?" he scolds. "That was very dangerous."

"Helping." We sit at one of two little wrought iron tables that are on the sidewalk.

"How do you know that he won't just spend the money on drugs or alcohol?"

"I don't and I don't care."

"How did you know he wasn't going to hurt you, or try and rob you? And how did you come by the money you gave him?" he quizzes like an authority figure.

"You were standing right next to me, Rhys. And not that it should be any of your concern, but it was my emergency money. 'A lady always has an emergency twenty tucked about her at all times,' words to live by," I tease. He eyes me with confusion and amusement.

"How do you know that you won't need your emergency money?"

"Will you abandon me in Downtown Miami, *friend*?" I smile. He chuckles, a hearty belly chuckle.

"You are very sweet. And painfully naïve," he offers, squeezing my hand. He turns to the lively table next to us and launches into a conversation with the old men. They are flip-flopping between Spanish and English and I only catch a few words here and there. Watching Rhys carry on, just passing the time with these charming old guys is engrossing, he is polite and kind. The woman calls out to Rhys and he goes to collect our coffees. The pastelito is delicious, flaky pastry filled with sweet cream cheese and guava, the coffee a perfect pick me up, just the way I like it; strong espresso, black with a cube of raw sugar. I stir it up and toss it back in one shot as is my coffee ritual. Rhys practically chokes as he sips from his cup.

"Did you not like it?" He questions, clearing his throat.

"It was perfect," I offer with a smile. "I don't really care for coffee, it is just a means to an end, really. That is why I like espresso, straight and to the point." I can't help but grin, taking the last bite of my pastelito.

"So, how is Kylie?" Straight and to the point. I lock him down and wait for him to offer an explanation. I lose a little nerve as each second crawls by, reminding me that it really is none of my business. He just smiles, holding the demitasse cup to his lips, eyeing me with humor, knowing that he is torturing me. He tosses his coffee back and puts his hands together in thought, fingers pulling at his full lips, deciding upon an answer. Slowly he lowers his hands to the table, covering mine. A jolt of current runs up my arms, traveling through my body at the speed of sound. His eyes are deep and clear.

"Kylie is fine. We were going over last minute details for the wedding." His smile is disturbed while he mulls his own answer. I don't say anything, waiting for him to offer some clarification, but he offers none. He takes my hands and leads me back towards the car. What business was it of mine? I had no right, even though I do care, more deeply than I want to. As we settle into the car, Rhys slides on his round tortoise shell sunglasses with a dazzling smile directed only at me, he flips on the radio and pulls out into traffic. The Buena Vista Social Club plays us out of downtown Miami, mimicking the beat of the city around us.

Chapter 6

We cruise along the Rickenbacker Causeway, surrounded by calm, crystal blue seas and cars that cost more than my apartment. The air is warm and the smell of the sea fills my nostrils. The road is perched precariously above the shallow waters, while supercars and super tramps cruise back and forth from one of the richest areas in all of Southern Florida, Key Biscayne. The village is quaint and charming. The same cannot be said about houses, each one bigger than the last, hiding behind manned gates and ten-foot privacy walls. The drive stretches and the houses become fewer and more massive, the narrow strip of land swallowed by sprawling gardens and manicured pool patios. A boat in every slip.

Rhys pulls into a curved drive that leads to an ornate wrought iron gate, adorned with fleur-de- lis. He punches a code into a post shrouded by oversized bushes and the gate swings open, slowly revealing the decadence that lies beyond. The drive is long and lined by tall sweeping palms, swaying in welcome, perfectly manicured grass expanses stretch to the water on both sides of the property. The house, if it can be called that, is imposing and commanding. Graceful archways anchor a wraparound portico, lending an air of

Mediterranean charm. The house glitters against the clear blue waters, whitewashed stucco and dark wood accents stand out against the tropical backdrop. Rhys is waiting, his grin wide and contagious, as he watches me take it all in.

"This is my family's house. The wedding will be here tomorrow. I thought you would want to see how it is all coming together. Please," he offers his hand, gently pulling me from the car.

Electricity flows between us, sending my pulse racing. The gentle tug of his hand pulls at my deepest recesses. Rhys leads me through the heavy front door, holding my hand possessively, and into a glimmering marble entrance hall, a vast chasm around which the rest of the house seems to radiate. The marble is cold and colorless, but the dark wood is warm and carries its age with grace. Museum quality art adorns the walls on either side, an impressive collection that even an art novice such as myself would easily recognize. Colorful watercolors of blooming hills, lazy rivers, busy Paris streets and the beautiful sun soaked south of France. Monet is well represented. I remind myself to return to these paintings for a closer look, their beauty so powerful, every brush stroke draws you deeper. Rhys leads me through to the inner atrium, flanked on either side by grand curved staircases leading to a dramatic balcony and more, fine, collectible artwork. It is like nothing I have ever seen, I can only compare it to the inside of Tara, expecting a weeping woman to come sweeping down the staircase at any moment. The grandeur is more than I can comprehend. He pushes open a pair of heavy, intricately carved wooden doors, revealing a buzzing scene.

"This is the ballroom where dinner will be served and then dancing." He scans the room, checking each and every employee that is hard at work preparing every little detail for the impending celebration. Round tables are being set up all around the perimeter of the room, while a group of women flutter about the swaths of blush colored organza and silk, creating a dreamy canopy above what will surely be the dance floor. At the back of the room a pair of French doors leads to a wide open patio overlooking a large lawn of perfect emerald green grass.

I hear a faint melody, familiar, floating about. I reach into my hidden little pocket to find my phone ringing. I almost forgot it was on me, the damn thing hasn't gone off in days. I reluctantly remove my hand from his and excuse myself to take the call. I look down at my phone to see an unfamiliar number, but it's from my home area code so I answer.

"This is Sophie."

"Where are you?" The voice is smooth and controlled, yet the current that flows beneath is pulsating with frustration. "I drove all this way to see you." Honey laced with poison.

"You shouldn't have because I told you to leave me alone." My pulse breaks into a sprint.

"I think we both know you didn't mean that, you never do. Now, where are you?" His tone is clipped and icy, losing patience.

"It is none of your business." Barely able to bite back the frustration, hearing his controlled even breathing, undercut by his smug assumption that he can walk in and out of my life whenever he feels the urge. My toe taps on the stone patio, nervous energy and anxiety building with every measured breath. It has been over a month since he contacted me last, I had hoped it would be the last time.

"Oh, wait," a threatening pause sends my pulse racing, "here we are, an invitation to Olivia's wedding, so you are in Miami, huh? Oh, and look a copy of your itinerary. Good, so I will see you at the airport."

"Are you in my house?" I can feel the bile rising in my throat, thinking about him moving through my home, the home we used to share.

"*Your* house? This is *our* house. Why didn't you tell me you were going out of town? I can only assume it is because you knew that I would not approve."

"I don't care what you think. What I do and where I go is none of your business anymore. I do not want to see you. I want you to leave me alone. Please leave your key and get out of my house, and stay out of my life!" Tears threaten to spill over, standing at the edge of reason.

"You are very bold when you are so far away. I wonder if your resolve will be equal when you are in my arms. I know how to make you agreeable, Sophie, and I am sure I can help you to see things my way. I will see you at the airport on Sunday." The last statement a demand before he cuts me off and the line goes dead. I turn the ringer off and shove the phone into my pocket, unwilling to be caught off guard again. I am left shaking and angry, momentarily unaware of my surroundings, and my uncomfortable company.

"Sophie?" Rhys' soft, cautious voice a stark contrast to the bile-filled conversation my ears just endured. I wipe the singular proof of my pain away from my cheek and turn to him with an overzealous smile. "Are you alright?" He moves a step closer, slowly, careful not to startle.

"I'm fine." Pushing back anxiety and worry, I paint myself cheerful and change the subject. Unwilling to let the momentary distraction ruin my time with Rhys, I hook my arm into the crook of his elbow and ask him to finish showing me the grounds. A beautiful distraction is surely the best remedy to a horrible ex-boyfriend.

Rhys' wheels are turning, clearly pondering

what he had just overheard. His face is set in a gracious, practiced smile, that does not meet his eyes. His eyes are hard, shadowed by a furrowed brow. He takes my hand in his and tightens his grip as we follow the stone patio that circles the back of the house. It all leads to a small circular stone portico and then splits into two paths, one leading to a second level, surely offering amazing vistas of sunsets and the incoming cruise ships. The second leading down a short pathway to a sunken patio boasting a half moon infinity pool, the edge perched over the seawall, melting into the surrounding azure waters. Directly in front of the portico is a perfectly laid stone path that winds through a ghostly veil of overgrown weeping willows and heavily blossomed wisteria, leading to a perfect spot overlooking the water, where two men are hard at work putting the finishing touches on the arbor Olivia and Matthew will stand beneath.

The chairs are being set up in a half moon formation around the arbor, mirroring the shape of the pool and the shoreline, lending a beautiful fluid curve to the whole scene. Rhys' hand is possessive around mine, leading me, demanding I follow. The caress of his finger against the inside of my hand is calming and erotic. The rest of my body hums, wishing the caress went beyond my lucky, lucky palm. He stops and sighs before turning me to him, placing his hand on the small of my back, anchoring me in his sights.

"Please forgive me for asking, Sophie, but is everything alright? You seem upset. Is there anything you need?"

"Everything is fine." I look into his eyes and he strips away any falsehood I had hoped to offer. The truth is bubbling to the surface and I cannot stop its flow, he has cast a spell. I sigh in resignation and launch into the highly edited version of events. "That was my ex. He likes to throw his weight around. All bark and no bite."

Rhys' face is impassive as he listens to me divulge information I really don't want to share. I try and slither from his grip, uncomfortable talking about the past with Mr. Right Now, but he refuses to let me back away, his palm gently locking me in his sights. He patiently waits for me to open up, his eyes never leaving mine.

"I guess I was hoping that this week would wipe it all away, that I could hide for a while. That maybe I could forget about it, reinvent myself, be somebody else."

"How is that working for you?"

"Life has a funny way of forcing you to be who you are."

"And who are you?"

"An idiot."

"I don't think so. You are no idiot, Sophie."

"I didn't protect myself. I knew better, but I

91

still let the wolf in the house."

"And now you will know better."

"Will I?" Looking into his crystal clear eyes, I am not sure. With this wolf I will surely make a host of mistakes.

"We live and learn, Sophie. You of all people know that. Don't let someone else's weakness become your downfall. You are too special, too strong." He brushes a curl away from my forehead with his finger, tucking it behind my ear, lingering about my lobe. I am completely floored, his words floating around me like smoke, dissipating into thin air. I want to grab them and shove them in my pocket, take them with me wherever I go. Yet in a blink they are carried away, the proof evaporated.

"I don't always feel strong."

"You are strong," he interrupts, his voice ripe with frustration and something that sounds like concern. "Look at you. On your own, you are strong and smart and very tempting. Any man who would make you second guess yourself is no man at all. Excuse me if I have overstepped, you need someone who knows what you need, someone to show you some respect." The words clearly do not relay the true weight of his feelings about what he thinks he heard. He is clipped, controlled, but unsatisfied.

"Like a friend?" I poke him with my words.

He seems inclined towards a speech when a tall, thin young man appears in the doorway behind us, clearing his throat to announce his presence. He is younger than Rhys with ginger hair and a heavy swath of freckles across his pink face, but his eyes are familiar, warm green like a rolling Irish hill. He grins at me, confident and crooked. Rhys turns his eyes to him and scowls, effectively erasing the young man's impish grin. Before I know what has happened, they are in a playful embrace, slapping one another on the back, frantically shaking one another's hands.

"Sophie, this is my cousin Charlie. He is here from Ireland, he just finished school and has come to work for me this summer." He turns to Charlie with the look of a proud older brother "Isn't that right, Charlie?" This is the first I have seen Rhys be so familiar and warm with anyone other than Matthew. I had come to consider him a man unto himself, an island. Now, to see him with family is endearing and revealing.

"Sophie, if you will excuse me, I just need to speak with Charlie. Please, feel free to look around, I won't be but a moment."

I watch the men finish the arbor as the gardeners begin to prune bushes for tomorrow's event. Large urns filled with wisteria and lacy tropical foliage anchor each row of chairs, as the aisle is marked out and cleared. I find myself pacing, wearing a path in the stone, uneasy being away from Rhys. I decide to head inside and look around while I wait.

"Quick and clean, Charlie."

"Not a problem, Cousin. If there is nothing else, I will make the call for the plane and we should be on our way within a couple of hours." I peek around the corner of Rhys' large office door to hear him wrap up his conversation with Charlie. He nods at me then quickly turns to dismiss Charlie.

"Keep in touch."

"You can count on me." He nods at me, tipping his newsboy cap like a proper Irish rogue, his freckled cheeks aflame as he leaves us. "Lass." The heels of his shoes click on the cold marble floors and echo through the vast foyer.

Rhys' office is warm and cozy and not what I would expect in such an ornately decorated home. The desk is heavy old wood, clearly well worn. The polish dulled by years of hard work, daily frustrations scar the surface. Every wall is covered in floor to ceiling bookshelves, packed with cloth covered volumes, leather bound classics and rows and rows of biographies, broken up only by two large sunny bay windows. Were it not for the windows, the room would be much darker and heavier. Looking closer I notice an entire wall dedicated to megalomaniacs, tycoons, billionaires, leaders of men and builders of empires, a wall of ego unparalleled. The thought of Rhys among those men, powerful and cunning, taking what he wants, never being satisfied, rattles my mind. I turn to find him, settled in his overly large, leather chair, casually reclined, fingers laced, the picture of intimidation and authority. Looking like he would fit comfortably among the shelves, nestled between the biographies of John D. Rockefeller and Howard Hughes. He brushes his fingers against his lips, watching my every move, his eyes probing. I tear my eyes away, the threat of spontaneous combustion looming heavily.

His shelves are hung with pennants from his favorite teams, trophies from his own triumphs, worn rugby balls, framed jerseys and other random male paraphernalia. A window into his mind, these must be things that make him feel comfortable, things that are important to him. The thought makes me want to explore, discover more, find out what makes him tick. I rake the shelves, up and down filing away interesting titles and books we have in common when I cannot help but stop and stare.

On a shelf high above Rhys' chair, behind his big beautiful desk, a beautiful woman commands my attention. She would command anyone's attention. Even from way down here I can tell that she is fierce; long, shiny golden hair, dazzling smile and a body that would make a Victoria's Secret model sick with envy. She is not alone in the picture, but she is so captivating that she is all you can see. Searching the picture for other beautiful people I notice the man holding her, a strong arm around her tiny waist, casually claiming ownership. His demeanor is easy, his beauty a match to hers in every way. He smiles crookedly at the camera, while her eyes are locked on him. They are perfectly suited to one another, love evident. I swallow so loudly I'm sure everyone in the house can hear it as I try and peel my eyes away from the photograph of Rhys and the most beautiful woman I have ever seen.

His eyes follow mine to the impossibly perfect photograph. For a moment he mulls the photo before returning his attention to me, the crooked smile firmly in place, disarming and distracting. He stands from his chair and moves around the desk, closing the gap between us, charging the air. He comes to stand in front of me, casually leaning against his desk, his form still easily looming over my meager frame. Relaxed and loose, he captivates my every thought. I look down at his powerful legs casually crossed at the ankle. A kick of my toe and I could move between those strong thighs, invite myself into his space and let him burn me up from the inside. Just a step and I would be in, so close I could rest my palms on his rock hard thighs, run my hands over the fine fabric of his slacks, warm him with my fingers. All I have to do is take a step forward, and into his arms. His scent fills the room, spread by a sudden breeze pushing through the large windows and my mind goes blank. I catch myself from falling into his eyes and pull back from the brink. Realizing that I am in grave danger of willfully jumping down a rabbit hole that I may never find my way back from, I still. It is easy to see why so many women are drawn to him, he can be so disarming. I cannot explain what is happening, or how I got here. I just know I want to be here.

Rhys is just the best man, a beautiful man, but just a man. I have been with boys but never with a man. A man with money to burn, a man who exists in a different sphere than my humble self. I would be remiss if I failed to remind myself of that fact. He is someone I would never know if it weren't for this wedding, someone who would surely never be interested in knowing me. And now he stands before me with his dazzling smile lit up just for me, his eyes alight with humor as he watches me overanalyze and roll it all over in my head. The corner of his mouth twitches and curls like a Cheshire cat, he winks and wrinkles his nose.

The buzz of my phone startles me, pulsating relentlessly against my leg, pestering like a begging dog. I try to ignore the unwanted interruption and focus on Rhys but to no avail. Reaching into my pocket I pensively remove my angry vibrating phone, looking down on a desperate text message. Angry Caps shout through the screen. A fog sets over my eyes as I stare. Words of hate jump out at me, slapping me, begging me to lose control, to reveal my pain. Rhys' strong hand extends in want of my phone. I look into his eyes and he takes it from my trembling hand as I sink into the chair before him. Casually he pops out the battery and sets the two pieces of angry technology on the desk, sliding them behind him and out of sight. His steely gaze intimidates, but a slight smile puts me oddly at ease.

"I'm going to need you to focus on me and in return I promise you my undivided attention." He never looks away. His focus is precision, sharp and unyielding. He stands and casually saunters behind his desk before taking a seat in his oversized throne of industry. He turns towards me, fingers steepled before his cupids bow. He is clearly in negotiating mode, he looks like a shark behind his oversized desk, powerful, distinguished, and not to be crossed. A shiver runs down my spine watching him in his seat of power, commanding, intimidating and sexy as hell.

"Sophie, I may have been wrong about us." He pauses with a thought that hangs from his lips. "Olivia thinks we should date."

"I got that. Subtlety is not her strong suit."

"No, well," he chuckles, leaning back in his chair. "I am not interested in dating." Why do I feel like he is about to let me down easy? What a presumptuous ass. I gird myself for a battle, readying my tongue to lash back. "I would like to spend the night with you, Sophie. I just cannot offer you any more than that." His words hit me like a Mack truck, knocking the wind from my chest and the retort straight from my mouth. I should be appalled, insulted, affronted at the very least. I let his words settle, heavy and low in my belly, and they don't sting as they should. "You need a man to properly navigate those curves."

His dishonorable intentions tickle my ears and the pleasant flutter in my belly grows into a hungry growl. I narrow my eyes on his wicked grin and nod. Yes, I could use a good fuck. And that is what I wanted, right? Who would it hurt? I would get what I want from someone who seems rather sure he has what I need. A quick war rages in my mind, what to do? Do I allow myself to be lured into his one night web? Should I be insulted and refuse, or agree, and go against my very nature. He is beautiful, and rich, with a reputation like a stud horse. Who am I to say no? I collect my thoughts, and slowly craft my response, leaving him to wait.

"And you think you're up to the job?"

"Oh, I know it." His eyes twinkle with ego. "Aren't you curious?" Oh my, his words are a baptism in sin, delicious, dark and twisted sin. "It is clear to me that you are worth the risk."

"What happened to being just friends? I

thought that is what you wanted." I reply before my mind can talk me out of it.

"I do want to be your friend. I also want other things. I cannot stop thinking about what's hiding under that dowdy little dress," an insult and proposition in the same breath. His smoldering glare burns down my defenses and I am ripe for the taking, completely unguarded and unprotected. "I am not feeling very friendly right now. I want to taste you, Sophie. I cannot think about anything else. I will kiss every inch of you until you whimper and beg." My heart speeds up to Mach one. My mouth is dry, but my pussy is sopping wet. "But I just want to be clear about what this is. What it will be. If we can both agree, then we can have a bit of fun and nobody gets hurt."

"And what of your rule?" I prod. He leans forward, whispering across the desk as if sharing some secret.

"Breaking the rules is part of the fun, Sophie."

"I could use a bit of fun." Which is a massive understatement, as reflected in my now damp panties. God knows the last time a man touched me in a gentle way is far beyond the reach of my memory. The thought of his deft hands traveling over my skin, his hard body pressed against mine. There are a million reasons to say no. I don't know this man. I am not generally so forward or casual about sex. But one good reason shines above all,

100

screaming, YES, to the heavens. I want to. With every fiber of my being, every inch of my skin, I want it. Ramifications be damned. I will be gone before we get too close, I won't allow myself to get hurt. "What exactly are you suggesting?" His eyes light up and he leans forwards, resting his elbows on the desk, a wide grin pulling at his perfectly full lips.

"You just agree to spend the night with me and leave the rest up to me." He leans back again, pleased with himself, crossing his legs. "I think that's what I need. You definitely need it." I am tripped up by his casual declaration that all I have to do is show up, like a prop. Immediately a chip of doubt erodes on my shoulder. What am I getting myself into?

"Leave it all up to you?" The first chill of warning trickles down my spine, like ice water, cooling the fire he just lit. I will not relinquish control to anyone, much less a man I have just met. I will never make that mistake again.

"I will have my way with you, Sophie. You just let me take care of you, and trust that I know what you need. I know what I like, Sophie. Do you?" I suppose I should steel myself for more of these probing, personal questions, but it suddenly feels invasive. How dare he insinuate that I don't know what I like. Do I know what I like? I know I don't like to be used. I know I don't like to be hit. I know

101

I have never been able to explore what I like because I have always been so hell bent on pleasing someone else. So deathly afraid to recognize, or put into words the things that my body calls for deep in my dreams, for fear of ridicule and shame. And with that thought I know I will do it. I know that I will be safe, he can't hurt me, I won't let him.

"I want you, and I promise I will make you forget all about him. Trust me, give yourself to me, we would be amazing together, I can feel it." I pick my jaw up off the ground before I can form a solid thought. Give yourself to me? What is this an old Dracula movie?

"So, I am to be added to your collection?"

"No, I don't believe that you belong in a collection, Sophie. You are a treasure unto yourself, unparalleled." A giggle escapes my throat before I can catch it. Such a seedy proposal crossing sweet lips is surely an anomaly. He frowns and waits for an explanation.

"You make it sound like I am giving you some sort of gift. I don't know that I can give myself to you, to anyone." The crack in my voice betrays the calm I try to exude. Control is something I have fought tooth and nail for recently. The thought of handing myself over makes my blood run cold. Yet, in his eyes, the way he looks at me, I want to believe that I can handle this. There is nothing resembling calm running through my body. My mind breaks into a sprint, unsure of my capacity to trust. But Rhys' intense glare grips me and demands an answer. I am exasperated, insulted, intrigued. Frightened and exhilarated. It is a heady cocktail of conflict, wanting to be with him so badly I can almost feel his hands skating across my skin and being frightened by the prospect of what he has in mind.

"You are a gift, Sophie. I cannot wait to watch you come undone. I cannot wait until you give yourself to me. And you will, because deep down, you want to. It is written all over your body." He licks his bottom lip and it rings deep in my belly. "I thought you may react this way, which makes the prospect all the more delectable. Don't say a word. Let me escort you to the dinner tonight and we will see what happens."

"Dinner?" Why is my mind so many beats behind? Catch up!

"Yes, dinner. We all need to eat." He winks and his lopsided, panty busting grin leaves me no choice. I would gladly let him to take me anywhere, no questions and no clothing necessary. He is like a controlled substance, slowly building in my veins, a lingering high that keeps my mind high above reality. The pain that this man must cause will surely be exquisite, the implied ecstasy worth every moment of impending agony.

Chapter 7

We arrive back at the hotel just as the sky begins to blush, the sun going down, hovering on her horizon, teasing the edges of the day. The elevator ride is quiet and charged, like two teenagers shy and anxious, anticipation stretched between us, quieting the verbal back and forth. Rhys is careful not to touch me, his hands firmly in his pockets. He just grins and winks as the car comes to rest on the sixteenth floor. I turn to him before I exit the elevator. Holding the door open he backs me against the wall and leans in. Flecks of gold sparkle in his eyes, captivating my attention, his breathing is even and controlled, his face soft.

"I will be down in two hours to collect you. Think about it." He softly brushes a rogue curl from my face, the back of his fingers leaving a trail of heat across my cheek. He pulls his arm back and retreats into the elevator, the doors closing on his crooked smile and my frozen form. How could I not think about it, his tongue and lips all over my body? My aching skin, begging for his attention, whimpering, begging, it is all I can think about.

A cold shower, a good all over buffing, and I am alert and excited, yet completely unprepared. Rhys' mysterious draconian offer swims through the muck that has mired my mind for longer than I can remember. His offer rings on high, louder than any other thought in my head. The echoes of his silky voice drown out my questions and doubt. I rub at my scalp with a fluffy white towel when I hear a knock on the door. My heart takes off and I search for a clock. How long was I in the shower?

"Sophie, are you here?" Olivia's voice crosses the door as she knocks again. I let her in and she makes herself comfortable on the bed, watching me towel my hair and lay out my clothing for the evening.

"Sophie, I am so sorry we haven't had more time together. I miss you." A pout on her full lips makes me grin. Her pout is potent and practically irresistible.

"Liv, it is fine. I have kept busy. I am really sorry for ducking out on the festivities last night. It was getting a little too hot in there."

"Oh. Please. I'm sure it got much worse after I left. Fortunately, Matthew showed up and swept me away. Some of those girls are wild, to say the least, fuzzy boundaries and all that sort of stuff." She waves her hand about, dismissing the 'stuff' like yesterday's news. My curiosity is peaked, what is the 'stuff'?

"I tried texting you after we picked up my parents. Where have you been all day?" I flash back to my phone in pieces on Rhys' desk. Shit!

"I was with Rhys." I peek out from under the towel to read a shocked face.

"What?"

"Is that so strange?" It stings to hear my own doubt reflected back through her shock. Olivia bounds from the bed and has her arms around me in a moment, pulling me into a hug.

"Oh, sweetie, it's not. It's just that Matthew said there was some emergency that took him from the bachelor party. He was supposed to go back to New York last night. I thought he would be gone until tomorrow."

"Well, he was here last night." Liv releases me and fiddles with my party clothes, fluffing the skirt and smoothing the shiny taffeta. I chose the outfit in her honor, a pale green taffeta skirt with a high waist and pockets (a must) and a tiny white tank. I know how much she always wants to glam me up. 'Put on a party dress and slap some makeup on that face girl, we are going out!' is a tag line she should trademark.

"I know he has been working on something big, but Matthew said that it is falling apart. He is always working." I reflect back on the powerful man surrounded by talking heads, watching me like prey from his leather throne in the Admirals Lounge.

"Maybe it is resolved." I can feel unanswered questions crawling up my back, tapping my shoulder, prying at Pandora's box of insecurities and self-doubt.

106

"Maybe. But, who cares. What is going on between you two?" Her eyes shine with anticipation, hungry for details.

"I don't know. I mean, nothing. We talked for a long time, and he slept here." I look to her for insight, but she offers none, hanging on my words waiting for a juicy tidbit to slip out. I hold back the details she so desperately wants. "I woke up this morning and he was gone, but he left me this note." I toss the note into her lap and walk into the bathroom. "He took me for Cuban coffee and pastries this morning and then to his family's house to see all the wedding stuff. Olivia it is so beautiful." Seeking a reaction and still getting none, I continue. "Then he said he wanted to spend the night with me and offered to escort me to dinner tonight."

"Huh?" Her face twists in question. Little does she know the true extent of his proposal, or of my almost complete surrender.

"Yeah, huh? He actually said '*give yourself to me*!' Can you believe that?" It is clear by her avoidance and wide eyes that she knows exactly what he means. But she shies away, a conspicuous non- reaction on her face.

"He must like you," her answer so matter of fact yet, childish and unsatisfying. It's clear that she is holding back, there has to be more. I know he wants me, he said it plain as day, but what is he expecting?

"Liv, tell me what I am getting myself into." Reluctantly, she takes a seat next to me on the bed. She grabs my hands and squeezes before releasing a long, heavy sigh. The struggle in her eyes is evident. I know she wants to protect me, not let me wander into the dragon's den. And men like that don't just randomly take interest in women completely against type. It is not in the nature of man to stray from what he knows and craves. I just hope he doesn't eat me for dinner.

"Powerful men like simple women, Sophie, receptive to their whims, willing and eager to do anything. Someone who won't complicate their lives. Rhys is no different. Just don't get too attached and you will be fine."

"Is that how you and Matthew are, Liv." She smiles, shaking her head.

"All men have a type and Rhys is no exception. He usually has a beauty on his arm, I won't lie. But I have never seen him with the same girl twice, with one exception." Her emphasis hangs, mingling with Rhys' earlier confession. A confession I thought to be a gimmick or a ploy. "And he has been pseudo single as long as I have known him." He likes the type of girl that I am not, I am a good girl. He said it himself. Why do I suddenly feel like the butt of a bad joke?

"Pseudo single, what does that mean?" She

shrugs me off with a lofty wave of her perfectly manicured fingers.

"You know, single and playing the game, but totally unavailable."

"I don't know about this." The more she doesn't say, the more spooked I become. *Simple women*, this is not a phrase I am comfortable with, I am not simple, nor will I allow him to belittle me like that. I want this, but can I handle it? I am beginning to doubt my ability to keep up with him, to please him. Not to humiliate myself.

"Do you like him, Sophie?" What a simple question. He is gorgeous, clever, mysterious and rich. How could I not *like* him? Like is not the right word. I want him, deep in my soul and far in the back of my mind. I ache for him. No. Like is not the right word at all. She has volunteered so much, yet revealed nothing. I still have no idea what it really means, or what he really wants or expects from me. I could never *give myself* to anyone. I have never been that kind of girl. My soul stirs and twists, the effect that Rhys has over me could be very hard to resist. Already he flows in my blood. What has he given up? And what has driven him back to his mystery vice?

"It's one night, what could it hurt?" She turns to me with a bit of worry in her brow. "Just don't let things get awkward."

"What do you mean?"

109

"I mean, if you sleep with him tonight don't expect anything from him tomorrow. He can be cold like that. I have seen it. And although I love Rhys, I love you more and I don't want to see you get hurt." Running the straight iron down my hair, she pauses, and pins me with her gaze in the mirror. "And, not to sound selfish, but I don't want it to affect my wedding. I mean, it is my special day."

"I won't get hurt. I am a big girl, I can separate things. Besides, I'm only here for you, Liv. Whatever it is, it's temporary. I'm sure that he just wants to use me like a rag doll, not that I am wholly opposed to the idea, but still. He is an addictive man, I have barely spent any time with him and already he is under my skin, and in my head. I swear sometimes he can see right through me. He is dangerous, I can tell."

"Sophie, this could be good for you, let loose for a change, take a risk. Don't deny yourself the opportunity to do something new, out of fear. You can't use your parents as an excuse forever. You have to live your life. Live it, don't just endure it, you deserve so much more than you have allowed yourself." I know that she is right. I know that I should let loose, follow my instincts, and stop being scared of my own shadow. Stop being afraid of what could happen.

Unsatisfied and frustrated by the lack of illumination, I change the subject, asking about last

110

minute wedding prep. It does the trick and we relax back into old friend skin easily.

She helps me get ready, like a big sister coaching the little on the expectations of a first date. I feel like a little girl, full of butterflies and fear. But this is no ordinary dinner date. I want to probe her about his pseudo single past, the beauty in the picture perhaps, but think better of it. All he has shown of himself seems in complete contrast to the whisperings of the women around him. I chose to let him reveal himself. Listening to them, one would surmise that Rhys was a sexual predator. One they would willingly surrender to, some of them over and over again. And he is coming for you! I push the fear aside and resolve to just be. I think back on that last night in my room and his musings on first impressions. Yes. I will allow him to make his own impression upon me. And with that, I banish the chatter and suspicions to the furthest dark room in the back of my mind and lock the door. Olivia finishes putting the final touches on my hair and pinches my cheeks before she is gone and I am left alone with the sound of my pounding heart, and a beautiful stranger in the mirror.

I smooth my full skirt, fluff my breasts and check my reflection. If I hadn't watched the transformation I wouldn't believe that was me staring back from the mirror. My hair is sleek, straightened by Liv, an asymmetrical curtain, teasing my bare shoulders. Make-up light and natural, an argument hard fought and won. I look down at my legs to my poor, poor feet, in sky-high, nude Loubitons. Olivia insisted that I borrow them. They are spectacular, and make the outfit, but whether or not I will be able to walk anywhere is another issue. I twist and turn in the mirror, admiring the sexy woman I see before me, wondering where she has been all my life, when a knock at the door bowls me over. My pulse breaks from the gate at full speed and I have to remind myself to breath.

He stands before me, one perfect gardenia blossom rolling between his fingers, my favorite flower. The scent swirls around us both, twisting and tightening, pulling us together. He shines in his pale, crisp shirt and slacks, like an angel, freshly fallen. His grin sideways and wicked betrays that devil within. His eyes wash over me, heating every inch of exposed flesh, taking in the sight of the stranger from the mirror. Voices in the hallway distract us both as Melissa and Kylie are also set out for dinner. His smile straightens as he steps forward, casually closing the door behind him with a tap of his foot, while they crane their necks for one last peek. I am sure the sighting will not go unnoticed.

"You look beautiful, Sophie." His voice is hungry and low, bringing me back to the moment, back to him. He brushes my hair back and tucks the gardenia behind my ear before closing his eyes and taking a deep breath from the flower. I catch myself closing my eyes along with him, letting his scent flood my nostrils, citrus and musk and gardenia. They complement each other nicely, strong and soft, heavenly and earthly. I feel his hand leave my hair before I open my eyes. His grin turned to amusement.

"We are quite a pair," he says, spinning me around to the mirror, he stands behind me with his hands resting on my bare shoulders. I think I may melt from the casual contact, when I see what he sees. His pale green button down linen shirt mirrors the shade of my skirt. I can't help but smile and reflect back on the couples Olivia and I used to see at the country club we worked at when we were young. They would match their golf outfits, shoes, club covers, visors and all, even the pom-poms on their socks. We would call them "Biff and Buffy" collectively, and always promised to never let one another fall into such a situation. At this point I would gladly don a silly visor and pom-pom socks if it meant I could remain one half of the pair I see reflected back at me.

The woman in the mirror is put together, confident and lovely under the warm gaze of such a potent masculine man. His hands rest gently on my shoulders, while the rest of my body tightens and

113

twists, humming with anticipation. He is calm and cool, smiling at me through the mirror. His thumbs caress the base of my neck before he slowly slides his warm hands down the length of my arms, leaving a telling trail of goose bumps. A naughty grin arises on his face and he swats my behind, stepping away from the mirror and towards the mini bar.

"Let's have a toast, shall we?" Not waiting for an answer, he pulls a bottle of white wine from the mini bar. The vibration from his gentle tap rolls through me in waves. He hands me a glass and holds his aloft, humor bubbling at the surface of his carefully manicured façade. He flashes a wolfish grin. "Here is to breaking the rules," I scoff; he grins and clinks my glass. The words echo in my head. The wine does little to cool the fire that is smoldering deep within me. Every trivial thing that the man does chips away at the walls I have built. Walls I prefer to hide behind. I like to keep a comfortable distance, but he inches closer to me with every breath. Can I do this? Do I want to do this? YES!

***

Dinner is held in the hotels steakhouse, and Matthew's father has reserved the wine cellar for the celebration. The dinner is intimate, hosting only

114

the wedding party and parents of the bride and groom. I am on a march to the unknown as Rhys holds my hand and leads the way. He draws circles on my palm with his finger and I loosen and relax under his gentle coaxing. Thoughts of Melissa, gossip, and my earlier phone call fall away. He makes me feel better, happier.

The wine cellar is cool, but the warm wood and priceless bottles make up for it. A long table anchors the room with ornately carved wooden chairs. Delicate white linen covers the table dotted with white votive candles that warm the slightly stagnant air. Everyone is moving about the room, greeting one another, buzzing about the coming event. When we cross over the threshold I swear you could hear a pin drop, a brief moment that was instantly swallowed by zealous greetings and the first of too many toasts.

Rhys' grip tightens around my hand as we make our way around the room, sending my pulse racing. He introduces me to Matthew's groomsmen, Mark, Matthew's younger brother and Wes, who looks as out of place as I feel. And I am not wrong. He is from a small farming community in New Zealand, but made it all the way to St. Andrews to play rugby. He is witty and brash, startlingly masculine and comfortably adrift in this sea of money. As I look around the room, I can't help but think that if things had happened differently Wes would have been the type of guy I would connect with here. Bawdy, beer drinking, foul mouthed and fun. Not worried about appearance or net worth.

I glance at Rhys while he talks with Matthews' father. I could never fathom a man like him being interested in someone like me, he has traveled the world. I've hardly been away from my home town. He is highly educated, well-mannered and refined. I would not use those words to describe myself, even in my wildest dreams. Just as the thought invades, he turns his soft eyes on me and smiles. Completely wiping away whatever was in my thoughts just the moment earlier. The effect he has on me grows with every circle of his fingertip, erasing everything but him and his touch. A quiet sigh escapes my lips and he gently squeezes my hand. I notice Olivia's father giving me the stink eye from across the room. I reluctantly reclaim my hand from Rhys and gesture towards Olivia's parents. He nods mid-sentence and releases me.

"Hi, Mr. J."

"Sophie," his tone is reproachful and parental, "what took you so long to get over here? You know better than to keep me waiting." His rosy cheeks and sparkling blue eyes betray his stern greeting. He rises to give me a quick hug and commands me to sit. His short stature in no way a reflection upon his character, he is a giant of a man. He always expected the best, not only from his children, but from all who crossed into his home, and if you were not keeping up he would surely let you know. Never one to mince words, he always tells it straight, even if it hurts. But he does it with love.

"We haven't seen you in quite a while, Ms. Noelle. What do you think about this wedding? Quite the extravaganza wouldn't you say? Don't get me wrong, Soph, I am not complaining. Lord knows I wanted my girl to find someone who could take care of her, and my little Liv certainly did well for herself, but this is some big time money." He lifts his empty glass and shakes it at the waiter.

"I went out to Key Biscayne today and saw the house. It is amazing! I know Olivia and Marie are going to love it. Where is Marie anyway?"

"She is outside, pretending not to smoke. Why don't you go say hello and drag her ass back in here." He turns and launches into a conversation with Mark about the superiority of American Football over "soccer" he mocks with finger quotes.

I find Marie, her slight frame easily hidden behind a tall trellis overgrown with bougainvillea, smoking her cigarette like a rebellious teenager. Ron hates smoking and never lets a chance go by to tell her so, but she continues, much to his dismay. I peek around the flowers and she exhales a slowly swirling plume of smoke before she grins ear to ear and hugs me, a warm motherly hug.

"I didn't want to startle you, or for you to think

117

that Ron was sneaking up on you."

"The man doesn't have a subtle bone in his body, Sophie, you know that. He would never sneak up on someone. And deny himself the opportunity to announce his arrival? No, he doesn't sneak. But I do know that he sent you." Her smile is so warm. She straightens the gardenia blossom behind my ear and scans my outfit for approval. Like mother, like daughter. "You look beautiful, Sophie. You girls are both so grown up." She chokes just briefly on the last word and I can see her eyes glisten in the moonlight.

"Oh no, none of that," I put my arm around her shoulder we head back in. "It is way too early for tears and if you cry I will cry." I turn to her and grasp her shoulders. "Let's get a drink, and no crying, not yet." I wink, she laughs and the tears are on hold. When we walk into the cellar most have taken their seats. Olivia and Matthew share the head of the table with his parents on one side and Liv's dad on the other, frantically gesturing towards Margie to join him.   Momentarily flooded with panic, not sure where I belong, I search the room and find Rhys' soft eyes, calling to me. He winks and pulls out my chair, tipping his taut jaw at me, inviting me to his side. The panic wanes with every step, replaced by hidden glee at his focused attention. He watches my every step as I round the long table, and so does Melissa, her eyes burning a hole in my back. I see Rhys turn his eyes from me to her and they instantly burn with something far more dangerous. His face is like stone and he radiates discontent, but it only seems to affect Melissa, she drops her eyes and turns away. Nobody takes notice of their exchange, but me, and I am shocked by his control over her and his immediate shift in demeanor. He stands and pulls out my chair. In the very next moment I take my seat next to him and he turns that sexy crooked smile on me, every ounce of anger drained away in an instant.

He puts his warm hand on my bare leg and fireworks ignite over my skin, leaving a delicate pink flush for all to see. My body hums next to him, on heightened alert. All my senses are aware of him, acutely tuned in to his every movement, every touch. All through the toasts and friendly banter his hand remains, lending a gentle squeeze every once in a while to renew the pale flush he seems to enjoy across my heated flesh. Waiters begin to file into the room with platters. Petit filets and gargantuan rib-eyes move around the table, finding their homes. Not surprising that the two largest steaks are set in front of Mark and Wes. Their eyes bulge like two hungry bears and they compare the girth of their respective slabs of beef. Matthew's father watches the boys and shakes his head before whispering something to his wife, who looks horrified by the lack of manners coming from her youngest son. She takes a leisurely sip of her wine and shakes off her husband before replacing her practiced smile.

Matthew stands and says a few words of thanks, professes his love for Olivia, again, and commands us all to eat, drink and be merry. Waiters continue to file in and out of the cellar with shining silver trays lined with ice, crowned with raw oysters, stone crab claws and chilled shrimp. Another procession brings delicate bone china platters with roasted asparagus and truffle fingerling potatoes.

The gentile crowd digs in as best they can. Talk, eat, drink and repeat. I quietly cut into my filet and listen to the chatter around the table. I briefly catch Kylie and Melissa whispering about Wes, watching him like two hungry lionesses. I feel sorry for him for being on their late night menu, although I cannot imagine that he will protest. Kylie stares at her phone, intermittently tapping away as they giggle and plot until Melissa catches me watching their exchange. I cannot avert my eyes fast enough and she glares at me with ferocious white hot hate. Her eyes quickly drop the instant Rhys turns his attention to me. He brushes his fingers along the inside of my thigh, traveling dangerously close to the fire, I squirm and he stills, turning those emerald eyes on me.

"You are being very quiet, Sophie. Is everything alright?"

"Just watching, and listening." I love the way his tongue rolls around my name. I can't help but think of that tongue rolling over my body, smooth like silk teasing and torturing my skin, lighting me up, yes please. As if he could read my mind, he smiles that crooked smile.

"Oysters?" He gestures towards the silver tray and the beautifully flawed shells, perfectly shucked, revealing their plump offering of briny, sensual deliciousness. He places two of the shimmering shells on my plate and hands me an oyster fork. "Do you know how to eat oysters?" I answer before my mind has approved the response.

"Of course I do, I am not completely uncultured." He stifles a chuckle and squeezes my knee again.

"Very cute." I am more embarrassed than proud of my unintentional pun, but I play along and smile in return. I loosen an oyster with the little fork and tip the shell to my lips letting it slip down my throat. Rhys watches me with hungry eyes and then does the same. He licks his lips and hums his approval as I loosen another and slowly slide it into my mouth. I have always enjoyed the buzz I get from oysters. They make my mind and body hum, almost as loudly as Rhys does. The combination of the two may be more than I can handle, but I am willing to take my chances with both. He tosses back another and I do the same. It's a battle of the mollusks, a battle I wager we can both win. As I tip the last shell to my lips, I see Kylie's eyes grow wide as she stares at her phone. She tips her head to Rhys and hastily pushes her chair out, the heavy wood scraping horrendously on the cold stone floor. She makes her way around the table and whispers something to Rhys.

"Sophie, please excuse me." He pushes his chair out almost as quickly and is gone before I can reply. The work of the best man and maid of honor are never done apparently. I turn back to my plate and the table. No one seems to have taken note of their departure, with the exception of Melissa, who wears an expression of sheer glee as she sips from her wine glass. Ten minutes later Rhys quietly slides back into his chair. His mouth set in a hard line as he winks and takes a long sip of his wine. The air around him is tight, his fingers rigid around his wine glass.

"Everything OK?" I ask, wondering what sort of wedding business could elicit such tension.

"Yes, all is well. I'm sorry to have left you." He rests his free hand on my thigh and the fireworks reignite under my skin. His fingers splay across my bare flesh. The feeling is intense, as if the weight of the world is in his fingertips. His warmth spreads slowly across my skin, under my skin and I am rendered speechless by his hand sliding like silk across my flesh. He breeches the hem of my skirt, his fingers ringing in my blood, leaving trails of searing heat in their wake. The hint of a smile crosses his lips and he knows exactly what he is doing. His eyes twinkle in the candlelight as the edge fades from his face and my heart breaks into a sprint as my breath gets shallow and labored.

The last hour passes in a haze of oysters, toasts and strong, warm fingers stroking my thigh. His other hand wound behind me, fingers grazing my neck every so often, keeping me alert and humming. By the time we are waiting for the elevator my head is buzzing, my body is loose, and my tongue even looser. I turn to Rhys feeling confident and sexy thanks to his sensual attention and casual manner. Adrenaline surges through me, propelling me towards what I know I have wanted since I first set eyes on him, I want him wrapped around me. But he says nothing, he stays stiff and faces forward, not even offering me a sideways glance as I open myself up, offering what he asked for. He just stands there, and I freeze.

Chapter 8

The elevator doors slide open. Grabbing my hand with promising ferocity, Rhys tugs me inside. Before the doors close, he has me pinned against the glass, a hand easily wound around my wrists, trapping them behind my back, holding me still.

"You are very eager." He presses his hips into me and his lips cover mine in an instant, kissing me with a pent up passion. There's the electricity I was hoping for, coursing along the edge of my body, searing in my veins. He takes the opportunity to explore my mouth, his tongue dipping in, swirling and retreating. Over and over, his tongue swirls and retreats as he sucks on my bottom lip and plants soft kisses on my greedy mouth. His lips are rhythmic and hypnotic, I am utterly afloat in his arms as he kisses me fiercely again, crushing my lips harder this time before an erotically pained growl quietly rumbles through both of us and he abandons me, pressing the button, sending the elevator upward. Meeting my pulse beat for beat, floor for floor as we soar towards heaven, and my room. His chest falls with the release of a deep and ragged breath. He grabs my hand and draws painfully slow circles on my palm, twisting my flesh, charging every nerve.

"I am going to do things to you that will make you forget your name," he whispers, "but not tonight." And my heart stops. "I am sorry to say that something has come up that will not be ignored." He holds my hand, drawing circles on my palm as we walk silently to my door. He turns to me, hunger brimming in his eyes. His hands are in my hair twisting and pulling me towards him, bringing my lips to his, covering me with such gentle ease. He licks and moves to a rhythm he creates, our mouths a perfect union of twisted tongues and bitten lips. Everything falls away with each flick of his tongue, and there is nothing but the two of us, dancing in an inferno. I am lost in his hands while his mouth invades at such a leisurely pace. He rolls his hips against me, pressing me against the wall. My head swims in his arms and I think he is lost to me, too. He sighs as he kisses, softly yet, each kiss softer than the last until we are staring into one another's eyes, ablaze, and transfixed. I couldn't turn away if I wanted to. The building could be burning around us and I would not care, the hotel could crumble at our feet and there would be nothing but Rhys looking at me like that, like he wants to devour every inch of me. He closes his eyes and catches a breath before slowly backing away. "Until tomorrow." He winks, and my libido melts to the floor.

I am dumbfounded, speechless and strung out. Did he really just kiss me like that and leave me standing here? Trapped in a vacuum, my heart is racing. When I open my eyes, he is sauntering down the hallway. I fill my lungs with the breath he left behind and fumble for my key. My senses splattered across the hallway. I flip the light on and flop down on the bed, seething from his kiss. The room swirls with a different air from this morning. It is charged and hot. All the way to my toes, his lips reverberate, pounding in my blood. My mind hovers, still high above, hardly able to look down upon me, sitting alone on my bed. This is not how I saw this evening playing out. I thought for sure he would be making me purr by now, instead a ferocious need crawls across my skin, clawing at me. I need to feel him, his weight, his touch. Maybe this is all part of his seduction. Part of his need to keep within the parameters that he has set, to maintain control.

My body is humming intensely, and it's hard to catch my breath. I touch my lips and the spark he left reignites. Oh, he is wicked, leaving me wanting, writhing in my own skin. He is well practiced. I think to put out the fire, but fear I may only fan the flames he has set. My hands won't feel nearly as good as his will. The thought of how much more explosive it will be if I wait circles my mind. I will save myself for him, this fire, it is his doing. He must be the one to put it out. Slowly I peel myself from my tank and skirt, holding the mood he has left me with, feeling seductive with no outlet. I light a row of stark white pillars that stand next to the tub. I run myself a bath, filling it with the heavily scented hotel bubble bath. The room is filled with a heady combination of gardenia, hot, sticky steam and flickering candlelight. God, I wish he was here right now. I slide slowly into the bath, letting my naked flesh slowly attune to the scorching hot water. When I finally settle in amongst the bubbles I let my head fall back and think of Rhys, and his crooked mouth. He dances behind my lids, teasing me.

***

A gentle breeze rouses me from a heavy sleep, and I wake as the sun is just cresting the horizon. I call to make sure she is awake and head down to Olivia's room. The morning passed in a haze of wedding preparation and last minute crisis. My body still slightly humming from last night, and Rhys' all-out assault on my senses. All the while Olivia is calm, more serene and giddy than any bride I have ever seen. The chaos swirls around her and she sits with a glass of champagne and the most contagious grin plastered across her face.

Kylie sweeps in and out of the room, assuring Olivia that all is going smoothly. She and Melissa move about the suite gathering Olivia's luggage and makeup, packing it all up to move to the estate on Key Biscayne. I take the opportunity to pull Olivia to the side. She pours me a glass of champagne and I move to take a seat on the bed, a pang of emptiness echoes through my hips and core, evidence of the previous evenings tease. I close my eyes for a moment and absorb the memory of Rhys' hips rolling against me and my pulse spikes, sending a shiver down my spine. My mind wanders to Rhys and how stunning he will surely look in a tuxedo.

Marie flutters about the room, picking up the clothes that Olivia has tossed about. Olivia was never very tidy, but Marie lives to clean. They complement one another. She pulls the duvet off the bed and a small nappy bunny falls to the floor, Olivia's bunny. He is gray from time, missing both eyes and his fluffy bunny tail, but he has gone everywhere with Olivia since we were girls. Her mother picks him up and begins to quietly weep. For her daughter's new life, her lost youth, it's hard to know. But, thoughts of my mother creep in while watching Marie weep for her daughter, tears of happiness at her upcoming wedding and a bright future. Tears my mother will never shed. I turn away, pouring myself a glass of OJ, thinking better of the champagne so early and on such an emotional day. Suddenly Marie turns her motherly eyes on me, as if she could tell that I had just been thinking about my own mother. Her mother's radar is in full force this morning.

"And what about you, missy? You need to find someone who will take care of you now." She pulls me into a hug and squeezes until I grin.

"I can take care of myself," I offer back. "I don't need anyone." I know Marie means well, but I am tired of people looking at me with that pity in their eyes. The poor girl has no parents. That look makes my hair stand on end, provoking the deepest need to prove everyone wrong. To stand up and scream at the top of my lungs I can take care of myself!

"Oh Sophie, you don't always have to be strong. We all need someone to take care of us, someone to love. Olivia said you finally got rid of that Collin." She waits for confirmation. I think she hated him almost as much as my mother would have, if she had ever met him. "He was a real asshole, Sophie. You are far too good for him." I turn to Olivia and almost give myself whiplash in the process. She puts her arms around me before I can explode.

"I told her everything, Sophie. My mom loves you, and your mom would want someone looking out for you. Please don't be upset." My mind reels at the array of sorted and humiliating details that Olivia could have shared with her mother. And she doesn't even know the half of it. I would never share my failures and shortcomings with anyone. Weakness is not a virtue I admire. I don't want people to know that I was so blinded. I was a sad fool. Now I feel foolish all over again.

"Come now, there is no reason to rehash painful memories. Now is the time to go out and get what is yours, Sophie. Olivia found her match, and yours is out there waiting for you."

"Everyone doesn't get the perfect happily ever after, Marie." The words fall from my mouth with ease, soliciting a crackling silence. She quietly leaves the room as Olivia twists around in a whirl of wavy blonde hair and wide eyes.

"You're a little snippy this morning."

"I am sorry, Liv. I will apologize to your mom. I'm just feeling a little high strung."

"Obviously. I assume you and Rhys didn't hook up last night." She sits at the foot of the bed and waits, eager and curious. "What happened? I thought you two hit it off. It looked like you were going to tear each other apart last night when you left the wine cellar."

"He kissed the hell out of me and then left me standing there, alone, like an idiot. I swear I almost exploded it was so hot." Her face falls slightly, churning over the words of casual encounters. "Maybe I am a little frustrated."

"What happened?" She pats the bed beside her. I take a seat, taking a deep breath.

"I don't know exactly. All night he was touching me and teasing me. When we got in the

130

elevator I thought for sure. But he just left me alone. He said not tonight, that something had come up that couldn't be ignored, and that was it. I assumed it was something for the wedding."

"So, he left you reeling all night? He is playing with you!" She teases, pushing my shoulder with hers. "Don't let it get to you. Rhys has been pursuing you, Sophie, not the other way around."

"What are you talking about?"

"Sophie, are you really so blind? He has been with you every free moment. Rhys does not deal in flattery and fakery. If he wasn't interested in you he would not be wasting his time. It is not his way. Obviously he wants to drag it out, spend more time with you." A knock at the door distracts Olivia and I am left with more questions than answers.

"Matthew! You are not supposed to see me!" She giggles as Matt pushes the door open and sweeps her up into his arms. Rhys steps in and closes the door behind him.

"One last look before you are mine forever woman!" He kisses her so deeply the air in the room stops, before he sets her back on her feet. Rhys' eyes call to me and I catch him watching me impassively. His eyes are hard and his crooked smile is nowhere to be found, like he knows we were just talking about him.

"Ladies, we just stopped in to let you know that the cars will be ready in two hours. Everyone should meet downstairs and we will all depart for the wedding together." He is all business.

"The boys and I are going to hit a bucket of balls before we leave. You ladies have a wonderful morning. And I will see you at the altar." Matthew cups Olivia's face in his hands before planting the sweetest kiss on her forehead. I watch Rhys' face, like stone looking right through me, his mood undefinable. I wish I could hide my emotions so easily. My heart lives squarely on my sleeve. They turn to leave and I want to scream. He is impossible to read, refusing to let anyone see what he doesn't want seen. How can I believe that he is interested in me when he can act so cold and detached? I want to chase him down the hall, demand his attention. Last night I was ready to give him everything and now he denies me.

Chapter 9

The girls are giddy, waiting to pile into one of the two stretch limousines that have been sent to take us all out to Key Biscayne. Excitement about the wedding is palpable, but Olivia is as cool as a cucumber.

"Nervous?" I tease, bumping her shoulder.

"Not one bit, Soph. I know this is the most perfect thing I have ever done. I love Matthew so much." You can see it written all over her face, the bright reflection of love shining through her bright blue eyes.

"You two are going to be so happy."

"I know," she offers, matter of fact, climbing into the car. She is followed by Marie, then Kylie and Melissa. I envy her clarity. Her raw, almost infectious optimism. A soft hand winds around my arm, stopping me from getting into the car. I turn to find Rhys; impassive face; his eyes betray the stone set of his jaw. He pulls me back and pops his head into the limo.

"Ladies, I will be stealing Sophie for the ride. You can have her back once we arrive."

A thrill surges through me at his commanding manner. I turn to Olivia to see a grin spread across her face as she winks with a shrug. He pulls me towards the sleek black Town Car parked behind the limos. His silence is unsettling, sending my pulse into a tizzy as I duck into the back seat. Rhys slides in after me, shutting the door, cutting us off from the outside. I shift to the opposite side of the car, waiting. I struggle to remain stoic in the face of his stone cold gaze, unsure of what I am to say. He watches me shift uncomfortably under his scrutiny, before his face softens slightly. He leans forward, resting his elbows on his knees, closing the distance between us. His fingers lace together, pulling across his lips, those plump, perfect lips. A momentary flash of his mouth on my flesh sends a jolt of pleasure pulsing through me. I feel the flush in my cheeks giving me away. He grins, fully aware of the effect he has on my body.

"I dreamt of your sweet lips last night. I am eager to taste the rest, and I must say that I woke feeling famished." A moment passes before my mind catches up with him and I choke, a flaming red flush climbing up my body as I clutch my chest, his raw words leaving me breathless and startled. My mind races through the pages of my sexual past flashing upon painful memories of asking him for that, just to be ridiculed and mortified by the results. And here Rhys is, a powerful sexual being, charged up from my lips and he thinks I am sweet. My stomach flips at the thought of him, between my legs, teasing me like in my dreams, tasting me, lapping at my flesh. I cringe quietly before I look into his eyes and shake my head timidly, afraid to disappoint him.

"I don't really… umm." Every broken syllable is more painful than the last; I cannot make the words come. I cannot bring myself to tell him that I can't let him do that to me because I am ashamed and afraid of what he will think, afraid of my own body. No, I cannot do that with Rhys. An ashamed nod of my head and I avert my eyes, not wanting him to see my embarrassment and fear.

"Hey, what just happened?" He tips my chin with his finger, raising my eyes to meet his. Concern and confusion flash in his emerald green eyes. "Did I *offend* you?" The slight edge in his voice begs me to assure him otherwise.

"No! No, of course not," I drop my eyes, wanting to shrink away from it all. But Rhys won't allow it, his finger turns my head back and his eyes demand my attention.

"Then what is it, Sophie. Tell me."

"I'm just not comfortable, with that." The words barely a whisper, but in my head they echo, never ending. He searches my face while he holds my hands, looking right through me. Invading my thoughts, trying to gain access to the restricted section, where I hide behind big talk and a smart mouth. It was so easy for him to just walk right into my mind, just as easily as I stepped into this car. And now he waits. Waits for an answer I cannot give, a rational explanation why a woman of twenty four is so uncomfortable and unfamiliar with her own body. Why?

"We are going to have to do something about that," he declares, righteously. "I have to taste you, Sophie. If I don't it will drive me mad." Lightning strikes at my core as the heat of his words crackle and pop in my ears.

"I'm sorry." I shrink away from him and with every second my boldness fades, leaving an awkward emptiness. How quickly everything turned. I was ready to wrap myself around him and ride him until dawn, and now we sit hand in hand, miles apart. Pulling my hands away, I turn back to face the window.

"Oh, no you don't. Don't be sorry, just be ready. I have plans for you. I have been waiting for this. I told you, I want to have my way." His voice is warm and slow. He lowers his forehead to mine, and places his hands on my shoulders, reigniting the flame beneath. "Do not worry your pretty little head about it. We will start slow. I am going to make you come so hard you won't know what hit you." His promise burns right through me, dark and hungry need pooling in my loins.

"Yes, please," my breathy plea the invitation he was waiting for. His hands are on both sides of my face, leading me, kissing me frantically, thankfully. His fingers wind in my hair while his hands rest on my cheek, soft and tender. Our lips twist and turn around each other, dancing to the quiet music of traffic, his hands soft on my face. He winks at me through thick dark lashes and sits back against the black leather seat across from me, gazing out the window.

"Did you and Olivia have a nice chat this morning?"

"I don't know what you mean."

"Come now, Sophie, I know you girls like to talk. What did you tell her?"

"I…" My mouth snaps back shut, not sure that I should divulge. "I didn't tell her anything."

"You are not a very good liar." His cool tone sends ice through my veins. "But, I won't hold that against you. How are you this morning? Not too frustrated I hope." The crooked grin at the corner of his lips is sharp. My mind is blank sitting in such close quarters. The smell of his skin teases my senses.

"I am fine, how are you?" I quip back, trying to keep pace with him.

"Anxious, and *hungry*," he grins "Are we still having fun?" His eyes twinkle with mischief. I nod my head in agreement and try to recollect my thoughts.

"I,….um." My tongue has disappeared and left me to fend for myself. What is he asking? I look into his eyes and a jolt of electricity grounds me to the spot. I am without any weapon to defend myself. His mere presence topples my defenses and brings me to my knees.

"I just want to make sure we are on the same page."

"I am under no false assumptions, Rhys. I know what this is. I also know that I am booked on a flight tomorrow, so don't you worry about me getting too attached. I will be leaving on a jet plane," I wink. "I see you, and I will not be one of those girls, begging for scraps of your attention. I don't usually do things like this, but believe me when I say that I can handle myself. So don't worry about me." I rush the words, unconvinced of my own declaration. "This whole rule thing makes me feel a little disposable. I don't want to be humiliated or used, but I can reconcile what this is."

"Ouch." The comment presses him into the seat. He crosses his arms and cocks his head. "I am using you, Sophie, and you are using me. As we all use each other. It is the human condition" The wind is sucked from my lungs. Like a punch to the gut, his words remind me of the deep chasm that lies between his reality and mine. He is right, I have nothing of value to him, nothing that he cannot find elsewhere. I am just a body to play with, something to quell his boredom. Disappointment cripples my smile, and it's hard to hide the hurt in my eyes.

"I am not using you," I whisper.

"Sure you are." His response is swift, sliding

across the seat, trapping me with his body. I want to say I told you so, to call his bluff. I open my mouth to speak when he kisses me, hard. Crushing his lips against mine, leaving me breathless, shaky and wanting.

"I want this," he mutters against my mouth, "and so do you." Pulling away from me, his face aflame with a challenge, he cups my face in his hands and swallows me with his eyes. I am lost in the green pools, warm from his lips and eager for more. "I will use your body to make me feel good, as you will use mine, and it will be glorious." I wind my arms around his shoulders and pull him to me, desperate for his touch, his kiss, him. "Believe me when I say you are not disposable. Now, let's just do what feels good," he coaxes, gently wrapping me in his arms, his tongue sweeping along my bottom lip before pushing into my mouth. His tongue dances against mine, teasing, until my head spins. The car ride is swallowed by the back and forth. Moments after he pulls me into his lap we are pulling into the circular drive of his family's house, our bodies desperate for more, he twists his hand in my hair and pulls my head back exposing my neck, holding me still. His lips are hot and moist against my throat.

"You are mine tonight," he murmurs. The vibration of his words leaves me breathless, his promise too good. "Say yes," he demands.

"To be used?" I whisper as the car door opens and the light of day spills in. He blinks up at me through those thick, dark lashes, a genuine sparkle playing on the gold flecks of his eyes.

"Stop thinking so much," he pleads, his vice grip tightening around my hand. My body relents, softening, humming with anticipation. My mind, however, is dragging.

Olivia prompts me from the car, following the wedding planner who is calling out orders like a drill sergeant. "*Ladies in the house for hair and makeup, men in the pool house.*" I turn back towards Rhys' waiting eyes, knowing that I am ready to surrender, at least for now. I want to, I need to.

"Yes," I mouth, being pulled from the car. I follow the parade of dresses and women, all the while watching Rhys. His face lights up, a triumphant grin curls his full lips. The force of that grin bores straight to my core and a lovely memory crawls up my body from my toes, gaining momentum as my mind is wiped clean by the thought of his weight upon me. He winks before disappearing around the side of the house, with Matthew and the others. As soon as he is out of my sight, my mind reels at what I have just agreed to; to be used, and to use him.

Chapter 10

The suite is teeming with activity. Olivia and her mom are inspecting the dresses while the wedding planner drones on about the minute to minute schedule. Kylie and Melissa sit in front of a large vanity in the expansive bathroom. One woman paints each of their faces while another coifs their hair, messy buns with smoky eyes and a nude lip. They sip their champagne from silver straws and whisper quietly to one another, giggling and groaning in unison. I decide to clear the air between us. They both clearly have a past that involves Rhys in some capacity, that which I really do not want to know. Feeling strong and newly confident with Rhys' desire hovering around me, I will not let her intimidate me. I step into the large bathroom and bring the silence with me. Both women stop chatting and look at me in the mirror. Melissa's eyes are cold, rimmed with kohl. The gold flecks in her eyes sparkle against the dark eye makeup while she scrutinizes me. Kylie flashes her whitened teeth and excuses herself from the tension filled room. I take a seat in the chair next to Melissa and pin her down in the mirror.

"How was your night?" She sips from her silver straw, offering nothing, watching me, waiting.

"My night was amazing," she bites back, so certain, so easily distracted by a roll with Wes, I assume. I take a moment to chew my tongue and collect my thoughts. She huffs at my non-reaction and hops out of the chair, grabbing her sippy cup and phone before sauntering out of the bathroom, leaving me alone, and confused.

We form a circle around Olivia to help her into her dress. It is delicate organza and silk, billowing in the air like a cloud above her, as we all help to pull the dress over her head. The top is sheer with a dramatic boat neck, capped at her shoulders. The embroidery over the bodice is delicate and detailed. Tiny Swarovski crystals cover her chest and cascade down her narrow hips, with a satin sash at her waist. The skirt is full, layer after layer of blush colored organza with a slit up her thigh. The finishing touch is her ballet heels, with satin wrapped around her ankles. The dresses she chose for the bridesmaids are equally delicate and ethereal. Tea length blush organza skirts with the sheer V-neck top, capped sleeves and equally beautiful embroidery. Olivia pulls me aside and hands me a gift bag.

"What is this, Liv? I am supposed to be giving you a present. Not the other way around," I squeak, embarrassed by her generosity when I have nothing for her in return.

"Just a little something sassy to go under your

dress. I know how you are, Sophie, you don't treat yourself enough. I bought you some things to make you feel good. Wear them tonight and I promise Rhys will lose his shit," she whispers with a sly wink and a nibble of her lip. I open the bag to find a contraption I have never seen. A small swath of nude lace with dangly bits, another, even smaller strip of matching silk, and a pair of what looks like stockings. I look up into Olivia's eager eyes and cannot help but laugh. "It's a garter belt, stockings and a thong," she whispers. My heart leaps into my chest. I have never worn lingerie, never even tried it on. I have always been a cotton panty and bra kind of girl. I am going to look ridiculous in this. Panic must have shown on my face because Liv immediately went on the defense. "Trust me, Sophie, you are going to look so hot Rhys won't know what to do with himself, not to mention they will make you feel so sexy. Trust me. Now, go put them on." And with that she shuffles me into the bathroom to figure out the puzzle.

The rest of us get dressed and we share a toast to Olivia and Matthew before Kylie excuses herself to check the details. I am glad that I am not the Maid of Honor. Olivia was worried that she hurt me when she didn't ask, but I know it is for the best. I do not have the time or capital to be a proper Maid of Honor at a wedding of this caliber. I am just glad to be here, sharing her wedding day. I watch her primp, as her mother fusses over every detail of her delicate dress when a soft rap on the door catches us all by surprise.

Rhys enters the room and all logic and reason goes out. Giddy like a school girl, I jump for joy silently and grin, like an idiot. He wears a tuxedo like he was born for it. He is perfect, comfortable, self- possessed, a gripping combination of elegance, sex and power wrapped in Armani crepe. Watching him cross the room and engage every woman like a true gentleman is mesmerizing. His eyes dance at the sight of Olivia in her dress and he compliments her as he hands her a small black box.

"A gift from Matthew, something new," he offers, pulling a velvet pouch from his pocket. "And this is from me, something blue." He grins at her, innocent and genuine. "You look beautiful, Matthew is very lucky." She smiles and he kisses her cheek. She opens the box to find an Art-Deco diamond and pale blue sapphire bracelet. Rhys helps her secure it on her wrist and then opens the pouch, dropping the contents into Olivia's open hands, two delicate diamond and sapphire drop earrings, set in the same fashion of the bracelet. The blue of the sapphires mirrors her clear blue eyes and are the crowning touch. She glows from within while her newly acquired decorations sparkle. She starts to tear up and pushes Rhys away like a brother, admonishing him for jeopardizing her perfect makeup.

He turns his attention to me, and I nearly melt. The force of his gaze is enough to knock me off of my feet. He licks his bottom lip and brushes my cheek. "You look lovely," he whispers with a warm smile, running his thumb along my mouth. I part my lips and nip at the pad. I don't recognize myself. I am brazen and bold, but I cannot stop myself. He makes it so easy, oozing sex and control. It would be a crime not to revel in every last drop of his sexual prowess. And he reads my mind without difficulty. That beautiful crooked grin raises the corner of his mouth and he winks.

"Tonight," he murmurs before he gently kisses the back of my hands and turns to leave. As he makes his way to the door Melissa emerges from the bathroom. Rhys turns to her and she shoots me a look of triumph. My heart sinks watching him whisper something to her that first elicits an unnerving smile. She watches me, hoping for a reaction as he shares an intimate moment with her in front of me. But, her wide smile quickly falls and her eyes fall away as he wraps it up. He backs away from her, locks her in his eyes and nods, as if asking if she understood. She drops her gaze to the ground and nods in response, before returning to the bathroom, closing the door behind her. That is the second time I have seen him shut her down. It is as if he has some power over her; power she seems eager to surrender. I try not to focus on her, or their odd relationship. He has made it clear that he wants to be with me, here and now. It is temporary anyhow, so why think too hard. Just lie back and enjoy the ride.

"Rhys, wait," Olivia calls to him as she pulls a small package from her luggage. Wrapped in gold foil paper and tied with a large tartan bow, her gift to Matthew. "Please tell Matthew that I cannot wait to be his wife," she tells Rhys handing him the package. He turns to me and winks before taking his leave.

***

Everything about the wedding was flawless. The low hanging wisteria created a breathtaking canopy over Olivia as she walked down the aisle. The ocean breeze gently released tiny blossoms as she moved towards Matthew, showering her with thousands of tiny flower petals. Each time I glanced across the aisle, my eyes were dazzled by a Rhys' crooked grin. I could feel him watching me as I stood behind Kylie and Olivia, Melissa hovering behind me, his eyes daring me to look, roping me in, trying to tangle me up. Every glance felt intimate, private. Reminding me of last night, and the promise he made in the car.

After the ceremony there were cocktails on the

pool deck, pictures with the photographer and a private moment for Matthew and Olivia. We were all led into the opulent dining room for a formal sit down dinner and dancing. All night I have been sitting next to Melissa, yet she has not said one word or even looked in my direction. I watch her walk out towards the powder room and decide to follow her, unwilling to let her unwarranted judgment of me go unchecked. I duck into the powder room after her and shut the door quietly behind me. Following her to the vanity, I know she is aware of me, but she acts like she is alone.

"Melissa." I try my best to remain calm and fill my tone with an undeniable power, but it just comes across as weak and unsure. "What is your problem?" She flashes her fiery eyes at me, a wide grin spreading slowly across her sour face.

"You have no idea what you are in for do you?" She turns on me, a shifty fire in her eyes. "Whatever you *think* is happening with Rhys is sadly temporary you know that right? You will never have him, no one can have him. He is unavailable, unreachable." She moves to the mirror, gazing at her reflection with a perverse admiration. "And you better hope that you are not around when she shows up, and she will show up, she is already here. She will make you wish you had never laid eyes on our beautiful Rhys Slate." She finishes her speech with a swipe of fresh lipstick and a quick pop of her fiercely red lips. Turning away from the mirror, she faces me, humor, pity and something else seeping from every over done pore. "You are way out of your league." She chuckles to herself and continues. "You think he likes you? You think you are any different from the rest of us? He just wants to tie you down and fuck you. That's what he does. He will take a piece of you for himself. You were an easy mark. I'm surprised you have lasted this long, must be some kind of record." She doesn't wait for a response; my fallen face says it all, while pleasure paints her gloriously triumphant. "He is playing with you and you don't even know it. You are nothing, just a number. " The triumph of her tone stings, she shakes her head and laughs. "He has never loved anyone but himself, and that twisted bitch Nadja." Reaching around me she pulls the door open, stepping into the hall.

"What are you talking about?" A wicked smile paints Melissa's face while she watches the dawn rise behind my eyes.

"Yeah, welcome to the club." With a wave of her hand, she disappears around the corner leaving me reeling. Her laughter lingers long after she leaves the room. I am stuck in front of the mirror, trapped again with a girl left out of the loop. I gather my emotional strength, put on a happy face and return to the reception. I wander around the perimeter of the room, watching couples dance and laugh. I catch Melissa's eyes while she writhes against Wes on the dance floor. She looks me dead in the eye with a wicked grin and I will her to combust, on the spot. Right there on the dance floor in front of everyone, I will her to burst into flames.

Leaning on my fingertips, I push on the receiving table and feel my mood sink and anger rise, coursing through my veins. *What the fuck have I gotten myself into?* I close my eyes, fighting back angry tears. Pulling in a deep breath, willing myself to calm I feel a warm breath on the nape of my neck. A shudder runs down my spine as a strong finger traces the line of my shoulder.

"I would like a dance with the most beautiful woman here." Rhys. His whisper like silk and sandpaper against my already assaulted nerves. Turning on him with fire in my eyes, bile rising in my throat, I push him away.

"Leave me alone, Rhys." I wave my hands around, emotion dripping from my fingertips, losing any grip on my emotions. "Stop toying with me." Rhys' face falls, hurt briefly passing before his crystal clear eyes. My head is swimming, his proximity pulling me under. I push past him, his solid form offering no resistance and he follows me quietly out of the room, his energy pulling at me like an anchor. I push through the double doors out of the lavish dining room, away from the party and into the darkened foyer. I sink into an antique

149

fainting couch in the far corner, hiding my face in my trembling hands. A deep and painful sigh escapes my lips, my eyes taking in the sight of Rhys' wingtips, polished and perfect. He stands in front of me, passively. I look up into his eager eyes to find them liquid, warm with concern.

"Please, Rhys, don't," whispering my plea for mercy and reprieve. "I don't want to play."

He moves around and takes a seat next to me, elbows propped up on his knees, his hands joined, fingers resting on his full lips. He turns his heavy gaze on me, unleashing the full power of his deep pain filled eyes. His chest falls as he exhales deeply, the side of his mouth pulled into a wicked grin that could melt the ice caps.

"Oh, I haven't begun to play with you, Sophie." Looking up into his waiting emerald eyes I can't hold back. The truth is undeniable. I am just a toy to him, a plaything that he will quickly tire of. How did I convince myself that I could handle this enigma? There are too many unknowns here to count, too many pitfalls to swallow me up. Yet he disarms me so easily, just a look and a slight grin is all it took. I ache as he caresses my cheek with the back of his fingers.

"Why does that sound like a threat?" Caught, with his guard down, he clears his throat and wipes the playfulness from his face. I wait with baited breath for him to offer an answer, an explanation.

He strokes his chin shaking his head.

"I don't know what you mean." His mask so easily slides into place.

"I just had a very enlightening conversation with Melissa, about your reputation." He winces at the mere mention of her name.

"Look at me," he demands, tilting my face with a finger. "My past has nothing to do with you. We talked about this. I thought we were just having a bit of fun?" He uses my words against me. Every soft plane of his face reflects the truth, but Melissa's elusive language and innuendo will not fade away. "I will deal with Melissa," he declares. "And I do not want to hear another word about it. What we are doing is between us, no one else. Do you understand me?" He is done, closed the conversation without question. He winks and I cannot help but smile. He quiets all the chatter in my head. Every vile word Melissa said falls away. There is no one but us, and I like it, even though the idea is flawed.

"That's better, you are beautiful when you smile. Now, come. I want to dance." He pulls me to my feet and leads me back to the reception and onto the dance floor. The crowd parts for him like the Red Sea. Once in the middle of the floor, he twirls me around, easily passing under his arm, he pulls me into his chest, his hand across the small of my back anchoring me to his rock hard form,

151

controlling my every move. The band begins to play "Lover Lay Down." A striking redhead with finger waves and an old fashioned satin sheath softly croons about spring's sweet rhythm.

Rhys is a skilled dancer, gracefully gliding us both across the floor. I am completely lost in the dance and the song. I look over and see Olivia and Matthew slowly swaying in one another's arms, barely aware of another soul, so happy, so in love. Uninvited emotions bubble to the surface and I press my cheek to Rhys' hard chest to stifle a sob and hide my face as he moves me to words of love and wanting. The emotions of a wedding, intense heart pounding lust, exhausting female gossip and the glamor of the whole scene is beginning to weigh heavily on my heart, and head. We move slowly to the music as a saxophone cries and launches into a lovelorn solo. Rhys lowers his head as the music begs and puts his lips to my ear, his warm breath sending a shiver down my spine. In unison with the breathy singer, he whispers in my ear "Oh…. Please..", a question, a promise. The simple lyric shatters my resistance. He places his finger under my chin and raises my face to meet his. A single tear betrays my carefully contained façade. He casually wipes it away with the pad of his thumb and smiles warmly. Easily melting the last pockets of icy resistance I have tried to hide away.

"Come." He grabs my hand and leads me off of

the dance floor while the saxophone laments. Leading me out of the dining room, he swings me around so we are face to face, bending down so we are nose to nose, and grips me with his eyes. "There is something I want to show you."

Chapter 11

He leads me out into the yard where a swath of blush colored silk covers the perfectly manicured stone path, a brief storm having liberated dozens of wisteria blossoms, now scattered across the aisle, a fitting footpath. The weeping willows sway lazily above, while thousands of tiny wisteria petals dance towards the ground, floating and twirling in the gentle sea breeze. The moody canopy is draped in thousands of twinkling lights, softened by the tendrils of dripping moss. The view is breathtaking. Water still, like glass and alight with all the stars in the sky swimming languidly upon the surface. I am momentarily lost, all of the drama of the wedding slowly fading away, leaving only me, Rhys and the glassine sea. His warm hand on the small of my back pulls me from the moment, his pulse building to an exquisitely torturous pace as he leads me around a large breakwater, onto an expansive dock. Walking onto the planks my sight is overwhelmed by the sleek, gargantuan yacht in front of me. I have to pick my jaw up off the dock. I have never seen anything like it. Rhys is clearly pleased with my reaction, a huge grin slowly spreading across his perfect face.

Pulling me into his powerful arms, he wraps me in his warmth and whispers. His moist lips against my ear, is almost too much to bear, "One amazing night." The magnitude of my lust for this man is beyond anything I have ever experienced. My entire body changes the moment he touches me, molds to his will, bends to his whims. I feel all that I have been missing, in his caress. His touch is all knowing, familiar and eager.

"Come." His one word command is enough to get me moving as he takes my hand to lead me on board. He is excited and his energy is infectious. He is like a little child showing off his new toy, I'm just not sure I can give him the reaction he is hoping for. Being surrounded by all this wealth and opulence is polarizing. Never have I been around such wealth or excess. The deck is sleek and dark, lit only by dozens of candles that circle the banquette. Very little is illuminated, other than Rhys' sparkling eyes. "Well?" he asks.

"It is amazing. Is this all for Olivia and Matthew?" He huffs at the question, and creases his brow.

"This is all for you." He winds his fingers between mine, leading me quickly across the shadowy platform and down below deck. "I thought since this was our one night together that we could stay out here, away from prying eyes and ears."

"Rhys." I tug his hand and look into his eyes wanting him to hear me, to understand. "Shut up," I whisper with a grin that he matches, "you're ruining it". He pulls me through the cabin with urgency and

I am sure he is not even listening. It is larger than I imagined. A large living area with a white bar and white leather couches, dominate the central cabin. A white baby grand piano sits in the corner. He leads me through the living area into the kitchen and through an unexpectedly large dining room, down another deck and through a solarium before he swings me around and pins me to the wall. His hips pressed against me, I rock back on my heels and almost lose my balance, saved only by the anchor of Rhys' hips, and the smooth wall at my back.

"Good, because I am done being *friendly*." His eyes burn with intensity and the resonance in his voice sends lightning across my skin. He rocks his hips against me and I feel his anticipation press into my belly. Brushing my hair to the side, he licks and nips at my neck while his hands make quick work of the slight zipper that lies at the small of my back. His hands slip beneath the sheer fabric of my bodice and my skin is aflame with the burning lust of his touch. "I hate waiting."

"I need to look at you. It's all I can think about," he demands, opening the door, rolling me around the corner into a large suite. I'm awed by the room, and the massive bed that dominates. It floats on a platform, above the rest of the room, an island of crisp blue linens, pale and tranquil, reflective of the sea. Chocolate brown pillows are tossed about the bed and surround the platform. I hear Rhys slide out of his tuxedo jacket before he steps up behind me, sending a shiver of anticipation down my jelly spine.

The cabin swirls with heavy sea air, all polished wood and salt. It is charged and hot. He moves swiftly through the space, lighting rows of stark white pillars, the mirrors they stand upon amplifying their flame, reflecting upon his beautifully, dangerous face. He beckons to me with a mere flick of his finger and I go, willingly, achingly. He turns to me, hunger brimming in his eyes. His hands are in my hair twisting and pulling me towards him, bringing my lips to his, covering me with such gentle ease.

He closes his eyes and catches a breath before slowly backing away to throw open the doors to the narrow veranda, inviting a gentle breeze to cool the crackling air. Moonlight streaks in over the bright linens on the bed, illuminating the entire surface and bouncing off the wall of mirrors on the far side, onto my frozen face. The reflection in the mirror could ignite a frozen lake, from across the room, I watch him slowly stalk towards me. He is looking only at me, and I watch him through the mirror, the only buffer between his fiery gaze and my highly flammable body. His broad shoulders roll under his shirt, while his hips gently sway side to side, rocking his form closer to me. He steps up behind me, placing his hand across my belly, watching my every move in the mirror. He buries his face in my hair, running the tip of his nose up my neck, the vibration practically rattling my teeth.

"You smell amazing." He gently runs his tongue along the crest of my ear before sucking on the lobe, all the while his hands are still and strong, holding me to him. His fingers splayed possessively across my belly, stone chest heaving against my back, his heartbeat slow and steady. I watch him in the mirror, worshiping my neck, lighting me up. He is so cool, comfortable in his role as seducer. He moves a hand to my neck and his fingers easily wind around my throat, the simple contact so erotic. Tipping my head back with his thumb, he opens me up for his mouth to devour mine. The kiss is deep. He tastes of scotch and cigars and the sea. I want to turn into his arms, but he holds me still, watching me slowly melt. Shining a white hot, crooked grin back at me, I swear I can hear the mirror shatter into a trillion tiny pieces from the force of his smile. An eager shudder rolls through me.

"Are you scared?"

"No."

His eyes sparkle in challenge and he pulls me into him with such ferocity that I lose my footing and he crushes me against his rock hard abs, growling into my ear. His hips rock against me while he grinds himself into my lower back. He is hot and hard.

"We are going to have to go slow. Or I may tear you apart." His casual, carnal promise sends shock waves through me, fanning the flames he lit. I don't know whether to beg or scream. I have a feeling I may end up doing both. "Now are you scared?"

"Maybe," I barely whisper.

"Good." Sauntering over to the bar I silently follow, watching the muscles in his back dance against the fabric of his shirt. That shirt needs to go. He pours a drink and watches me back up against the counter. He hands me a glass and I play with the amber liquid swirling it around and around watching him, watch me.

He radiates heat, wrapping around me, twisting like a serpent, luring me to the fruit of my undoing. Electricity teems in the air, crackling in my head, loosening my grip on reality. He tips his drink, but I shake off the offer. My head swimming as it is, no additional plying required. Taking the drink from my hand, he abandons it to the counter and drags his hands through his hair, rousing the thick dark curls. I drink him in, every languid inch of predatory heaven, inching closer, his casual pace falsely comforting. Strong hands grip my waist, raising me to the counter, the cold granite on my bare flesh quickly forgotten as he takes his place, coaxing my thighs apart, closing the empty space between us. His hands float like clouds over my swelling curves and settle to the cool counter on either side, teasing circles on my hips with his thumbs. His hands sneak under the edges of fabric spread across the counter and hover just shy of my bare flesh. Heat radiates from his fingers, teasing. I shift, called by nature to do so. I want his hands on me. I want him to tease me, touch me, kiss me, feel me. I want him inside of me. His face is impassive while he watches me squirm. He doesn't kiss me or say a word, just watches my temperature rise. I close my eyes and focus on the circles he draws in flame across my hidden skin, a few quietly deep breaths and the sound of blood rushing in my ears calms to a dull roar. I feel his eyes, waiting, appraising the results of his teasing. I slowly raise my lids and that beautiful mouth twitches into a stunning grin before his hands are around my bare backside, pulling me to the edge of the counter, forcing our bodies together.

"Are you wearing stockings?" he murmurs against my throat

"Yes," I breathe in his ear a warm whisper.

"Mm mm…I love that."

My hunger grows at his approval and I wrap my legs around his waist, pulling him closer, wanting to feel his chest against mine, rising and falling in time. I run my hands up the back of his neck, and bury my fingers in his inky black hair. His hands move to my face, pushing my hair back and his mouth is on mine. His hands gentle, while his kiss is urgent. Holding my head, his fingers tangled in my hair, twisting and pulling as he presses his soft lips to mine. I part my lips to him and his tongue dips into my mouth, gently probing. He teases my bottom lip, gently licking then biting before he retreats his hands still firmly wound about my hair, lips swollen and unsatisfied. If ever there was a mouth made to kiss me, surely it must be his. His mouth is perfect, so easily reading mine. His eyes are heavy and sexy as hell. He places a tender kiss on the corner of my mouth, and another before he backs slightly away and demands my attention.

"Tell me what you want, Sophie."

"You." I offer shyly, unsure of what he expects.

"Well, that goes without saying," he smirks, winking.

I hop down from the counter, inching towards him with my eyes firmly focused south of his sparkling eyes. He is so powerful, shoulders broad and strong. His chest surely as beautiful as the rest of him, I tug on his bow tie and watch it slowly unravel. There is something so sensual, so sexual about an undone bow tie, all that it implies, all that it promises. I begin to unbutton his shirt slowly, not saying a word, not looking at him. I just listen to his breathing, heavy, while his taut muscles rise and fall in the wake of his attempt at control.

I spread his collar to see a tiny gold cross lying at the base of his throat. I pick it up and twirl it between my fingers, the metal warm from his moist skin. I look down into his face, in awe of the unexpected talisman, but there is nothing pious reflected in his gaze. His smoldering eyes are hungry and promise sin. The last button sits just at his belt and I peek up at him to see fire in his eyes. I unbutton the last button and run my finger across the leather, pressing it into his flesh watching his eyes jump.

"I've never been asked what I want." Our eyes are locked as my hands move under the lightweight fabric of his shirt. I run my hands up his torso, my thumbs flicking and teasing his nipples before cresting his powerful shoulders and pushing the pesky shirt off of his back. The sight is breathtaking. Every plane and muscle perfectly honed, peppered with striking black hair. His waist is lean with a dark and dangerous trail that dips between those muscles that make me lose my train of thought. "I don't know how to answer. I don't know what you want me to say." I place a gentle kiss amongst the dark hair in the middle of his chest and he closes his eyes.

"I want you to tell me what you want." His mouth is slack as I place a kiss upon each perfect blush colored nipple, before running my hands across his abs, resting them on his hips, hovering across the edge of his pants, between heated bare flesh and the cool, supple leather of his belt.

"I want you." In the space of a heartbeat, his face changes, becomes soft and safe. He cups my face so softly in his hand and strokes my cheek. Leaning into his palm, I lock away the memory, the feeling of his hand on my face and his eyes so soft. It is like heaven.

"You got me." He pushes my dress from my shoulders and runs his fingers over the crest of my breasts, swelling within their delicate lace cage. "Beautiful," he mutters, his hands skating across my flesh, leaving a trail of heat, he nibbles my throat and slips the straps from my shoulders. "Turn around." The hot whisper sends a shiver down my spine. I turn towards the mirror and watch him. He slowly turns his nimble fingers to the hooks on my bra. I let it fall to the floor in front of me as he sinks to his knees and slowly pulls my dress into a pool of shimmering pale gold on the floor. I am utterly exposed, save for the tiny strip of silk that covers my aching sex and the garters holding my silky stockings.

"You are so soft, Sophie. Like a rose petal. I want to stroke every inch of your skin until it glows pink under my fingers." An appreciative groan rolling through him, while his hands roam over my feverish skin, pulling and kneading my wanting flesh. He pulls one of the garters and lets it snap back against my sensitive skin, sending a jolt straight to my core. "I imagine this is what Botticelli's beauties felt like. These curves could distract a man for days." The words hang hot and heavy in my mind as his deft fingers skate up my legs, tracing my every outline, coming to rest on my bare hips. His thumbs teasing at the dimples at the base of my spine, his lips feather light, placing a kiss on each, before he slowly rises to his feet, keeping his hands on my flesh, skating up my sides, drawing a shiver to the surface.

"So soft." His hands are everywhere, twisting me to the heavens, pulling me down into the dark, his mouth hot and confusing. His touch is too hot, too soft. My mind floats above in disbelief, watching me writhe beneath his fingers. My nudity reflected is a stark contrast to his fully dressed form. Rhys pulls and twists my nipple, coaxing it out, pinching and rolling. His hand rises to the base of my throat, fingers gently stroking my jaw. I am putty in his hands, silently willing at this moment to do anything he asks of me. He turns me around and I have no need to cover myself as I normally would. His eyes are so hungry and appreciative I want him to look. I want him to stare at me until I fall to pieces. Hell, I want to look at myself. The creature I see staring back at me, wearing nothing but stockings and garters, she is wildly sexual and beautiful.

A sly smirk paints his beautiful face before he sweeps me up, and moves to the bed. Sinking amongst the layers of down and duvet covers, I watch him lose his shoes and socks in an instant. Standing at the end of the bed, he undoes his belt. My mind races at the thought of what lies hidden in those slacks, waiting to '*tear me apart*'. He pulls the belt through each loop slowly until it lies in his hands, doubled over. He arches a dark brow at me as he casually pulls on the belt and it snaps so loud it echoes through the room. I jump at the sound and he grins. I see the thoughts turning over in his mind as he quietly snaps the belt again before tossing it aside.

"Gentle," he mouths, raising his eyebrows and dropping his pants. The evidence of his arousal strains at the seams of his sexy designer boxer briefs, that pesky serpent and his forbidden fruit. My pussy clenches and I bite down on my lip to stifle an excited gasp. The sight of him has my mind swimming. He hooks his fingers into the waistband, teasing, before he decides to keep them on. My face falls in disappointment, a child whose toy is taken away. He grins and slowly climbs the mountain of down and linen, inching towards me. Sliding under my leg, he hitches my thigh up on his shoulder and plants a feather light kiss on the inside of my knee, I flinch at the contact of his warm lips on my cool, neglected skin.

"Just a kiss," he murmurs his lips hot against my thigh. "I want to savor every moment," crawling up my body planting a kiss with each word. "I want to savor you," he places a gentle kiss among the curls at the apex of my thighs. "I want to taste you," a kiss on my hip. "I want to tease you," a kiss on the other hip. "I want to make you shake." His finger slides the silk to the side and gently grazes my slit, the contact too brief and fleeting. He runs his finger up the length of my body and rests it against my lips, heady with promise and proof of my need.

"I have been able to think of little else," he mutters before kissing me so deeply my head swirls. His words wash over me in the most delightful shower. My heart aches in time with my core and I am instantly wet and needy. His fingers slide under the garter and snap, snap he has them undone in an instant. Rolling the stockings down my legs, one by one he manages to touch every inch of my skin, lighting little fires everywhere he goes. He pulls at the tiny string that holds my panties together and tugs them over my hips and down my calves. I point my toes as he pulls them from my body. I run my hands down his powerful back as he takes his place hovering above me, the weight of his body the only thing keeping me from floating away.

Rhys moves painfully slow, grinding against my flaming thighs, his cock hard and ready. His fingers twist and pull at my flesh scattering desperate kisses across my breasts, whispering his approval. He nips and suckles at one nipple while tugging at the other. The dance of push and pull, soft and hard ripples through me, my hips rock and roll seeking relief. I grasp Rhys' ass and pull him into me, wanting more, more of him, flesh to flesh, sharing heat. He groans in approval as my fingers dig into his flesh, pulling down his boxers I run my hands around his waist, and dip my fingers in among his curls. He gasps as I wind my hand around his rock hard cock and squeeze, slowly, rhythmically. He stills in my hands and closes his eyes, surrendering to my touch.

This is what I am good at. I may not know what I want, but I surely know what he wants. He rolls to the side and my hands go with him, slowly pumping his hot flesh until the skin strains against itself, hard as a rock and ready to ride. He raises his hips off the bed so I can pull his boxers down and out of the way. He looks like heaven, lying back amongst the clouds, his body chiseled and perfect, and his perfect cock throbbing for me. I rock back onto my heels and take him all in. His eyes twinkle with well-deserved ego while he watches my hands stroke his length, up and down. He gasps and his eyes roll as I squeeze at the base, rolling my thumb over his thick pink head, spreading the bead of pre cum around and around. I watch him slowly coming apart in my hands, and the power is intoxicating. I have complete control over the control freak. Just as my ego begins to swell his eyes open, aflame with purpose and restraint. He sits up in a flash and has my mouth in a tangle. Slowly he gets to his knees and pulls me onto his lap. He rocks back on his feet and I wrap my legs around him. His cock rests heavily between us, throbbing against my belly, echoing in my loins.

He holds my neck and kisses me, slowly, with practiced restraint. I wrap my arms around his neck and rock into him, inviting him to slip inside of me. The friction of his staff against my slick folds becoming unbearable, I reach between us to slip him in but he stops me. His eyes are black as coal, dilated and heavy.

"Not yet," he scorns, placing my hand on his heart, holding it there. His heart rate is even and strong, while mine is frantic. The connection calms me and I feel my pulse slow, meeting his. "Slowly," he mouths as his hand dips between us and he gingerly swipes at my slit, one, two times before pushing a finger beyond the folds. Drawing circles around my clit with his thumb, he slides a finger into my waiting sex. Then two fingers before swirling them around and around making me dizzy from the sensation. Heat rises from my toes as he draws torturous circles, over and over again until I cannot take another moment. My entire lower body tightens in response, trying to fight back the eruption. My legs tighten around his waist and my eyes screw shut while I focus on the crashing waves in my head. A low moan escapes his lips and it is almost my undoing. He continues until I think I may burst. Circle after circle twisting me tighter. Every instinct tells me to fight it, but Rhys won't let me.

"Come on, Sophie, let go."

"I can't," I pant, breathless.

"I can feel you. You want it, now give it to me."

"No," I shake my head stubbornly trying to fight.

"Come Sophie, NOW!" His thumb and fingers assault me in unison pressing every button. Rolling my clit while his fingers stroke the inside of my throbbing sex, I lose control. I shudder all around him, gripping his shoulders while the most beautiful white noise fills my head. Rhys' fingers don't stop, he twists me higher and higher until a second crack sounds in my head and I am utterly lost. My body clenches and braces, as another orgasm rolls through me like thunder. With no thought of anything my head flies back, I open my mouth ready to scream, but manage nothing more than a fading "…. Fuck!" moaned to the heavens, grinding into his hand, forcing more pressure, more pleasure. My chest heaves, struggling to catch my breath as my body hums in delight. My body feels alive and heavy. He brings me gently down, back into his hands, back into my body. I had no idea my body could do that, I felt like I was being torn apart, but it was so, so good. I release a last heavy breath and open my eyes, sweat rising on my brow. Rhys swipes it away with the pad of his thumb and brings it to his lips.

"And so we begin."

Chapter 12

He places my hand upon his chest covering it with his own, holding me flat to his heart. He places his other hand on my heart and stills us both.

"Keep your eyes on me." He gently flexes his hand over mine and I feel him, flow through me. A surge of his energy, mixing with mine exhilarates my blood and our pulse becomes one. He is breathing slowly and deeply, channeling his energy and I can feel every ounce, pouring over me, into me. My head hums while my eyes are locked onto his, holding on for dear life. Every measured breath brings us closer together. Sitting in his lap connected by our hearts and hands, nothing has ever felt so intimate. Our breathing begins to synch with the beat of our hearts and he begins to sway, slowly at first, building a rhythm with every revolution until we are rocking back and forth in unison. He picks up the pace and kisses me, lips gentle and soft. Pulling my hips closer to him, he rocks against me, pressing his hard member between my folds. He pulls me into him and rolls my hips forward. His cock slides up and down my slit, teasing.

"You are so wet for me, Sophie, so soft." His visceral tone propels me forward and I wrap my arms around his neck and crush my heated skin to his, our hearts racing towards each other through the thin veil of sticky skin. All the while his eyes are locked upon mine. I slide up and down his shaft, spreading myself all over him. My blood is boiling from the heat and vibration. I want him inside of me, every pulsating inch. My hips sway of their own accord, and my head rolls from the rush of blood, but he pulls me back, back down to earth, back into his orbit. "Stay with me," he insists, "make it last."

He covers my breast with his warm mouth, kneading and kissing until the flesh is swollen, then he moves to the other side and continues his assault. A frustrated moan grates in my throat, his eyes travel back to mine and they are serious, feral. He slides his hand between us and grazes the inside of my thigh before taking himself into his hand.

"The things I would like to do to you. I am going to lick you and kiss you and suck on every part of you until you weep, Sophie." His words hang in the air, his lips moving to mine, kissing me so softly it flutters in my chest.

"God damn, Sophie," he hisses my name and it spikes through me, ripping through my tight, empty core, leaving me unabashedly eager, and dripping wet. He takes my hand and wraps it around his straining shaft, the veins roped around, pulsating and hungry. He guides my hand up, then down, up, then slowly down, squeezing my hand as we twist around the root. His eyes are heavy, watching me stroke him, guiding me in his pleasure, igniting my own. I uncoil my fingers and graze his heavy balls, pulling at them as he slides our hands back up his rock hard shaft. His eyes flutter and he hisses through gritted teeth. "Look at what you've done to me, Beautiful. I have been hard for days."

The praise goes straight to my head and my hands go straight to his hair, pulling him into me, crushing him to my naked skin. I pour myself into a deep, toe curling kiss. Every ounce of need, every ache, and every flutter of my heart since the moment I laid eyes on him floods through me. I want to climb inside of him and wrap myself around his heart, the way he has wound himself around mine. Every inch of me is burning for his touch, my center aches and throbs where he should be, filling me, and possessing me. I feel more connected to him now than I have ever felt with anyone. The way his eyes lock onto mine, he sees right through me. He knows what I need, and I need him to give it to me.

I rise up on my knees and hover above him, slowly stroking my wet lips over the tip of his cock. I look down into his flaming eyes for a sign, for permission; permission to take him in. He bites his lip and groans in approval. His eyes twinkle with mischief while his hands fit perfectly upon my hips, guiding me over his thick, hard dick. He plants a slow wet kiss on my forehead, a tender kiss to the tip of my nose and a soft kiss on my chin before he

173

flexes his hips and his head dips into my greedy pussy. One last deep breath and a scorching look before he sinks into me, filling me up. He pushes me to the hilt, until I don't think I can take anymore.

"Sophie you are so tight, just a little more," he hisses through gritted teeth. "Relax, Beautiful."

He pulls me down as I let out the last breath, filling every empty inch. We have merged, our bodies wrapped around each other, his body filling mine. His skin is warm and sticky, smelling of sweat and sex and him. My breasts are crushed against his chest, the smattering of black hair tickling my sensitive skin. His lips are soft on my neck, while his powerful hands rock my hips forward, swallowing space and time. He rolls me forward and back, building friction and heat. I am exploding with need, aching from the inside. A tremor rolls through me, a delicious shudder, as my muscles tighten and grip his cock. Pulling him deeper, I roll forward wanting more. He stills me, his hands on my hips, before fluidly flipping me to my back and covering me with the weight of his beautiful body. He rests on his arms, trapping my shoulders on either side as he slides slowly out of me, rolling his hips in circles above mine.

"You are driving me crazy," he whispers before thrusting into me, filling me to the bone, forcing the breath from my chest. The fullness is euphoric and

174

my head swirls as he plunges into me over and over again, pressing me into the mattress. His breathing is ragged and clipped, moving above me with such force and animal grace. "Talk to me, Sophie."

"I….I…" I stutter with each thrust. I don't know what to say. I just want to feel this, the exquisite slide of his cock, the press of his hips. The agony of waiting falls away, leaving me raw and hungry.

We move slow and steady, our bodies entwined and in tune. His weight feels natural, each thrust is welcome and his warm breath ignites a fire across my skin. The slow burn gives way to building heat, my tight walls flex and curl around him, pulling him to the depths. My hips rise up to meet his, matching his every thrust. He slides slowly out and rolls his hips, making shallow circles, while he teases my clit with his thumb. A tremor builds under the tight bundle of nerves, and he circles her mercilessly, stroking around and around until I feel like I am going to fall apart. Thunder roars through my head, his thumb presses my clit as he pounds into me with such force I slide up the bed. My chest is tight and I hold my breath, stopping the onslaught. I try to tame the pleasure that is erupting within me as Rhys thrusts away, mercilessly claiming my body. His hips slam into me, faster and faster, reaching deeper with each explosive thrust. My whole body rattles against the building orgasm that I try to hold at bay.

175

My thighs lock around Rhys' form and pull him into me, trying to slow his building rhythm. He lowers his mouth to my breast and bites at my hard nipple, pulling it through his teeth, rolling it on his tongue and it is my undoing.

"Let go," his warm whisper fills my ear. I cannot hold on any longer and come around him. Like a single drop in a still pond, pleasure ripples through me while Rhys continues to thrust. Long, slow thrusts followed by needy grinding. He rolls his hips against me, rubbing his skin to my heated, tortured clit as he sinks as deeply as my body will allow. Then he rears up, his hands grasping my hips, and with a wink he slams into me. The fullness and impact pushes me over the edge and I shatter around him again as he pumps himself into me violently. Three hard thrusts and he pulls out. No! The emptiness is shocking, devastating. My body pulses and twists as he grasps his throbbing cock in his hand, he rests the other on my wet folds and swollen clit. He presses my clit, prolonging my pleasure as he pumps himself, three strong, slow strokes before feeding himself back into me, sliding balls deep. He rocks his hips and pounds into me with two heavy drives before he stills and he comes hard, filling me up. He collapses over me, a string of sweet and dirty nothings whispered in my ear. He rolls to the side, pulling the sheet around us before pulling me into his arms and cradling me to his chest.

I focus on the sound of his heart and the feel of his heartbeat. His pulse is racing and his breathing shallow as he strokes my hair and nuzzles my neck, teasing with his warm breath. This is the closest I have been to Heaven. His fingers so gentle on my heated skin, his breathing like a hypnotic mantra. We lay in silence, me engulfed in his powerful arms, his body wrapped around me possessively.

"How do you feel?" I hum with delight, unable to do much of anything else.

"High as a kite," I manage in a soft whisper.

"Good." His mouth closes over mine for a sweet shallow swipe of his tongue before he hops off the bed and struts into the bathroom. I drink in every inch of his powerful back as the moonlight dances across his form. I didn't get a good look at him before. I was too eager. Now I can focus, and he is gorgeous. Every inch of pale skin pulled tight over lean muscles, his legs sculpted and strong. Even his feet were perfect. He shines in the moonlight like a god, a god who just shook my foundation, one whom I could easily worship.

I watch him emerge from the bathroom with a washcloth and a bottle of lotion. His hips sway as he strides towards the bed and a shiver runs through me; those hips, which have so recently and thoroughly nailed me to the mattress. He gently wipes me clean with the warm cloth. His touch feather light over my swollen lips, he grazes my heated clit and a jolt of electricity through the oversensitive nub causes me to gasp.

"Shh." His warm breath glides across my hips as he rolls me over. His hands move to my back, gently warming my skin, exploring the dip and curve of my spine, kneading and rolling across sore muscles. His magical hands loosen every tight sinew, coaxing all the remaining tension from my body. The smell of the lotion is intoxicating. It swirls heavy in the air around us, filling my head with magnolia and luscious memories of Rhys' body, pressed against mine, filling me up. I close my eyes and surrender to his hands. They skate across my back, his fingers digging into my shoulders, untying long curled knots. He is careful not to let an inch of skin go without his tender touch. He caresses my shoulders and runs his fingers down my arms. He cups my buttocks and kneads the base of my thighs. He stops there and his fingertips make circles in the neglected flesh. I am loose and limp under his touch. He travels down each leg, brushing his lips across the backs of my knees as he kneads my tight calves, until he comes to my feet. I am painfully ticklish and flinch, rousing me from drifting into a sex coma. Rhys grabs my foot and pulls. He runs his thumb up the instep, pressing into my flesh riding the curve and it rattles through my loins. He does the same on the other foot and my head rolls as the sensation moves through me. Climbing my body slowly, planting feather light kisses on my backside. He grasps the back of my knee and hitches my leg up, pressing me into the bed with the weight of his chest.

"Shall I do it again?" His tongue slides across my ear.

"Please," I giggle, writhing beneath him. He pins me with his hips and slips a finger into my still swollen flesh, rolling around, before he adds another finger and plunges them into me softly massaging me from the inside.

"You are already wet. I like that," he purrs against my neck.

He slides his legs between mine and pushes my knee up farther before slowly sliding between my lips. He thrusts and my body accepts him like a missing piece. Every hard inch buried deep, rocking me from the inside. He moves slowly at first, sliding in and out, the rhythm painfully slow, making me desperate for more. I try and press up against him, forcing pressure, but he stills me with his hands on my hips. Holding me flush with the bed, he takes his time rolling his hips, stroking, taking my breath away. I whimper into the sheets and he takes off increasing his speed, pounding harder, his balls brushing against my hot flesh as he moans in my ear.

"You are so beautiful, Sophie." His hand

moves to my swollen heated lips and he starts to stroke. Long, slow circles around my clit, twisting the slick flesh around and around. My head swims, adrift in the sensation. He teases and circles, pressing harder, before the buildup washes me senseless and I grab a fistful of sheet and an orgasm rolls through me.

"Good girl." His voice is raw as he rears up and slams into me. Grinding against me, and then slamming into me again. His hands are all over me, grasping at my flesh, pulling me closer as he thrusts once more and empties himself. My walls close around him, pulling him deeper. He collapses over me, still connected in the most intimate way. I pulse around him, milking him for every drop before he rolls onto his side and pulls me with him. A sheen of sweat and sex covers our skin. He kisses the back of my neck and his tongue teases the rivulets of sweat that converge at my spine. He gently slips from my body and I slip into a sated, dreamless sleep.

Chapter 13

My body is limp, my head senseless and swimming in the deep pool of ecstasy that Rhys has so easily filled. My eyes flutter open to a room smothered in darkness, even the moon has disappeared. Rhys is coiled around me, his knees hitched up behind mine, forcing me into a fetal curl. Our fingers are tangled, and he has tucked my head safely under his chin. His breathing is slow and even, his heartbeat familiar and comforting, his arms strong and safe. How easily I slip into this intimacy, with no thought of what is to come. I slide out from under his arms and tiptoe out of the bedroom, snatching his shirt off the ground. With every step I regain myself, remember how I got here. I walk into the bathroom, pulling his dress shirt on over my head, softly closing the door behind me.

I flip on the light, illuminating the large bathroom, larger than you would expect for a boat. Staring back through the mirror, flushed and mussed, I am face to face with a new woman. Amazing what a few orgasms and the attention of a real man can do for a girl. I inspect myself, the healthy flush on my cheeks, the bright sparkle in my eyes and the genuine smile across my face. I can't remember the last time I felt this good, this happy. After years of self-imposed unhappiness, this is what I have been missing. This is a new freedom. In the space of a breath, my chest opens, my heart threatening to leap from my body and do cartwheels. Heat rises in my blood, eclipsing any rational thought. I see the sweet pink bruises on my skin from his perfect mouth, covered in sex and a growing sense of something I am unaccustomed to. I feel full. Full of myself, full of him, full of lust, I don't know. I just feel full for the first time. After years of feeling empty and unworthy, I feel full, but not yet satisfied.

As softly as possible I slide through the cabin, Rhys tosses and turns, softly breathing, but soundly sleeping, looking peaceful, satisfied. His beautiful body draped in heavenly white sheets, mouth soft and relaxed. I watch him for a moment, in awe that such a beautiful man would take me to bed. The mere thought of his warm mouth and hands roaming over my body send a tremor down my spine and my mouth goes dry. The lingering smell of his cigar smoke, and the faint taste of wine left upon my tongue summon a craving. A craving I thought long gone. A cliché craving that I must satisfy. I need a smoke. I fumble in the dark for a glass of ice water from the bar while plotting where to find a cigarette or perhaps one of his cigars. Heat prickles under my skin, and I drink deeply from the tall glass of water, sucking in a piece of ice, rolling it around on my tongue. I pull on Rhys crumpled, white dress shirt that had been unceremoniously surrendered to the floor. It smells of cologne and testosterone. I dance in the scent, willing it to wrap itself around me. I head out of the cabin, hoping that the late hour will afford me privacy. I'll step outside for a breath of fresh air on deck; perhaps it will crush my craving.

Basking in the afterglow, lost in my thoughts, I anticipate the first sweet swirl of smoke in my lungs. Sliding up the steps, I try and remember the winding path we took to get to our cabin. I pass the galley and a laundry before I run into a young woman I assume is staff.

"Can I help you find something?" she asks with a slight, indiscernible accent.

"I was hoping to find a cigarette or cigar, and the way up to the deck."

"I can help you with that, Ms." She pauses and waits for me to introduce myself.

"Oh, I'm sorry. I am Sophie." She turns on her heel.

"Ok, Ms. Sophie, follow me." She winds through the dining area and around the tall bar, pulling out a large humidor. She flips it open to reveal a full box of Cohibas. I take one and she closes the box, handing me a clipper and a lighter before prompting me again to follow her. Up another flight of stairs we emerge onto the deck.

"Thank you," I tell her as she disappears down the stairs and below deck with a curt nod. I wonder how many random women she has had to show around the yacht, how many conquests she has watched come and go. The candles on deck flicker and dance as they burn themselves out. I hear the faint sound of boisterous voices coming from the other side of the breakwater. I fumble with the cigar, dropping it to the deck. I bend over to pick it up and Rhys winds his hands around my hips.

"What are you doing?"

"I wanted some fresh air and a smoke." He shakes his head, but says nothing. Taking the clipper from my hand, he picks up the cigar. Concentrating too hard on snipping the end, he slowly lights it with long, drawn out puffs, creating a lazy cloud of smoke that wafts above him.

"Why didn't you wake me?" he asks, puffing heavily on it, covering himself in a cloud of smoke.

"I didn't want to disturb you, you looked so peaceful. Why do you keep shaking your head, what have I done wrong?" Watching me intently, he brushes the hair from my face with a sigh.

"I'm sorry, you did nothing wrong," he teases, tugging the hem of his shirt farther up my thighs. "I just thought…" He turns away, towards the sounds of the party which must have spilled out onto the lawn. Robbing me of the sight of his face, the opportunity to know what he is thinking. We watch as a few remaining party goers flit across the lawn and head for the pool deck, their high pitched squeals of play fill the dark night.

"Hey." I tug on his shoulder, needing to see his face, wanting him to look at me. Tipping the cigar at me in offer he raises an eyebrow in challenge. I take the long fat cigar, watching his eyes as I run my tongue across my lips and gingerly wrap my mouth around the tip. The tobacco is sweet and smoky. I take three short puffs and blow a wide, meandering smoke ring in his direction. He raises that wicked eyebrow and steps through the ring.

"Cigars?"

"My dad smoked cigars and drank scotch when he thought I was asleep. I like the smell."

"Ah." He towers above me as his wet lips take the cigar again, puffing and smacking on the now damp butt. "I like you in my shirt," he offers casually with a slight grin. "Sounds like the party is still going," He steps to the rail of the yacht and gazes against the dark into the large swath of grass that surrounds the house.

"Where did you think I went?" I tease, taking the cigar from his long fingers. A spark ignites between us as our fingers brush. The chemical reaction of our encounter rises to the surface, crackling in the air between us. The warmth of his casual brush spreads through me like liquid, filling me up, drowning me. He lunges forward and takes my face in his free palm. His eyes bore into me and his lips twist into a lopsided grin.

"I thought perhaps you ran, like a frightened little bunny." His mocking tone and hooded eyes don't fool me. The playboy has a heart.

"You give yourself too much credit. I am no frightened bunny. Maybe a hungry fox, and it would be a mistake to underestimate the fox, they're cunning and unpredictable."

"You are unpredictable. I will give you that." He takes a step closer and folds me into his arms, pressing his bare chest against me.

"That was incredible. But I'm afraid that it is not going to be enough. I am going to have to ask you to stay." He raises an eyebrow in question. I can hardly wrap my head around what I am hearing. He was annoyingly clear in his intentions, one night. I assumed that was a hard and fast rule, and that he was a stickler for his own rules. Yet, here we are. Moments after he has shown me what my body can really do and already wants more. His eyes sparkle in the dying candlelight and rising moon.

"I would like to tie you up," he whispers after a long silence. Fright climbs my back and hovers in my shoulders. Reflexively, I take a step back, out of his reach. No way, the thought of being tied up turns my blood to ice, the slow trickle cooling my body and bringing me down hard.

"How romantic," I scoff, trying to sound unaffected. He grabs my arms pulling me back to him. His fingers roll against my skin, flexing and

186

digging into my sensitive flesh. His face is stone, his eyes serious and expectant. He looks quite serious. "You're joking, right? You said no kink. French vanilla, remember?" I tease, hoping, waiting for him to crack, for a sign that he is teasing. Melissa's words eek closer to the surface of my conscious mind, '*He just wants to tie you down and fuck you.*'

"A little restraint isn't kink, and I don't joke about sex." He traces lines down my back with feather light strokes of his strong, nimble fingers. "This isn't romance, this is fun, Beautiful." His hand skates down my back, cupping the curve of my backside, where he pauses and murmurs to himself, groaning in approval while he squeezes and pulls at my begging flesh. "I don't believe in romance, it's so forced and phony." The thought hangs heavy in the air, seemingly unfinished. "Most importantly…" he ponders, his lips tracing a scorching line down my throat, peppering gentle kisses across my shoulders before quickly turning me away from him. His powerful arms wind around me, making my cage, his body heaving behind me. He places a hot, wet kiss to the back of my neck, sending a shiver down my spine.

"When I want something, I take it." His lips move across my shoulders before I can protest, a low feral moan rising in his chest. Disarmed by his moan of approval my face breaks into a lip splitting smile. I cannot help it. He has charmed me so easily, and now he wants more. "Mm, there we go, I love that smile, Sophie." A wolfish grin paints his face. "Now, will you let me have my way?"

"How can you be so sweet and threatening at the same time?"

"You are sweet," he teases, licking his lips salaciously. "I am selfish. Believe me. Just say you will stay, or I *will* tie you up." If only he knew how deeply that small, innocent threat pulled at the recesses of my weary mind. "Stay."

"I am booked on a flight tomorrow. I can't afford to change it."

"Stay," he insists.

"How can you break your own rules so easily? Perhaps after a little sleep you may change your mind. I am not interested in becoming an unwanted guest or worse, some pathetic hanger-on." This knocks him off balance, a noticeable shudder runs down his spine and he stills.

"I'm not as fickle as all that, Sophie. Do you really think so little of me that I could turn like that?"

"I just don't want to end up regretting this."

"Alright, I can respect that." Clearly exasperated by my bargaining and curiosity his head falls back, and he gazes at the emerging stars.

"What if I refuse?"

"I will cancel your flight personally, and tie
188

you up so tight that you can't escape for a month."
There is an edge, a promise in his eyes that sends a
chill down my spine. "So what will it be, Beautiful,
two days, or a month of bondage?" I cannot help
but crack a wide smile at him, completely entranced
by his proposition, by the promise of more time,
more pleasure, more Rhys. "Good, that's settled.
Now bring that foxy ass back to bed." And with a
casual ease, he puts the whole thing to rest, leading
me below deck, my throat cooled by the water, my
craving satiated by the shared cigar, and my body
ready for another ride.

Chapter 14

My head rests perfectly in the spot made for me under Rhys' arm, my legs wound around his, my arm flung heavily across his sun warmed chest. I can't help myself from running my fingers down his torso, my fingertips skipping over each ripple of perfectly chiseled muscle. His chest gently rises and falls with each long, sleepy breath. Here he lies, next to me, in a rumpled, torn bed. On a yacht! The thought is intoxicating, that I could affect him in such a base way. He looks peaceful, non-intimidating, and tempting. I reach out to pull at the sheet that teases me, slipping away from his powerful thigh, when he catches me in his grip. His long fingers wound tightly around my wrist, with a quiet force that resonates right down to my toes. A growl rumbles in his chest and he pulls me closer, cradling me against him. He has my hands folded in front of me, firmly in his grip. Caged by his hands and body, I lay still against his chest and listen as his heart rate forms a hypnotic rhythm.

"Not ready to wake up, this feels too good. Ten more minutes," his gravelly whisper rattles in my ear, echoes in my loins and I am of the same mind, yet I know our peace is about to be shattered by the post wedding brunch and Olivia and Matthew's departure.

"What about brunch? And the crew is probably

pacing outside our door. I am sure they need to get the cabin ready for Olivia and Matthew before they leave, right?" He groans and pulls me tighter.

"Alright, alright." A feather light kiss to the back of my neck sends a delicious shiver down my spine before he flips me over and kisses me until my head swims. "I'm up." Taking my breath with him, he hops out of bed and pulls a duffel bag from the wardrobe. "Here." He tosses me a flowered Lily Pulitzer sundress from my luggage. I look at him in question, but he answers before I can ask. "I had a bag made up for us, I hope that's ok?"

"So, now you are dressing me?" I tease, as he pulls on a pair of blue Dockers and a crisp white shirt.

"They are your clothes. I just picked one of the half a dozen dresses from your bag. Just get dressed. I have to check with the crew, make sure they are prepared for departure. I will meet you on deck." He leans in and kisses my forehead before slapping my ass and he is out the door.

***

I stand and watch the boat pull away from the dock. One last wave to Olivia and Matthew as Rhys shows the last of the guests out to the drive and a fleet of waiting cars. By the time the last guest is out the door it is almost four in the afternoon.

191

Stillness fills the house for the first time, and it dawns on me, standing in his empty house. We are alone, this is happening. A ripple of anticipation and nerves slithers down my spine. How will we fill the next two days?   "Sophie." His warm honey voice flows through me, pulling me from my thoughts. He stands right before me, yet I must have been looking right through him, lost in my own debauched head, considering the possibilities. "Are you hungry?" He runs his finger down the length of my arm.

"No." I shake my head and lock eyes with him. All day long I have wanted to peel those clothes right off of him. He is the picture of casual class and style in his slacks and white dress shirt, deceptively gentlemanly. Yet, beneath lurks a sexual animal of a caliber I have never known. A slight grin turns his mouth.

"Are you tired?" he teases. I just shake my head and fight back a smile. What I want is him, spread out naked beneath me, or me beneath him. "You want to go to bed." The dark twinkle in his eye says he knows my reply, and was not asking.

"Yes." Raising an eyebrow, his wicked tongue swipes across his bottom lip and my eyes grow wider.

"Oh, this is going to be fun." His crooked grin pulls at something deep within me. With his palm on the small of my back, he guides me slowly up the stairs. "After you."

"Take that damn dress off." The edge in his voice is new, and urgent. Something about the way he touches me, the way he speaks to me. I do as he asks without a thought, without hesitation. He knows. He makes me feel like I don't have to think. I just want to feel, to feel him. I let my dress fall to the floor and step out of it. Rhys steps in front of me, dropping to his knees.

The picture of carnal elegance, I relish the sight of him on his knees. I look down into his eyes to see myself reflected in them. He is waiting for me. I reach out to his shirt I undo the top button, spreading his collar open, running my finger along his collarbone, along the delicate gold chain at his throat. Every part of him is so masculine. Chiseled and hard, like stone. As I move my fingers from button to button, he watches with shallow breaths. I rake my nails across his chest, pushing the shirt open to revel in the beauty of his skin, scattered with dark hair. He runs his hands up the back of my bare legs, searing my skin with the fire in the tips of his fingers. Hooking his thumbs in the delicate lace around my hips, he slides them down my legs, leaving me exposed. All the while he remains cloaked in fine clothes.

I stand before him, alive, aware and aching with anticipation. He is crouched before me, his erection straining at the front of his crisp slacks, raking me over with his intense eyes, taking in every nude curve, every soft dimple. I stand before him naked and needy while he remains the picture of gentlemanly class. Yet I know there is nothing gentlemanly about what he is about to do to me. What I want him to do to me.

He buries his nose between my thighs, running his face along my heat slicked flesh, breathing me in deeply, a salacious grin tugging at his full lips. It is so dirty, so damn hot. I am already damp and hyper aware of myself. He looks into my eyes, rocking back onto his heels.

"This is all up to you, Beautiful." I waver under his scrutiny, swaying before I regain my balance. Sure that I want this, but tongue tied and twisted, I cannot find the words. My flesh is on fire, my heart leaping in my chest and my pussy is wet and waiting. "I kneel before you a starving man, Sophie. Feed me. Please."

I swallow the last vestige of doubt, knowing that I want his mouth on me. I need it more than air. Without hesitation, I surrender to the deep growling need within me. I close my eyes, let my head fall back and press my hips in his hands. In an instant his hands are heavy around my waist, a deep growl erupts from his chest and he tosses me backwards onto the large bed; every inch of animal hovers over me, hungry and excited. I drip with anticipation, his lustful aggression fueling the wanton trollop inside of me. He makes me feel alive, on fire. I am sexy, confident under his tutelage, able and so eager to learn.

He wraps his hands around my ankles and slowly pulls me towards the foot of the bed. I sit up to see him kneeling at my feet, his eyes full of carnal lust, his lips wet and swollen. It is all very familiar. His eyes are tentative, waiting for permission. I reach down and push the linen shirt and vest off his broad shoulders, running my fingernails up the back of his neck through his coarse hair. He closes his eyes and releases a deep moan, leaning his head into my waiting hands. Urgency clouds my vision as our eyes meet and lock in an erotic knot. My breasts fall free and into his waiting hands. He kneads and squeezes the heavy flesh, his finger and thumb twisting and pulling at my little pink nipples, making them pointed and hard. He leans in and takes one breast into his mouth, rolling my hard nub around with his long tongue. He nips at me with his teeth and looks to me.

"Aahh." He pulls my nipple between his teeth, and then begins to knead and pull at my flesh with his other hand.

"Spread your legs, Beautiful," he whispers. Slowly he pushes me back onto the bed and sinks back to his knees, his hot breath tickling the inside of my already warm thigh. His hands sit firmly on the inside of each knee, slowly pushing my legs wider. I am open and splayed before him, exposed and unsure. Yet he looks as if he is gazing upon a masterpiece. The reverence in his eyes surely should be reserved for some Renaissance painting or beautiful sculpture. Yet he looks at me with those appreciative eyes, alight with anticipation and worship. He pulls me to the very edge of the bed and dips his head between my splayed limbs, taking a deep breath of my scent.

"Mm mm," he hums, blowing a cool breath across my swollen folds; I writhe and shift my hips. "Don't move," he demands in a husky whisper. He stills me with his strong hands, wrapping one arm around my leg, resting my thigh on his shoulder, he strums my clit with his thumb and watches my face. His gaze is so intense, watching him take so much pleasure in touching me is surreal and I have to turn away. I close my eyes and let every movement wash over me. "That's it, Beautiful, just lie back and enjoy."

He continues to strum my clit as he dips a finger into my waiting sex. "Oh, you are so wet already, Sophie." My name drips off his tongue like honey. He slips two fingers in and begins to pump in and out, building rhythm while he presses on my clit with his thumb. The underlying tension in my body crescendos at his ministrations until my body moves of it's own accord, my hips sway, begging. I press against his hand, begging for more, raising my hips off the bed, lifting myself into his palm, wantonly waving my pussy in his face. I feel an orgasm building as he puts more pressure on that bundle of frantic nerves, slowly pushing his middle finger between my folds and massaging me, warming me up, making slow methodical circles.

His hands continue their slow torture and my head is swirling in a torrent of heat and pleasure. An explosion is building more intense than anything I have ever felt, my body is no longer my own, moving on its own accord, responding to every move he makes. His finger hooks and rubs a spot I have never felt, sending a shock wave through me. He lowers his head and gently begins to kiss and tease me with his mouth, licking and nibbling my most sensitive spot. Around and around his tongue swirls as his fingers push me higher. He blows onto my hot, wet flesh and then plunges his tongue inside of me, pushing and sucking the nectar he has coaxed. Into a million pieces my world shatters, my body humming and pulsing, waves rippling through me. Blood pounds in my ears as my body convulses in his hands. Slowly he lets me down; pulling his fingers from my sex he looks at me with dark eyes, licks his lips and sucks my juice from his fingertips. I am shocked and gasp in response, as a wicked, crooked grin spreads across Rhys' triumphant face.

He climbs my body like a lithe predator admiring his subdued prey. He hovers above me as I slowly come down, shudders rolling through me still, rocking my limbs and stealing my breath. I look up into his eyes just as he thrusts into me and gasps in pleasure as his eyes roll back. He doesn't hold back, pushing himself to the hilt, burying himself within my still quivering sex. I stretch and mold around him, feeling the delicious burn of his large cock ripping me open.

"Oh. My. God, Rhys," I moan as he sets a steady pace, rocking back and forth, in and out. He pulls back till just the tip of his throbbing cock sits at the base of my lips. He rocks his hips; shallow thrusts make me needy as his tip dips in and out of my swollen folds. A storm builds deep in my body, spreading like flood waters, threatening to drown me in pleasure.

"Oh please!" I gasp. Wanting more, needing the full length of him buried deep in my core. "Please Rhys." He teases me, watching me writhe as he slowly moves back and forth. "Harder!" I beg.

"Yes!" he roars before slamming into me, filling me to the hilt, our hips crashing with explosive force. "That's it Beautiful, talk to me." His frantic pace ignites a series of explosions that ring deep in my blood and steal my senses. "Pull your knees up!" he roars. I grasp the back of my knees and pull them to my ears just as he rears up and slams into me with such force that our bodies

198

converge in a crushed and tangled knot, writhing and grinding against one another. My body is alive with the echo of his assault humming in my veins. He slowly pulls back, leaving me wanting, aching for another. I whimper and that wickedly sexy, crooked grin pulls at his mouth, his eyes tease, and a devious sparkle betrays his intention. He slams into me again, and again, filling me, crushing him to me, every time, driving harder and deeper, taking more and more for himself. His eyes watch me, intent on witnessing my inevitable undoing, the undoing he is driving me towards, with every hot thrust. His hands pressed firmly against the back of my thighs, pinning me down, making me crazy, and greedy. I want more. I want him to climb inside of me, to fill me. I cannot take another minute, but I cannot stand the thought of him stopping.

He watches me come undone under the relentless onslaught from his powerful jack hammer hips. I don't think I am even in my body. Sophie left the room while some nymph is getting her brains fucked out by the god of sex himself. I watch myself scream for mercy and beg for more, completely out of control. Thrashing about as much as his strong hands will allow, unsure I can absorb anymore. I cannot keep still, my body is no longer my own, skipping on a note. I am barely aware as he empties himself in one deep and final thrust, his neck craned to the ceiling, eyes screwed tightly shut, growling through gritted teeth.

"Sophie!" He stills and drops to his forearms, resting his weight on my humming body. I look up into his eyes while my body slowly returns to earth. My legs are clamped on his shoulders, my hands tangled in a fistful of sheet and my own hair. The weight of his body, his heart pounding through his flesh pull me back to earth, back into his arms. I clench around him, unwilling and unable to release my stranglehold on him. He lies on top of me spent, sweaty, and panting. He winces as a gentle spasms roll through me, he releases my legs, and they fall to his sides, leaden and worn. Rolling onto his side he pulls me into his chest, pulling the sheet over us both. I lay, speechless against the soft, sticky hair on his chest and listen to his heart. The rhythm is familiar and comfortable. Like a lullaby. Caressing my heated skin, his fingers run up and down the back of my arm. My skin is littered with goose bumps, and streaks of heat that radiate from the trails he draws. I feel unable to speak, or move. I just lay in his arms, our breathing and mingled heart beats the only sound in the room.

His large room is bathed in a soft pink light from the sinking sun. The bed is in disarray, rumpled sheets and blankets scattered like remnants from a storm. Pillows tossed all over the dark mahogany floor, and I am spent. I hardly had a moment to look around before we fell back into bed, and got lost. I hardly have the strength to lift my head from the mattress to peruse my surroundings. The large bed sits squarely in the middle of a room that is larger than my entire apartment. A sitting area of chairs too nice to sit in circles the large bay window that lends the fading light. I roll my head around, more than a little delirious to see Rhys and his sparkling green eyes. Propped up on his elbow, he eyes me shrewdly, watching me slowly regain consciousness. A bolt of lightning strikes through me as he reaches out and grazes my shoulder with his strong fingers, I flinch, blinking up at him for a moment, floating in a soundless chasm, my body totally shut down. And he just smiles.

"Earth to Sophie." I close my eyes tightly, willing the world to return, for my mind to return to planet earth. When I open them I get my wish. The faint sounds of Rhys breathing and my own pounding heart, tickle my ears and I have returned to the land of the living, or rather to the land of the obscenely wealthy and bored. I roll to my side, pulling a sheet with me and wrap myself in it as I stare into the eyes of a man who just so thoroughly undid me, I can hardly form a coherent thought. All I can do is smile.

"You ok? I lost you there for a minute." He grins, knowing full well the answer. I just shake my head and take a deep, cleansing breath. I don't want to come back down. "I'm going to get us a drink. You just lay there and look beautifully spent," he teases, hopping out of bed like a lithe cat.

He pulls on a pair of pants from the floor, leaving me alone to recover. When he returns, he has a glass of water in one hand and scotch in the other. He sets the rocks glass down on the bedside table and hands me the water.

"Drink up." I gulp it down like a parched desert prisoner. He laughs at my zeal for refreshment, dropping his pants to the ground and climbs back into bed. Taking the empty water glass from my hand, he exchanges it for the rocks glass and sits up against the ornately scrolled headboard. "Who taught you to come like that?" I choke and splutter at his question. Is that something that can be taught? If it is, surely it is his doing. I just shake my head. "What's the matter, cat got your tongue?" he teases, taking a slow sip of scotch before offering me the glass. I sit up and take a sip, hoping my voice will return.

My voice is small and distant. "That was intense. I thought I was going to black out." I grin slightly from embarrassment. "I have never felt anything like it."

"That was your G-spot." He opens his arm and invites me to rest against his shoulder. "What a glorious reaction. You are so responsive," he muses, his fingers caressing my shoulder. "It won't be the

202

last time I hit that button," he says in into my hair, before taking the scotch from my hand. "What would you like to do this evening?" he asks.

"Stay here, just like this," I say, looking up into his seductive eyes. He smiles down on me and winks.

"Me, too." We lie in bed, sharing the scotch in relative silence. Comfortable, sated silence.

"Ask me something personal, Sophie." I am floored and more than a little intrigued. Suddenly he wants to open up. Is it the setting, what we just did? I don't care. There is so much I want to know. But, before I can contemplate and choose wisely my mouth takes over.

"What am I still doing here?"

"After one night with a woman it is evident what she expects, what she is hoping for. I know all I need to know. It is easier to keep the lines clear and concise after one night. If I were to see them again the lines would blur and I don't want that. I don't want anyone to get the wrong idea." Even as he says it, as if he is talking about someone else. I know he is talking to me. "But you, Sophie, I have no idea what you expect from me, I don't yet have all the information."

"Nor will you ever," I tease.

"Ah, therein lies the rub. I have to figure you out, Sophie. I trust you. I have known you for a blink of an eye and I trust you more than some women I have known my entire life. You fascinate me."

"Fascinate? That is a heavy word. There is nothing fascinating about me. I am just a simple girl, no worldly knowledge to speak of, and no high powered job to brag about. Just Sophie."

"If that is truly how you see yourself then you need to take another hard look. Because that is not what I see." Immediately I want to deflect, redirect the conversation. I don't like it when people try and hold a mirror up. Insisting that you see what they see. I know what I am.

"Have you ever been with someone more than once?"

"I don't make a habit of it."

"Why is that?"

"I don't like to be tied down," he says with a smirk

"Ironic, don't you think?"

"I suppose."

"You are so cryptic."

"I am a very private man, Sophie. So much of my life is dedicated to public things. The few parts I can keep private, I am fiercely protective over. You can understand that. When you let people overstay their welcome, they start to insert themselves into your life. I cannot have that." His voice is distant, contemplative. "This is completely new to me." He twirls my hair around his fingers, absent-mindedly.

204

"What is?"

"You. Wanting you to stay. You drive me to distraction. In two days I have become besotted. I have developed an obsessive need to be near you, to touch you." He grins, tracing soft lines down my spine. "To be on you, to be *in* you. I just want to be all over you," his hot whisper in my ear almost pushes me over the edge.

"Stop, be serious." His confession is magical.

"OK, serious," he says, backing away, taking his deft fingers from my needy flesh. He looks at me and his intention is clear, baptism by hot and heavy words. "I want to know what you are thinking, how you are feeling. I want to know every part of you." Something in the way he looks at me makes me feel like I am about to fall. Or burst into flames. Or turn to liquid.

"This is supposed to be about you, remember?"

"Right. OK, ask me something else."

"When was the last time you said 'I love you'?"

"Wow, OK," He pauses for a moment a shrugs, taking a sip of scotch. "I can't remember. Not since I was a child, if I'm honest. When was the last time you said it?"

"This morning to Olivia," I say matter of fact. "You should tell people when you love them. Tell them every day. Who would not want to hear that they are loved? I think it's important to say it, if you

205

feel it." I watch his face change, in a way I do not recognize. I expect him to clam up and squirm. But his gaze is intense and open. There always seems to be more hiding behind his eyes than he ever lets on. If his eyes could talk I would know him so much better. "What about your mom, or your dad? Don't you tell them you love them?"

"No. I do. Love them." The words do not come easily. He pauses for a deep breath and a pull from our shared glass. I take the glass from his hand a swirl the amber liquid around and around, the distinct smell of peat wafting from the crystal rim.

"What about a woman? Have you never said '*I love you*' to a woman?" A minute nod of his head tells me he doesn't want to go there. But he asked for personal, and I seize the opportunity, before it's lost. "Have you ever loved anyone?"

"Maybe, although I think it was worship, not love." The planes of his face adopt a sharp edge as his jaw flexes and he grinds his teeth. "I don't like to throw those words around. They come with a lot of weight, and expectation." His pensive gaze roams my face before our eyes meet.

"Are you afraid of what people expect from you? Or are you afraid of not getting what you expect from them?" I pour the remaining drops of Dalwhinney over my tongue and let the burn slide down my throat. "Giving love is easy. Accepting love, that is different. But give and you shall receive, that is what I think." I set the glass down and wait. He just shakes his head the way I have become so accustomed to and his lips curl into that crooked grin. I love the way his lips twist. That grin pulls at my hips.

He climbs over me slowly, pushing me down on the bed. He laces my fingers with his and pulls my hands above my head. Brushing his lips across my neck, he raises goose bumps all over my body. He affects me so easily, my body language, he knows it already. My body is like an open book to him. I feel free and open. With one hand solidly pinning my wrists, he winds his fingers in my hair and pulls it to his nose, taking a deep draught.

"You smell like heaven." I smell like sex and scotch, and Rhys. Winding his fingers around my throat, he pushes my head back, grazing my chin with his thumb before pushing it into my mouth. My first instinct is to bite down, but I quickly pull his thumb into my mouth and wind my tongue around. He pulls it from my mouth, but not before I nip the pad. Running it along my bottom lip, he scorches me with those heavy eyes and whispers, "Give and you shall receive."

Chapter 15

I lie wide awake next to a rare creature, a woman that does not make me regret my lust. Sophie is soft, sweet, smart and funny. And that mouth, I need to fuck that smart mouth. From the first time she said my name. Every moment with her has been so easy, so comfortable, and familiar. I want to wake her up, get lost in her again. I love the sound she makes when she comes, the way her skin flushes, a pale swath of pink rising just under that freckled skin. But I think better of it. I know I have exhausted her, pushed her farther than she has ever been. I let her sleep, with the thought of checking some emails, catching up on work for an hour or so while I let her recover. The house is quiet after all the wedding noise. All the houseguests are gone, only a skeleton staff remains. I pull on a pair of silk pajama bottoms and head down to my office, running into Marta, the full time maid, at the bottom of the stairs.

"Good morning, Mr. Slate. Can I bring you your coffee?"

"Yes, please, Marta. I will be in the study."

I drop into the large leather chair behind the well-worn desk that my father passed down to me. It is marred with the frustrations of three generations of Slate men. Each a captain of industry, leader in business, pillar of their

208

community. This desk reminds me of all I have to live up to, all I am expected to achieve, the mark I am expected to leave on this world. It is a tall order for a typical young man to face, but I have been groomed for this my entire life. I turn on the computer monitor and set straight to cleaning out my Inbox. Scanning down the page I look for the financials for Viktor Vladova. I want to get this deal done. I don't want to be forced to deal with Nadja, and where her father is, she is never far behind. His company is on the verge of a hostile takeover and looks to Slate Holdings to bail him out. He and my father were partner's way back when, but I knew when my father put me in charge of the deal that he wanted to distance himself from the possible fallout. I am knee deep in a development proposal for new building in China Town when the door swings open. I expect Marta, but get Nadja instead. She holds my coffee, Marta trailing behind her.

"I am sorry, Sir, she insisted."

"It's OK, Marta, thank you." She turns and walks out, while Nadja slowly closes the door, intention written clearly all over her smug face. She is wrapped in a short navy blue trench coat, tightly sashed about her waist. I can guess what is underneath. Her body language screams for attention, so needy and high maintenance. She strolls casually to my desk, placing the coffee at the edge. Sliding around the desk, she steps before me, leaning back on the desk and our knees meet. I push back in my chair, unwilling to play, but aching to watch her try. I pull at my bottom lip, examine her and rock back in my chair.

"You are awfully casual for a Monday morning." Raking me over with her eyes, they linger too long on the silk pajama pants I pulled on, like she is trying to make me hard just by looking at me.

"And you are as hard headed as ever. Twice now you have disobeyed me. I told you that I would see you on Thursday. You are not supposed to be here."

"I had a shoot last night. Are all of your guests gone? I thought you may be lonely. I'm lonely." She unties her coat, letting it fall casually open. I know her too well, she is so predictable. She pulls the coat open resting her hands on her hips. She is on display in a lacy black corset, her small breasts spilling out, and dark red nipples cresting the edge. She drops the coat across my desk to reveal her stockings and garters. Everything about this used to drive me wild, it never occurred to her that I would ever move on. But I have, wholly. Sitting here with her standing in front of me dressed like that, willing and able, practically begging. I feel nothing.

"What are you doing here?" I ask, knowing full well. She is predictable. Predictable and completely out of control most of the time. She drops to her knees in front of me and pushes my legs open, sliding between my thighs. The light in her eyes is dull, tired. Her bony hands are cold, slithering up my covered legs like a serpent. She tugs at the elastic waistband of the silk pajama pants I threw on, but I give her nothing. I will not grant her access to any part of me, no more. She tugs hard again, pulling them out, revealing the dark patch of hair above my still sleeping cock. It doesn't rouse for her, not even a jump or twitch. It took me years to master my body. To control my urges, hold them down, bury them deep. But I no longer have to do that with her. It is a vacant spot. The place she once held is now empty and dark. Comfortably, easily empty. My mind drifts to Sophie. I bite down a smile at the thought of her draped across my bed like she was last night, a writhing ball of limbs and moans.

"I want to play. I miss you. I miss this," she whines, rubbing her palm across my crotch, clearly thinking the secret smile was for her. She tries to elicit a response, to make me hard, to force her suit. I grab her bony wrists, pulling her to her feet. Kicking the chair out from behind me, I stand before her. I will dominate the situation, not her; I don't want her thinking that we are playing. I shift on my feet and square my shoulders. Her eyes travel to my cock and a wicked, mean spirited grin lifts her face. "What's wrong with you? You are not even *hard*."

"I am busy, Nadja." I walk around the desk and she follows.

"Don't you think you're taking this hard to get thing too far, Rhys? It's very tiresome." Her hands travel over my chest, skating over my scar, through my chest hair until they rest just at my collarbone. Her fingers twist the cross at my throat with humor and disdain. I always hated her mockery of my talisman. She drops the cross against my skin, placing a slight kiss at the base of my throat. My lips curl in disgust, my stomach lurches and I push her away. Holding her at arms-length, I pull the sash from her waist and cinch it back up, closing her coat, hiding away her wanton attempt at seduction. Normally a corset and some stockings would perk me right up, but the sight of her does nothing. Oh, she raises my blood pressure still, but only in the most horrible, insipid way.

"This cannot happen again, Nadja. I am done *playing* with you, for many reasons, all of which you are keenly aware of. I will help your father, but that is all I will do for you. I do not want this anymore. Do you understand?" I wait for an answer. I need an answer, to know that she hears me; hears what I am saying, not what she wants to hear. She is not the kind of woman who takes no for an answer. I suspect that she has never had to take no for an answer. But there's a first time for everything. I wonder if I am her first no. I hope I am. I want her to remember it. Remember the sting, what it feels like to have the one person you thought you could count on, turn their back. The one person you thought you could trust with your heart, only to break it.

"You don't mean that, Rhys." She peeks up at me through her lashes, trying to be coy. The dark makeup around her eyes casting a long shadow down her sallow face. "Come on, Daddy, baby girl wants to play. Let me make it up to you." Her raspy purr grates on my ears.

"I do mean it, and you have to go."

"Do you have someone here?" She slows and looks me up and down, a spark igniting in her tired eyes. "Where is she, I want to meet her. Maybe we could use her." She demands heading towards my office door. Oh no, she will not meet Sophie. She will eat her alive, and then where will I be? With my chest pressed to her back, I pin her to the door, stopping her from pulling it open. Her skin is clammy and cold, even though the air outside is warm and sticky. Her shoulders are sharp, everything about her is hard. Hard, cold and contrived, she writhes against me, a small squeak crossing her lips, trying so hard. I do not want her here.

What would Sophie think about a half dressed woman coming out of my office? Would it be evident to her that Nadja is in a wanton state of undress under her designer coat? It was all too obvious to me, but then I know the vixen well. How would Sophie react? I wince at the thought, knowing how most women would react. With a deep sense of suspicion and betrayal, I am sure. No, I am not prepared to explain Nadja to Sophie. Not now, not ever, if I have the choice. I don't need the complication. "Are you afraid she may like me better?"

"That's it! You will leave, now. I will let you know when I know something about the deal with your father. We are on track for the Gala and in the meantime, you will stay away from here."

"How long has she been here, Rhys? This better not be the same gash from the wedding. You are breaking the rules for this girl. There must be a good reason. What is it?"

I open the door and lead her out of the office, my hand firmly at her back, pushing her towards the front door, giving her no alternative. We round the corner and come face to face with Sophie, standing as still as a statue at the bottom of the stairs. Fuck!

***

It's Monday, I think. Time has little meaning in Rhys' bed. Fuck, sleep, fuck, eat, drink, fuck, repeat. I am awake long before I open my eyes. The

214

sun is too bright, and inescapable. I take my time, roll onto Rhys pillow and pull it close to my chest. He lingers in the fibers, his musk and sweat. The smell of sex surrounds me and I bathe in it. Just the scent of him sends my mind wandering along a dark and lovely path. I rub my thighs together and I am already wet. He fucked me into a coma last night and the first and only thing I can think about when I wake is going back for more. Yikes. Maybe this is why he has to limit his interactions to one night encounters, lest he create a population of addicts. This is not good. I take a moment to collect my thoughts before I open my eyes. I roll over to see that it is much later than I could have imagined. He really did put me in a coma. I hurry out of bed and into the large master bathroom. I pull a pick through my hair and brush my teeth before throwing on a pair of shorts and a lacy tank from my luggage. I cannot think of anything but finding him, and slipping back into his blissful hands. He has created a monster.

Knowing he has been avoiding work, something Olivia said he never does, I head first towards his office. Hopping down the formal staircase, I slide around the corner, but stop when I hear Rhys' voice, and then the voice of a woman.

"Come on, Daddy, baby girl wants to play." The muted purr crawls across my skin and claws at my raw nerves. What the fuck? I know I shouldn't

listen but I'm locked in now. Who is he with? Blood is pounding in my ears and I know I should retreat. I shouldn't eavesdrop, but my feet will not budge. I am glued to the bottom stair. My ears are perked and my stomach is doing flips as Rhys' muffled voice gets louder, "*You have to go.*" My pulse is racing, frantic heartbeats drowning out a conversation that I want desperately to escape from, yet want desperately to hear. "*I want to meet her. Maybe we could use her.*" What the fuck does that mean? Oh god, is this how it all comes crashing down on me? I make one flippant choice, one misjudgment and the universe conspires to make a fool of me. What am I doing here? I want to run. I want to burst into his office and make my presence known. I want to disappear and pretend none of this ever happened.

"*That's it!*" Rhys' tone is ferocious and fear inducing. I hear the shuffle of feet and a few muffled words before the door is wrenched open and it's too late. I have nowhere to run, nowhere to hide. I try to make a break up the stairs, but realize I cannot get away fast enough. I turn around and try to make it look as if I have just come down when I almost fall backwards, coming just inches from running into a statuesque blonde, cloaked in a short navy blue trench coat. The blonde from the picture in Rhys' office, and she is more breathtaking in person. Tall and slender, her hair hangs down her back and shimmers like gold against her tanned skin. Her bright blue orbs, rimmed with kohl, inspect every inch of me.

"I don't see it," she mutters under her breath, before she flips a switch, blinding me with a practiced, disingenuous smile. "You must be Sophie." Her face is bright and friendly, but something in the way she thrusts her hand at me is off. Speechless, I offer her my hand. "It is lovely to meet you. I am Nadja." Her fingers are long and slender, and her cold, clammy skin sticks to mine as she shakes my hand a little too hard. My stomach turns at the sound of her name, and I take a deep breath, swallowing back a growing disdain.

"It's not like Rhys to keep his girls for more than one night. You must be doing something right." She winks at my souring face. It takes a tremendous effort to appear stoic and unaffected by her haughty presence. She clearly loves to intimidate, her hand still wrapped around mine. Like a cat in heat she is trying to mark her territory, a too tight squeeze of her hand tells me we are battling for control. She rakes me up and down while a slight hum oozes from her throat, leaving a poisonous sting in the air. I pull my hand from hers, taking a step back, away from the coiled snake so ready to strike. Her eyes are locked with mine while a predators' smirk twists at her pouty lips. "What's the matter, honey? Cat got your tongue?" Her fire laced giggle kicks me out of my own head, my tongue trying desperately to catch up with my mind, but failing miserably.

I turn to Rhys leaning lazily against the door of his office, a casual witness to our encounter, seemingly amused and unaffected. He grins, but it does not meet his eyes. There is nothing casual about him at closer look. His body is rigid, his jaw tight, teeth grinding slowly as he watches her. A slight shift in his demeanor, barely detectable, sends a shadow across his bright eyes. A brief twitch pulls at the corner of his mouth as I drop her hand and his eyes narrow on Nadja. His face is tense, an inscrutable expression perfectly in place upon his chiseled features.

"That is enough." He shuffles Nadja towards the front entrance with a curt goodbye. My leaden feet have me anchored to the spot, stunned by the entire exchange.

Chapter 16

"Come." He grabs my hand, pulling me behind him. He is distracted, tense. "I want to play." There's that phrase. My spine rattles at his words. My chest is struck with a strangling fear as he bounds up the stairs, taking them two at a time. His pull is urgent, but every step brings me closer to something I know I am not ready for. She provokes him, Nadja's effect is left all over his tense form and his uneasily silent mouth. Trepidation courses through me with each heartbeat, growing stronger. I try to fight back the fear, but it wells in my throat erupting in a shocking unprovoked declaration. He tugs at my hand, but I plant myself and tug back.

"I don't want to be tied up!" He slows and turns on me, hovering a step above me, his form even larger and more looming than normal. His eyes narrow as he exhales a deep held breath, pulling me reluctantly over the landing.

"I haven't decided what I am going to do with you yet, but don't fret. I will be gentle. Remember, I am supposed to be having my way, Beautiful." Pushing the bedroom door open he crosses to a chest of drawers, pulling a length of shock provoking silk from the bottom drawer.

"I never agreed to that." I am transfixed by the rope, hypnotized by its menacing color and ominous length as he pulls the bundle back and forth over his open palms. I am unable to look away.

Disappointment dulls the sparkle in his eyes. "You have a fair point. I see that I will have to remember to tie up all the loose ends with you, Sophie." His tone is clipped, and icy.

"You seem out of sorts. Maybe we should wait." I take a seat at the foot of the bed, careful to remain as far away from the headboard, or anything he could tie me to. He is like a caged animal, eerily calm, but in a dangerous state of mind.

"I am fine, just a little frustrated. I would like to take that frustration out on you." His fingers trace a scorching trail down my cheek, sending a shiver down my jelly spine. "Have you ever been tied up?"

"No." I have never done anything adventurous or kinky. And I have never craved anything like that. Being tied up or tied down illicit a serious flight reaction, the thought makes me want to run for the hills. Far away from this man that has made me feel so amazing.

"How do you know you don't want it?" His wicked question churns deep in my mind.

"I don't know."

"I think you're afraid."

"Should I be?"

"Do you think that I would hurt you, Sophie? Do you think that would bring me pleasure?" I shake my head, unsure of my own mind. He watches me closely, waiting for me to spook. I have never felt the way he makes me feel. I feel driven to please him. I want to trust him. But the thought of being at someone else's mercy, trusting him not to hurt me, I don't know that I am capable. It is too soon.

"What scares you about being restrained?" His tone is silky and measured.

"Not being able to get away." My voice is small and quiet, and I struggle to stay in the moment. Not to let my mind drag me back into dark memories.

"Don't you trust me, Sophie?" His face is serious, a shadow of doubt clouds his eyes and I fear I have lost him. "Do you really believe that I would hurt you, or make you do something you didn't want to do? It is an exercise in freedom. You would be free to feel and enjoy everything I do to you without having to think." And that phrase is the clutch for me, 'everything I do to you'. To me, not with me.

"I….I'm just not ready for that."

"If you don't trust me we shouldn't be doing any of this." He pulls the ropes roughly through his palms once more, squeezing and kneading the swaths of shiny, blood red silk before whipping them back into the open drawer. "Trust me when I say that if I ever do bind your hands and legs, and I hope I do, you won't be going anywhere."

"That sounded like a threat. Your sales pitch

221

leaves something to be desired."

"Oh, there is plenty left to be desired, Beautiful." Shoving the drawer closed with his foot, the discussion is closed, I challenged him and I lost, even though I got what I wanted.

"I thought we were going to play?" my voice strangled by disappointment that catches me off guard.

"I've changed my mind," his voice is resolute. I sulk, sinking into the bed, pulling a pillow across my lap, covering myself. "Don't pout, it's not becoming and it will only strengthen my resolve. You need to recognize your value. You are more than a plaything, Sophie. You don't have to do anything you don't want to do. And you shouldn't do something you are not sure of, even if it is to please me." Moments ago, he was ready to tie me up and fuck me silly, now he admonishes me like a parent. How can he demand my independence and submission in the same moment? How did this become about my self-worth? I thought this was about him.

"You are angry."

"No, I am not angry." I don't believe him. He stalks into the bathroom, returning with a towel that he slings onto the bed next to me.

"Then what? What have I done?" Knowing full well that I haven't done anything, except turn him down.

"I am just frustrated, with myself." He is at war with himself, the evidence written all over his face. His brows knit together, forming a deep valley between them, his mouth set in a hard line and his body is tense. I move to the end of the bed, closer to him. But he shifts away, moving from under my advancing hands. He stands, looking down on me, crystal green eyes full of doubt and something else, something unreadable. Something I know, deep in my gut stems from Nadja, and her visit. It seems she has left him teetering on the edge, lost in thought, and now the suggestion of the ropes? I thought he had been kidding. At the very least, when he said tie me up I thought of a little wrist restraint, maybe a tie, something I could easily escape. But those ropes were long. They do not look like a prop, the menacing shade of blood red and uncomfortably smooth silk was intriguing but more frightening than I had imagined. At that moment all I could think of was being tied up and left, or worse. The thought was too much to bear, too scary to hide. And now he is distant and pulling away. Rifling through his drawers he pulls out a pair of running shorts and a faded green tee shirt, with St. Andrews Rugby scrolled across the chest.

"Rhys?" He turns to look at me and I almost drown. He is far away, getting further by the minute. A wave of fear crashes in my belly, swirling around me, threatening to pull me under.

"Did I do something wrong?" I can't say where it came from, the fear that welled up inside me, but it was there, and it was cold. And I knew that I could not let him walk out with his frustrations in tow. Something told me that if I let him walk out, everything would change. He was retreating. It was evident in every stiff move of his body, every terse word from his mouth. *She* was pulling him down. I need to pull him back up.

"You haven't done anything wrong, Sophie. I'm going for a run." Eyes cast down, he heads back into the bathroom, closing the door behind him, shutting me out. I can't let this happen. I cannot let him shut down. We have had such a good time up until now. I will not let Nadja take that away from me, now I am feeling selfish, determined. I hop off the bed and stand at the closed door. I set to my shoulders, hold myself straight and tall, hoping the outward appearance of strength will influence the inner limp noodle. I open the door without a knock and find him leaning against the counter, staring at himself in the wall size mirror.

"Hey." I rest my hand on his forearm. He turns his face to me and we stare into one another's eyes. He doesn't say a word, just watches me, his eyes darting over my face, from my eyes back to my mouth.

His jaw relaxes ever so slightly, the crack in his façade that I was looking for. I reach up on my tip toes and place a soft kiss on the corner of his mouth, the stubble from his beard barely a tickle against my cheek. It takes him a minute. A very long minute, before he allows himself to thaw. Hauling me into his strong embrace, he crushes me to his chest, his heart beating frantically, drumming against my ear.

I press myself closer to him, wrapping my arms around his waist. The muscles in his back move and roll under my hands. His heart slows gradually while he holds me. All the while placing feather light kisses in my hair. His hands are wound around me like an anaconda. He cups my head in the most protective gesture, tilting my chin to the heavens he stares at me, studying my face before the corner of his mouth twirls into a perfectly crooked grin. There he is. He leans down and takes my mouth with such force that my legs wobble. He catches me behind the knees swinging my legs up into his arms so easily. I wrap my arms around his neck, press back and slide my tongue into his mouth, flicking at his lower lip. He lifts me onto the counter, setting me on the cool marble top. Pressing his thighs between mine, he spreads my legs and fills the void with his hard body.

"Please don't be angry with me," I whisper. Pulling away from me, his look is one of utter shock, and resignation.

"Sophie, I could never be angry with you. *I* am

sorry." Shaking his head with a huff, he buries his head in the crook of my neck and gently kisses me, his tongue dipping into the hollow of my throat. His mouth is warm and soft, plying me with every soft brush of his lips. I bury my hands in his unruly morning curls and tug hard, pulling his face back, looking him in the eye.

"What was she doing here?" I need to know.

"She just came to rattle my cage," he says with a violent shake of his head.

"Well, it worked. Who is she to you?"

"Nobody of any consequence." His glare is hard, dilated and unwavering. It is clear by every atom in his body that he does not want to rehash what just happened. So I am left to work it out on my own, or wait out his frustration. Either way, I know myself well enough to know that I cannot let it go. The way she called him *Daddy* and the way she sized me up. Every fresh memory conspires to make me ill. But I push it back, for his sake and mine. We will revisit. I will never forget the ring in her voice, "*maybe we could use her.*"

"What are we going to do today?" I ask with a sly half grin, hoping that he is thoroughly distracted and willing to talk. He smiles a whole, true crooked smile and it's clear that the toxic Nadja cloud is lifting, and we will be as we once were.

"Let's go out. We will go to the beach, do some shopping. Get out of this house for a bit."

Chapter 17

After a long day of lounging on the beach under the hot Florida sun and Rhys' insistence that we window shop and walk for what felt like hours, I was spent. A deep, heavy sleep pulled me under the moment he slipped from my body and I was trapped in dark dreams. I wake strangled by a familiar fear. Sliding out from beneath his heavy arm I make my way into the large master bathroom, locking the door. Needing a moment to collect my thoughts and examine myself without the weight of his gaze.

"Sophie, are you alright?" Rhys' soft voice and a faint rap on the door startle me from my self-examination. I unlock the door; the light shocking Rhys' sleepy eyes. His hand flies to his eyes and he reaches around to flip the light off, leaving the ambient under cabinet lighting to illuminate the small room, and my fallen face. Grateful for the silken pajama pants that he has pulled on. Although I fear the distraction stems not from his body, but from his very presence. He consumes the air around me, trapping me. I drown in his eyes while he leans against the counter.

"I just needed some water."

"Come back to bed." He grabs my hand and leads me back into the bedroom. I climb back among the cloud of pillows and down while he pours me a glass of water. Sliding in behind me he peppers feather light kisses across my shoulders. I reel from the contact. It is hot and heavy and so soft. Continuing his delicate assault on my cool flesh, his hands travel to my breasts and my head rolls back onto his shoulder. He teases me, caressing me gently with his palm, wiping my mind of worry. Now both hands are on me, kneading and squeezing my now rapidly heating breasts. His fingers pull and twist at my nipples, rolling them around and around. "Aahhh." I moan into his neck and he continues pressing and pulling at my flesh, and then he is gone. His hands have abandoned me, the only proof of him is his rock hard chest against my back, his rhythmic breathing against my spine.

"Something is on your mind, Beautiful." He laces his fingers with mine, wrapping our arms around me.

"Hmm?" The only thing on my mind is his hands, warm and knowing. *Please, put them back.*

"Tell me what is bothering you," he pleads, placing a kiss at the curve of my neck. The spark he ignites propels me, and I know that this is my chance. To seize the opportunity to reveal the deep insecurity this woman provokes in me. I have to unburden myself, she has dominated every thought since she sashayed out the door this morning. He wants to know what is on my mind. I will share. Turning in his lap, I catch him by surprise. My eyes are wide and clear, and I mean to be open.

"Nadja," I say, looking dead into his eyes, afraid of the light I expected to see at the mention of her. But there was no light that crossed his eyes at the mention of her name, just a deep, dark, shadow. Snorting in indignation, he swipes my hair away from my neck. So adept at distracting me from my course, fingers trace the curve of my spine before they grip my hips, lifting me atop his folded legs. He drops me into his lap and cups my face in his hands. "She is perfect, and a little scary," I mutter, afraid to look him in the eye, afraid that if I look directly at him, he will see right through me, straight through to the cowering, insecure girl that has slunk into the corner to pout.

"Scary… yes. Perfect…." He laughs a humorless, bitter laugh. "No, she is far from perfect." Irritation paints his tone.

"The effect she has on you is…" I am unable to finish the thought. "What happened?" He looks bewildered, bothered by the inquisition. A stony silence fills the moment, stealing my breath. Do I really want to know? Too late now. His fingers twist and turn in my hair. Brushing my cheeks rhythmically with his thumbs, he pulls his bottom lip through his teeth. His eyes are dark and pensive, pondering his answer.

"We were young." He frowns, lines crinkling across his forehead, the corners of his eyes creasing ever so slightly.

"That's it?" He is not offering anything.

"That's it." His jaw is flexed, his mouth set in a hard line. He has effectively ended the conversation before it even began. I get nothing. "You were very impressive this morning. She is a force and she labors to intimidate most women. To be honest, I thought she might eat you alive. I was waiting for her to unhinge her jaw and have you for breakfast."

"So you set me up like a piece of bait?" I don't know what to say to that. Inside, she has played on every insecurity that I harbor, that we all harbor. But I knew how important it would be for me to keep it inside, to hide it from Rhys and from myself. "Was she the one? The one you have been with before you started making rules?"

"Yes, she is the only other one. And she is not happy to now share that title. But, you are my guest, Sophie. She is an unwelcome nuisance." It does little to quell my curiosity, but still I swell at his declaration. She was unwelcome.

"She pales in comparison to you," he whispers hotly in my ear before taking my mouth with conviction. After a long silence, I let my mind wander and my curiosity gets the best of me.

"Tell me about your cross." He picks up the delicate gold cross and twirls it between his fingers.

"It is the only thing I have that is real. It keeps me connected."

"I don't imagine you at church."

"It's more about family for me." He locks me in his sights and doesn't let me go.

"Family? I thought it was just you and your dad."

"My father's family, most of them are back in Ireland. I spent quite a bit of time there when I was young. My aunts practically raised me. I grew up alongside my cousins. We all went to Catholic school, I was an altar boy. I loved everything about it. It is the purest place on earth."

"You were an altar boy? Forgive me, but I cannot imagine it."

"I have been many things, Sophie. I can be anything I need to be. But that is as close to the real thing as I am ever going to get." He puffs lightly on a newly lit cigar. The smoke swirls in the air, a ghostly tendril reaching high above our heads. The moonlight bounces from the mirrored wall casting dancing shadows around the room. The molten ember of his cigar casts a light across his placid face. It strikes me as I watch him, his revolving demeanor, adaptive behavior. The calm he exudes, like he always knows what to expect, what will come next. Like a magician manipulating his audience, he creates the reaction and controls the room. It is all smoke and mirrors. Nothing is as it seems.

Looking into his clear green eyes, I want to believe that he is safe. I want to trust him. I know I

231

want to make him happy. And I know he was disappointed earlier when we debated the issue of the ropes. I am suddenly overcome with curiosity, fantasy. I want to know what it would be like. I want to surrender to him, I can do this. I move out of his arms and make for the dresser.

"What are you up to?" he asks with a perfect devious grin wide on his face. I pull the bottom drawer open and retrieve the folded length of red silk rope that he unceremoniously abandoned just a few hours earlier. It is smooth in my hand, cool and strong. I pull it through my fingers, sending a shiver down my spine. Yes, I want this. His eyes are wide with excitement. I bite my bottom lip, lower my eyes and walk slowly to the bedside, keeping my eyes cast down. I place the rope across his lap, running my fingers across the tops of his thighs and step back. He takes a deep breath, swings his legs to the floor and pulls me to him, his hands gripping my hips tightly. He tips my head up with his finger and searches my eyes. I am clear, and sure. Confident. And the smile that spreads across his face sets me on fire.

"What do you want, Sophie?" his voice is rough, but quiet. I look down into his face pondering the now familiar question. His lips part and he swipes that bottom lip with his tongue. It ripples through me, I need this.

"I want you to have your way," I whisper.

"And?" he demands. He will take his pound of flesh now.

"I want you to tie me up." I look him dead in the eye, watching the fire rise in his blood. Surely I can allow his excitement to eclipse the faint shock of fear that sits in my heart.

"And?"

"I trust you," I mouth, breathless and excited. That was what he needed to hear. Grasping the hem of my tee shirt, he whisks it off over my head.

"We will start slow." He drops the rope on the floor and moves to the dresser and a smaller drawer. He pulls a shorter length of black rope and tosses it to the bed. The weave is open, the feel is soft. It is not nearly as menacing as the long red ropes, but still ignites a spark deep in my belly.

"I do want to push you, Sophie, but slowly." He weaves the black rope between my wrists, over and under, until they are clasped together in a beautiful, symmetrical chain, he is meticulous, careful. "I will not tie you to the bed. We will save that. For now I will just bind your hands, and you will get the idea. What it feels like to be bound, to let go." Several tight, intricate knots run up the inside of both arms, my hands bound together tightly, blood pulses under the ropes. He moves me to the head of the bed.

"Lie down." I lay back on the pillows and he raises my hands above my head. "Grab a hold. And do not let go." I do as I'm told, grasping the cold metal scroll of the headboard. I wrap my fingers tightly, knowing that I will want to let go. My pulse is racing, my mouth is dry and he looks like an excited child. My hands are raised above my head, anchored by rope and will. He pulls me by my feet, so that I am stretched across the bed. Hooking his fingers into my panties he peels them off, slowly, making a meal of it. He winds his hands around the back of both of my ankles and yanks my legs open, a look of awe and hunger on his face.

"Take a deep breath and blow it out," he commands. I do as I'm told. I pull air deep into my lungs and release it. Rhys pushes my legs up high above my head as the breath rushes from my lungs. My feet are pressed against the headboard on either side of my hands. I fold in half. His arms stretched over the backs of my legs, holding me flush, his face hovering directly over my waiting sex. I am curled, with my ass in the air, when I feel him. The brush of his lips as he smiles, then his tongue runs like satin all the way across my seam. Like a lollipop, he licks me slowly from top to bottom, and back again, all the while holding my legs above my head. My hands are tied and anchored and my legs are like jelly. I have no choice but to absorb each gentle lick, every urgent flick. I could let go of the headboard, but I don't want to.

The sensation of the ropes and Rhys' mouth all

over me are more than I can handle and I shatter like a delicate piece of crystal. Fireworks explode behind my eyes, but I do not let go of the headboard. My hands grip the iron as my body rocks and rolls under Rhys' wicked mouth. His tongue rolls around my clit as his fingers pump in and out of me. He curls them into me and begins to stroke a button deep within that spikes my blood and sends me falling over the edge. The orgasm rips through me, shredding my senses, leaving me breathless and twitchy. The energy continues to build, higher and higher until a vicious explosion rings behind my eyes and I scream out for mercy, for more, I don't know. My body pulses around his fingers as his tongue continues to press and circle my nub. My ears are hot and filled with bright white noise and my hands grip the headboard for dear life. Afraid that if I do let go I will fall. He slowly lets me down, rolling my hips back onto the bed with a cheeky grin as he brings his fingers to his lips and sucks my essence from them. Before I can fully regain myself he shoves his fingers into my mouth.

"Taste yourself," he demands, pressing his fingers to my tongue. I am salty, sweet, musky and surprisingly pleasant. Moaning as I suckle at his fingers, I am shocked at myself, shocked at my wanton, dirty behavior. And more shocked that I love every minute, and want more. He pulls his fingers from my mouth with a pop and flips me over like a rag doll.

"Don't let go," he whispers hot against my ear before gasping as he thrusts his hard cock into my dripping pussy. His fingers dig into my hips as he pulls me back onto him. Each thrust deeper than the last. He is like an animal, lost in me, lost in his passion. I buck against him, pushing off and sliding back, slapping my ass against his chest as he growls. I feel him press his chest to my back and the weight on me feels amazing. Sinking his teeth into my shoulder, I arch my back and focus on my grip. His fingers slip from my sweat slicked hips as he rises up and flips me back over.

He drives himself deeper until we become one, liquid and replete. Piercing the celestial heavens with the heat and intensity of our lust for one another, the big bang erupts all around us and we are nothing but energy. Every cell in my body is alive, humming with electricity, reaching for him. Our auras are surely mingled as we are sucked into a vortex in which only he and I exist. The world is alight with our lovemaking, the sun jealous of our heat. He collapses in a sticky mess on my chest. His damp forehead pressed between my breasts. Breathing ragged and clipped.

"God, Sophie." His lips move against my skin, and he shudders again, the final tremor pulsing through him as he empties himself into me. He jerks and stills, exhausted and spent. We are joined by body, by mind, by sweat and tears. So tied up in each other it's no longer clear where I end and he begins, and it feels amazing.

Curled against his chest, I lay silent and satisfied to a degree I did not know was possible. His arms wound around me like possessive, creeping vines. Our fingers laced, twisted in knots. He draws slow circles on my palm, hypnotizing me. The ropes still securely wound up both of my arms, he fingers the silk, murmuring to himself, appreciative, admiring his handy work. It really is beautiful, I suppose. The silky black rope woven from my wrists to my elbows, it lays flat and smooth against my skin. Each cuff has a long chain braid running down the inside of my arm. The knots are intricate, finely made, it's clear that he has had ample practice. I run my finger across the rope, the throbbing in my arms evident under the sensitive nub of my fingertip.

I had been so distracted by what he was doing to me; I forgot to notice how tight the ropes are. My arms begin to throb more violently, blood pulses from through my veins, struggling against the tight black rope, fighting to get to my hands. I wiggle my fingertips, as they are beginning to numb. Rhys rolls me onto my back and pulls my hands to his mouth. He places a gentle kiss on each wrist, and begins to untie his artful knots. With every unwinding of the rope, blood rushes under my skin, satisfying, relieving. I rub my wrists and find that the sensation is sensual, erotic. Running my fingers along each line, I revel in the rush of blood and electricity. The evidence of his hunger, his passion is written all over my arms. I muse to myself about the possibilities the ropes represent. How else could he tie me in knots, what else could he do to me? How much can I take?

"Where did you learn to tie knots like this?"

"Just something I picked up." A sly wink raises the corner of his lopsided mouth and I giggle like a silly school girl. We spent the better part of the night chasing exquisite tiny deaths. He pushed me beyond the limits of my imagination, pushed Nadja out. But my body is in shock, unable to recover. My skin is sticky and hot and raw. A brush of his hand and I may burst into flames or turn to dust. I am spent and deliciously achy. He rolls off the bed, taking his magical hands with him.

"I need a shower. Join me?" He holds his hand out for me, but I cannot even raise my arm. I smile sleepily at him and nod, unable to peel myself from the bed, unable to take another sensual assault, which is surely what will happen if I get in the shower with him.

The shower roars to life and I decide to escape to the kitchen while he reluctantly showers alone. My body has been twisted and turned in ways I could never have imagined. I am sore and stiff from being tied up, something that frightened me until the first sensual twist of the rope. I rub at the rope marks that are seared into my skin. The indentations so fresh and tender, row after row of gentle bite, the braid of the rope still evident in my flesh. The slightest pressure and I can feel him all over me again. Anchored to the bed, unable to do anything but absorb all he could give me. He spread me open and made me feel powerful when all my power had been taken away. The rope marks will fade, but I will never forget that. I shake it from my mind and set to work gathering ingredients for waffles. Nothing better than a little sweet carb kick for recovery.

"What are you doing?" He shines like a god, freshly showered, inky black hair still wet, gently curling at his forehead.

"Making waffles. You earned it." I smile before turning back to my work, grabbing a block of sharp cheddar I found hiding in the back of the fridge. I grate the cheese over the bowl of waffle batter.

"Waffles at two a.m.? Do you know that you are putting cheese in my waffles?" he asks, wrapping his arms around my core, squeezing me tightly before kissing me gently on the shoulder. I shudder under the weight of his kiss. My body is still buzzing from each and every encounter, the intense high building upon itself until I go into some sort of sexual fit. He has turned me into a fully possessed white-hot flame of a woman. I don't think I will ever be satisfied, he just makes me want more. He makes me utterly greedy and licentious.

"It is my Mom's recipe. She always put just a sprinkle of sharp cheddar in her batter, said it made the syrup taste sweeter. She would always make them for my Dad after he went fishing." He stills behind me, pausing at the mention of my parents. I back up into him, circling my hips against him, wiping the comment away.

"I feel honored. Can I put on some cooking music for you, Beautiful?" Sweeping my hair out of the way he places a heavy kiss against my neck.

"Yes, please."

Skin still glistening from his recent shower, black silk pants dangle from his hips, torturing me as he walks across the kitchen to the bay of cabinets that houses a nerve center of technology. He grabs a small remote and closes the cabinets. He turns to me with a wolfish grin. Head cocked to the side, he starts the music and saunters towards me with his hands extended for a dance while Louis Armstrong croons for a kiss.

"Is this appropriate music for waffles?"

"Yes, I believe it is." I move into his arms and I'm swept away. Around the kitchen, we sway, moving across the cool marble floors, in our bare feet. Like Fred and Ginger. His strong arm wrapped around my waist, fingers tugging at my warm flesh.

His eyes are locked on mine, his hand pulling me closer to him, pressing me into his freshly showered skin. His fingers travel down my arm and stop at my wrist. He brings it slowly to his mouth and kisses the line of each rope mark, gently rubbing the pad of his thumb across the tender flesh.

"I think this may be romance. A girl could get the wrong idea." I look up into his eyes, clear green pools, safe and warm. He rests his forehead against mine, presses his hand to the small of my back and pulls me closer.

"Oh, I already have the wrong idea, Sophie. Perhaps I have decided that it is in my best interest to sweep you off of your feet."

"I believe you have successfully done that already. Several times in the last two days."

"Really?" He seems genuinely surprised. "You hold your cards tightly. How am I to know?" I am once struck by his inability to read me as I had assumed he could, and his ever burgeoning self-doubt.

"How about the fact that almost every time you touch me, I fall flat on my back." He smirks and twists his head.

"I think your waffles are burning, Beautiful." He turns me towards the stove and pushes me towards the smoking waffle iron. He laughs at me, removing a piece of coal in the shape of a waffle. "It's bad luck to eat the first one anyhow. Throw it away and start again." I manage to make two perfect waffles while he tries his damndest to distract me with his body, his eyes, his mouth. But I am focused on a hearty breakfast so we can get back to bed.

He sets the marble bar with woven black placemats, basic white china and silver, pours orange juice and watches me flip the last waffle out of the iron. I walk around the bar and take the stool next to him. He winds his arm around my waist and pulls me closer, stool and all. Pulling my hand to his mouth, he brushes his lips along the deepest rope mark. It travels up my wrist from the base of my hand to my inner elbow. His lips are soft and generous, planting feather light kisses on the sensitive skin inside my elbow. The effort echoes in my groan and I shift slightly on my stool.

"I love these," he muses, running his fingers along the deep rope marks that mar the delicate flesh of my other arm. "All right, little lady, let's get a taste of these cheddar waffles. I have never heard of such a thing, but here we go." He takes the first bite drizzled with dark maple syrup and pauses. He turns to me and a wide grin spreads across his surprised face. "These are delicious!" He declares

"Careful now, I might change your life," I tease, taking a syrupy bite. He stops and watches me intently, willing me to surrender my full attention. The intensity in the set of his shoulders sizzles and I nearly choke, taking a long, slow sip of juice before daring to make eye contact. When I look up he is pensive, watching me. Waiting.

"I have never been with a girl like you, Sophie." I don't know what to say, he has caught me in his cross hairs, unprepared, speechless and electrified by his casual confession.

"What does that mean? A girl like me?"

"Someone who makes me waffles at 2am." We eat in silence, savoring the sweet treat. His hand rests on my leg and my foot rests on his stool.

"This is nice." Looking up into his eyes, I am struck by how comfortable and familiar we have become in such a short amount of time.

"What?" he asks, his mouth half full of the last bite of waffle.

"This. You relaxed, not looming like a force of nature. Me, like this. It just feels good. I haven't cooked for anyone in a long time." He puts his fork down on his empty plate and turns to me. His eyes sharply focused on my face.

"I loom?" His brows knit together and I suddenly hope I didn't cross a line or hurt him. I drop my eyes and my voice follows.

"You can be very intense," I peek up through my lashes, hoping for a calm and kind reaction, "always flexing that alpha male muscle. This is a different Rhys."

"It's you, Sophie." He brushes an errant curl
243

away from my face, his finger lingering at my ear. "You have blurred all the lines. I am breaking my own rules." My heart skips a beat as a rush of pleasure surges through me at the casual manner in which he can talk this way with me. But, I never meant to blur any lines or force his hand in any way. Frankly, I find it hard to believe that little old me could affect a man such as him in such a way. It's not who I am, not how the world sees me, not how I see myself.

"Well, thank goodness for air travel. One more day and I will be out of your hair and all will be as it once was. Lines restored, rules reinstated. Tidy, just like you like it." I watch his face fall slightly before he collects the empty plates and drops them in the sink.

"Right, tidy," he murmurs, not looking at me.

Chapter 18

His fingers flow like lazy rivers down my back, coaxing me from a deep, exhausted sleep. I peek out from the safety of my sleep to discover a darkened room. It is still dark outside. Rolling out from under Rhys' hands, I curl up into a ball and bury my face in his chest.

"What time is it?" I murmur against his calm, steady heart.

"Time for a swim," he whispers, his voice smooth like velvet, coaxing a grin that tugs at my mouth before I ever open my eyes. "Come, we can watch the sun come up." He pulls away and I am bereft from the loss of his warm skin and intoxicating scent.

"Grab my suit."

"You don't need one, Beautiful."

"Um, yes I do. I don't want people to see me." Panic cracks in my voice, an exhibitionist I am not.

"It's dark, Sophie. No one can see us. Besides, a little exposure can be exhilarating." Oh, he is playing with me now, playing on the fear that is all over my sleepy face. I clutch the sheet tightly to my chest. Protecting myself from what's to come, covering myself now against the threat that I may not be able to cover myself later. He emerges from the bathroom, a pale green cotton robe hanging from his shoulders. He tosses another robe at me and tugs the sheets out of my hands. I slip the soft robe around my shoulders and stand up. Still sleep soaked and dazed, my knees buckle and I sag into his waiting arms. "The water will wake you up, or I will," he threatens, tucking me under the crook of his arm. We head out to the pool, and into the fading moonlight.

The pool is cool and calm. I dip my toe in and a shock runs up my body. It is black outside, the only light emanating from the bottom of the pool, casting a soft blue light across the water and the pool deck. In the distance, I can barely make out a few twinkling lights on the horizon.

"Cruise ships," he answers casually, reading my thoughts. We are alone. The thought helps calm my nerves, and I begin to untie my robe. Rhys drops his without hesitation and dives into the pool. His lithe nude form slips, elegantly beneath the water, illuminated by the pool light. He shines, like a deity of the deep, strong legs pushing him, roped arms pulling him. He emerges from the water and shakes his head, playfully spraying me with the rivulets that swing from his inky hair.

"Come on in, Beautiful. The water is cold without you." He splashes me again and I give in. There is no winning when he has made up his mind. Compromise and patience don't seem to be in his wheelhouse. If he wants me in the pool, I can either get in of my own accord, or he will make me. I drop my robe with a flourish, casting it behind me like a bathing goddess. I channel Rita Hayworth, imagining in the dull light of the pool that I am glamorous and confident. The thought is shattered by a face full of water from Rhys.

"Hop in," he begs playfully, "I am tired of waiting." So impatient. I slink into the pool slowly, letting my body acclimate. He watches me from the opposite side, his body hidden under the water, only his beautiful face bobbing above water line. His eyes are dark, hooded, and hungry. I stop just as the water hits the crests of my breasts, the quickness of my breath given away by the ripples in the water that roll off of me with every shallow intake. I am practically panting. In two fluid strokes we are nose to nose. He plants his feet below him and rises out of the water, hovering above me. He glistens, the dark hair on his chest grasping at drops of water. He runs his hands up my arms and kisses away a drop of water from my temple before he spins around, pulling me to the edge. Tugging me off my feet, he pulls me so easily through the water and into his lap. We hover on the edge of the pool. Water spills over the side of the infinity edge, seemingly swept into the sea. I feel like I am being swept away. My breasts are crushed against him, pressed to his skin, sticky and hot. I move in his hands, floating and twisting above him, before straddling him. My legs spread wide as I sit astride this slippery wet god.

My thighs lock around his core and he softly moans his approval against my ear, sending a shock wave, tearing straight through me. I am on fire. In the pool, dripping wet, I am burning to cinders and ashes. I surrender to the weightlessness of the water, push off the wall and lay back, letting the water and Rhys' hands guide me. Floating on the surface I sway back and forth, flying high above, peacefully at rest in his hands. Water laps around my head, kissing my temples, washing me clean.

The moon looks down on us, watching me, watching him. I am free. Never have I experienced the freedom to feel and be, like I have with Rhys. In his hands, I am able to let everything fall away. Insecurities melt into the warm Florida air. I am more myself now than I have ever been, or am I just who I think he wants me to be? Does it matter who I am? When I am in his agile hands, I am the girl I want to be, the girl I never knew was hiding deep within. His hands float over my body, silky and soft under the cool water. Pulling my nipple between his fingers gingerly he tugs and twists until they stand at attention before dipping his head and taking one into his mouth. I moan to the heavens, absorbing each gentle flick of his tongue, every soft tug of his teeth. I lift my head and his hungry mouth sends a shiver coursing through me, rippling through the water.

"Lay back, Sophie, just let me touch you. The

moonlight shining on your skin makes you look like an angel," his voice is low, hushed. His hands and mouth roam freely, teasing and warming my skin. Up and over my floating breasts, across my soft belly, his mouth, leaving a trail of heat and soft kisses behind. I watch the moon begin to sink, my head swimming in his hands. I loosen my legs and float away from him as he teases my belly button with his tongue, dipping in and sucking the water droplets out. He is slow and methodical, covering every inch of me with warm, soft kisses, a gentle swipe of his tongue and knead of his hands. When the first sparks ignite deep in my loins I am caught, between the cool water, his warm mouth and strong hands. I ride the slow wave of his ministrations, back and forth across my skin with his tongue, his fingers barely brushing my flesh. At the precipice of a deep valley, I sit at the edge, waiting for his final push. It comes as his mouth closes over my breast and his fingers slide inside of me, so gently I barely register they are there before my body opens up and I fall, silently over the edge. Slowly, falling into a deep cavern of a whole new pleasure; a calm, quietly-building tsunami. It creeps over my skin, through my blood and crashes quietly in my head. Ripple after ripple emanating from my skin, crossing the water, filling the pool with aftershocks of his quiet assault. Drifting on his fingers, I lay across the water spent from a fiercely silent orgasm that rolled through me without any warning. No frantic build up, no desperate need for release, just a slow, controlled burn.

He puts his hands under my neck and pulls me into his chest. The skin to skin contact is warm and soothing. I nuzzle into his neck, licking away the water from behind his ear. This is a new state of sated, a new state of being. Everything is gone, nothing can touch me right now, except for him. If the entire world evaporated around us it would not matter.

"That was…." Whispering in his ear I cannot find the words to finish my thought. There are no words for what that was.

"I know," he says, tugging on my hair. "Come, I want to get you upstairs." Planting a kiss at the base of my throat, he pulls me to the steps and out of the water. I stand boldly in the slowly rising sun, empowered by our carnal escapades. Feeling emboldened, brazen even. The thought that someone could have witnessed such an intense exchange, been a secret party to my pleasure sets a fire in me that I was not expecting. Just as I fully embrace the bold, sexual being I feel like, Rhys steps to my side, covering me quickly with my robe.

"That's enough," he scolds.

"I thought you said a little exposure could be exhilarating?" I tease him with his own words.

"Yes, well. Some things should be just for me,

like the pretty pink flush that colors your skin after *I* make you come. I don't like to share." He pulls his robe around his shoulders and then ties mine tightly at my waist, cinching the sash, pulling me close. Wrapped in his arms, standing in the dark, watching the stars fade away, I could get lost. I fear I may already be lost. He says these things, takes my breath away, and works my body like an expert. How does he know me so well, it's as if he has a road map to my body? The only copy in existence, he knows things I could never have guessed. He does things I would never know I needed. And he comes by it so casually.

We sleep through the morning after so many midnight interruptions. He tries to rouse me for a shower, but I am unable to lift my limbs, my body firmly planted in his bed.

"I have to check some emails. Take your time, Beautiful," he says with a kiss to my forehead. "I will be downstairs."

I lie among his scent and blankets for who knows how long before I can muster the strength and energy to rouse myself. Wrapping myself in the top sheet, I slide into the master bathroom and spy a new creature in the wall size mirror. A creature who has inched her way towards my surface with every encounter, now Rhys has invited her into the light. My eyes are bright, skin clear, hair mussed. But the smile that pulls unbidden at my lips is new, and welcome. I cannot tamp down the way he makes me feel. But I should learn to control it, remember that it is temporary. The thought rips a tiny hole in my heart, a slow trickle of pain seeps into my blood stream. It is all temporary. That is why it is so good. No pressure to continue, no wondering, *where is this going*. It is going nowhere. I would be remiss to forget that. One more day.

***

I slide around the corner, skating on the slick marble floors giddy from our early morning swim, when I come face to face with an ice queen. Yet another interruption. Statuesque in a Chanel suit and pearls, cold and hard as granite, she assaults me with her glare and wrinkles her nose in disgust, fingering the lapel of her jacket in judgment of my Old Navy shorts and tank.

"Nadja was too generous," she muses to herself, a look of amusement and familiar disgust paints her delicate features. Poking at the air, moving two steps closer to me, her stance defensive, but her face is soft and calm, a mask. It must run in the family. "Do not get too comfortable, your days here are numbered, little beggar." The words are almost melodic, wrapped in a faded French accent. Her eyes alight with a fire that could burn the house down. "Mother." His voice smooth
252

like silk, yet his tone offers no doubt as to his mood. "Sophie is my guest, and I will thank you not to speak to her like that."

He saunters out of his office and puts his hands around my waist, possessive and protective, pulling me into him. He nuzzles my neck, taking a deep draught of my freshly cleaned hair before planting a light kiss on my throat and releasing me.

"I need to speak with my mother, Sophie, why don't you go open a bottle of wine." He leans into my ear and whispers, "this won't take long."

His mother is trying to burn me down with her eyes, and Rhys is just rubbing my little triumph in her face. I can't say that the sight of that woman uncomfortable and defeated was painful, in fact, it felt good that Rhys would stick up for me. I leave the two of them as Rhys ushers his scowling mother into his office. Her voice searing with anger as she launches into a tirade, "Nadja said you had a house guest. You need to turn out that little pauper." The last words I hear before he closes the heavy door.

They emerge less than 20 minutes later, and I hear him show her out. He finds me in the kitchen, reluctantly nursing a glass of wine, and waiting. Sauntering across the marble floor, he glides or floats, my own personal, seductive angel.

"Let's go out for dinner."

No part of me wants to go out. Everything here is insulated and perfect and I don't want to be

253

reminded that there is a real world out there just waiting for me to return. Between his mother and Nadja, I would prefer to be locked away in relative safety. Those two women look like they want to snack on me with wine and crackers. He strolls around the island, slowly inching towards me. His eyes darken with every measured step. Just a look from him and everything south of my waist begins to beg. I take an involuntary step back against the counter, my throat suddenly dry. I drop my eyes, overcome with shyness. Why? Everything we have done, he has done. Shy is the last thing I should be feeling. But, there it is. He makes me feel like a shy girl, and a bold woman. Confused, that is how this is making me feel.

"I would rather stay in," I manage.

Peeking at him through my lashes, careful not to look straight into the sun, I bask in his gaze for a brief moment. Any longer and I begin to lose all sense of purpose. My lust for him is devoid of all virtue. It is hot and irrational, the sight of him makes me burn, his touch rages through me, an uncontrolled inferno. The slightest brush of his finger provokes a tidal wave of need. I ache to be beneath him, to be tamed by his body. I am washed of my doubt when he is inside of me. He has baptized me in sin and sensual delights. I am a convert to his cause. I belong to Rhys, every soft inch of my body that he has explored, every nerve, every drop of warm blood. I am his completely. He wipes my mind clean. His fingers melt into my hips, pulling me to him. He places a finger under my chin and tilts my head, looking straight through me.

"You have become greedy, Beautiful." He lifts me so easily and spins on his heel, placing me on the counter, the cool marble a shocking contrast to his warm hands. He kneads my backside, pulling me to the edge, pushing his way between my legs. I wrap them around him, pressing him to me with my heels. "Greed is a punishable sin." He brushes his lips across my shoulder before taking my face into his hands. He crushes himself to my lips. Hunger pulses between us, charging everything. His hands travel down my arms, leaving my skin hot, puckered with goose bumps. I rest my hands on his chest, his chiseled form a heavenly rest for my palms. His heartbeat is even and controlled, while my heart is trying to leap, with both feet. Every touch is more intense, it becomes more and more difficult to remind myself of the brevity of our association. We know each other so well, yet not at all. Our bodies are quite familiar. But the rest remains an unspoken backdrop. The rest just doesn't matter when we are here, tangled up in one another.

His lips twist and turn against mine, dancing the rhythm we have come to know so well. I have come to crave the taste of his tongue, the feel of his lips. Need grows heavy in my belly and I fist my hands in his hair, dying to get closer. I feel starved of him, hungry for anything he will give. I bite his bottom lip and a tremor rumbles through his chest before he smiles against my mouth and a small laugh escapes his tender, torn lips.

"You are beyond greedy, Ms. Noelle, you are positively insatiable. I think I have created a monster. But we need to eat, and a change in scenery could be interesting."

Chapter 19

His hand rests possessively on my knee, his strong thumb tracing mindless circles on the delicate skin inside my thigh as he scrolls through e-mails on his phone. I lean into him and watch the scenery go by the tinted windows of the Town Car. The sky is pink and orange, a wide swath of beautiful watercolor painted across the horizon, sinking into the dark gray waters of the Atlantic. I could very easily get used to this. Thank goodness for the long fingers of reality that reach out for me as we speak. Lest I forget where I come from and what is really mine. The city grows as we inch off of our private island. Traffic becomes heavier as we get deeper into Miami. The city is teeming with pent up energy. People spill onto the streets, bidding goodbye to the day. Patios hum with happy hour crowds, velvet ropes begin to go up. Miami is coming alive. We pull into a secluded drive surrounded by tall palms. A stark white tower rises out of the grove, bathed in sinking sunlight, glowing peach against the cloud streaked sky.

Rhys' face is bright with anticipation and it is infectious. He mouths "Italian?" as Charlie pulls to the velvet rope and the entrance to Cecconi's. The restaurant is beautiful, lit up with thousands of twinkling lights, white table cloths and candle light. Bold green and white stripes cover the concrete floor. The place is empty save a couple at the bar. They sit close, sharing a secret, gazing only at each other, the heat of their attraction slowly filling the empty space.   "We'll take the patio," he whispers, in the nick of time. I don't want to contend with that sort of love and affection all evening. It would drive me to distraction. Jason, the host, leads us to the Garden Room. It is outdoors and secluded. A single table is set up under the pergola that is dripping with vivid bougainvillea and muted little lights. He pulls out my chair and takes a seat across the table from me. Oh, he is so far away. Jason turns his back and grabs a bottle of wine from an ice lined silver bucket.

"Here we have the wine you requested, Sir, the Ruinart, Blanc de Blanc." He pops the bottle and pours two glasses. "Shall I give you some time?" he asks.

"I think we will have a few small plates, Jason. That way we can try more." He grins at me. "Let's start with the Carpaccio and the baked artichokes," he looks to me for approval, lifting an eyebrow. I nod in agreement, trusting whatever he orders. "And the Branzino. I think that will be all."

The table is covered with an assortment of mouthwatering food. A seductive conspiracy flares in his eyes, and my belly flips. The prospect of trying more with Rhys sounds almost as delicious as all this food looks.

"Is there anything else I can do for you?" the waiter asks.

"No, thank you. We have everything we need." Rhys looks to me and winks. We share the delicious assortment that Rhys has ordered in electric silence. He offers me a bite of Branzino from his fork, I feed him an artichoke. It is all very sweet, very intimate. Our quiet moment is shattered by the clicking heels of a blonde bombshell. She approaches the table and a knowing grin passes Rhys' lips. A tailored black jumpsuit hugs every ridiculous curve, her loose blonde hair floating about her shoulders. Her big brown eyes are focused on him, bright and wide, taking in the beauty that is Rhys.

"Mr. Slate, good evening." Her tongue rolls on his name, a sultry accent wrapped in a tight little package. "I had heard you were dining with us tonight. I just wanted to come and make sure everything was to your liking." The way her eyes rake him over, familiar, knowing. A knot forms in my throat. Her body language, everything about her screams familiarity. Jealousy blooms in my heart, and I struggle to hide it. He watches her squirm, swaying on her feet ever so slightly. She watches him with baited breath, fixed on him. I feel like an intruder, eavesdropping on a private exchange. He arches an eyebrow at her and lights up his best panty melting smile. His full lips, curved in the

259

most knowing, arrogant manner.

"Everything is wonderful, thank you, Celine." He turns his eyes to me, focused and intent, shutting her out. "We will have dessert, whatever is tonight's specialty." I watch the humor in his eyes as he knowingly robs her of his attention. She stands at the end of the table, speechless, fidgeting. I look up at her as he dismisses her with a curt wave and a request for an aperitif. Her face falls ever so slightly before she recovers herself, tossing me an inscrutable, hollow look.

"Are you enjoying yourself?" I ask, knowing the answer. "You are aware of the effect you have?"

He is fully aware of his power, and in no way resentful or denying. Bestowing a ray of his beautiful light on every woman he meets. No need for him to use force when he can dominate with the slightest brush of his fingers, or flash of that crooked grin. The twinkle in his eye breeds envy amongst the stars.

"I am aware, and I am glad that you are." I look up into his eyes and the challenge is clear. "I think you like that other women want what you have."

"I don't *have* anything. We are just using each other, remember? It's all temporary." Just as I say it, she returns to the table with two small glasses of Grappa, an Italian sponge cake with two forks and a wicked look in her eyes. She places the dessert in front of him, folds her hands in front of her, drops

260

her eyes and speaks in a hushed tone.

"May I join you later, *Sir?*"

I look from his impassive face to the wicked glint illuminating her dark chocolate eyes. I know that I have heard something I wasn't supposed to. But, her intention is clear, and deliberate. He doesn't give her a second glance, focusing all of his razor sharp attention on me, I'm trapped in his eyes like prey, unable to look away or move, even though the threat level has been raised. It is clear, I am about to be devoured, yet I stay. Wait for his prompt. Wait for his guidance.

"No, that will be all. Thank you." He dismisses her and her smile falters before she slinks away, but he doesn't notice. Waiting for a reaction, his expectant eyes are wide. My voice has been stolen as my mouth drops open, but not a sound escapes. I close my mouth with a snap before it falls open again. Is that what I think it was? Was she suggesting that she? That we? My mouth finally catches up, with little eloquence.

"What was that?" As the words escape my mouth, there is a part of me that does not want the answer. Afraid of what it may be. What I know it was. Add ménage a trios to the list, the growing list of Rhys' many talents and exploits. My head swims, and I catch myself rubbing my forehead, tugging at the bridge of my nose. It is mind-boggling trying to keep up with him. I am a grown woman. I thought I was secure and informed in my sexuality before I met him. He has been like a force of nature on me, my body and my mind. Forcing me to reconsider everything I thought I knew. Everything I thought I wanted and needed. This is a step further. The thought of him with that little spinner makes my stomach knot. A stabbing pang of jealousy and a green eyed monster stares out at him from behind my eyes.

"Nothing," he replies, his conviction noticeably absent. *Sir.* I play the word over in my mind. The way his eyes lit up when she said it, the way her mouth curled into that Cheshire grin. My eyes narrow on him. He is cool, unaware of the war raging in my head.

"This is the craziest thing I have ever done," I declare. I thought I was keeping pace. Clearly I am out of my league and miles away from my comfort zone.

"What are you talking about?" He is cool as a cucumber watching me squirm.

"This. This affair," I cringe, hating the word as soon as it escapes my lips. It is too adult, carries too much weight to be the name for this. Whatever this is, I don't know any longer. I let myself be clouded and confused, diluted into forgetting the reality of our situation. One more night with him is all I have. I can live with this information for one night. He told her 'No.' There is nothing to worry about.

Perhaps, a deep dark part of me gets a thrill from his kinky taste. I trust him, I just can't share him.

"This is the most outrageous thing I have ever done. There is so much that I don't know. You make me feel like a novice." I stop and take the last strawberry between my fingers, bringing it to my lips. A barely audible gasp and his eyes become dark and carnal. Slowly, I lick the tip of the strawberry watching his eyes. He bites his bottom lip before turning that one thousand watt, glacier-melting grin on me. I am no match for that mouth. "I do know one thing though. I don't like to share." I turn his words back on him and the humor is not lost. One night or a lifetime, I am not the kind of girl that can share. I know that about myself, had enough experience with having too many people in a relationship. And yes, for me sex usually comes with a relationship; more new territory that I am exploring with Rhys, the casual fuck thing. But nothing about this feels casual. Not anymore.

"We have already established that you are greedy. And you are no novice." His eyes twinkle in the dull torchlight. He likes to watch me squirm, to push me.

"You will be free from my greed tomorrow."

"What happens tomorrow?"

"I go home."

"You don't have to."

"What will you do? Tie me up in some unseen

room, tucked away to fuck at your leisure? I have a life, Rhys." He struggles to remain stoic, impassive. But the desire is written all over his face, in the slight curl of his lips, the devious glimmer that lights his eyes. No doubt at the thought of tying me up. Desire blooms, hot and heavy, deep in my belly at the thought and I realize I want him to push me higher. I want to push myself.

"Will it be so easy to leave me?" I pause on his query, knowing the answer, but not wanting to share the truth.

"It won't be easy, for me." I don't want to focus on how easy it will be for him. He most likely has a willing hostess or waitress at every hot spot. A woman anywhere he wants. And then there's Nadja.

"Will you think of me?" I ask. Some sick form of self-inflicted torture. *Masochist!*

"Without question, Beautiful. I cannot seem to get enough of you, you have me hooked. In fact, I need a fix, now." I am delighted by his answer, flushed and taken aback by the ease and clarity of his declaration. He rises from the table and I am struck by his beauty. He is so charming and sexy. Easy. And for one more night, he is mine. He steps behind me and pulls out my chair, like the gentleman he is. He drapes his jacket about my shoulders and pulls me close, tucking me protectively under his arm as we walk through the crowded restaurant and out to the curb. He tugs on my hand, a devious glint in his eyes. *Can I do this?*

"Come here." We round the corner, heading towards the back of the building. A small dock juts from the other side of the walk, a small fishing boat bobs on the wavy surface.

"I want you out in the open." My heart races. Looking across the dock I see no shelter, no privacy. But I know what he wants, he wants me exposed and raw. Pulling me along the back wall of the restaurant he pulls me into a small nook that is overgrown with bougainvillea. It looks like it hasn't been tended to in quite a while, which makes me feel better. Maybe there is no reason for anyone to venture back here. The clouds begin to mist, just as my blood is coming to a slow simmer. The dinner, the innuendo from the hostess, and now this. Rhys and me, in the rain, exposed. A shiver runs down my spine.

***

The rain is soft on Sophie's heated skin. I skate my hands down her arms, trails of goose bumps rising in their wake. A slight shiver runs down her spine and her bottom lip quivers. It is a delight to watch her bloom and open up under my hands. So easy to make her needy, she responds like she has never been touched by sensual hands, every release is more explosive than the last. I don't know how high I can take her here, outside. She is clearly unnerved by the prospect of getting caught, but she cannot resist. It is there in the deep dark irises that hide her green eyes, dilated, expectant. A bead of sweat rises at my top lip, mingling with the slight raindrops that have begun to spring from the sky. I lick the rain away from my lip and she lunges into my arms. I twist her around, one hand resting, pressing at the apex of her thighs, the other gently wrapped around her throat. I press my chest against her, feel the ragged tear of her breath and push her against the wall. Turning her face to the side, she presses her cheek to the wet brick and closes her eyes.

"Are you ready for this?" I ask, pressed heavily against her back. The friction and heat between us is enough to unman me. I concentrate on the brick, the cool rivulets of water that trickle down, through the cracks and mortar grooves. "We are not going to play or take our time. I am going to fuck you, fast and hard. Are you ready for that?" I hear her breath catch, she is always so quiet, but I know she likes it when I talk dirty. Reaching beneath her skirt, I run my palm across her tight cheeks, coaxing blood to the surface, warming her up. She sways her hips, pressing her back into my waiting erection, wagging her delicious ass in front of me. I raise my palm from her skin and wait a moment, before bringing it back down hard, across both alabaster cheeks. "I said, are you ready?" She squeals in delight.

"Yes." Her voice is breathy, heavy with lust, and I know I've got her. Hooking my thumb into her panties, I tug until they rip in my hand, a tiny shred of damp silk that I tuck into my pocket. Angry red lines mar her skin where the panties pulled and snapped, she will feel that later. I fumble against the zipper of my slacks, kissing her back and shoulders as she bows under me. The smell of gardenia, fresh rain and Sophie's musk wafts around me, and my blood is whipped into frenzy. Unzipping my trousers, I free my cock and it falls heavy into my hand, already throbbing, aching for Sophie's soft, yielding warmth.

"Turn around," I whisper into her ear. She turns and her eyes go straight to my rock hard cock, bobbing in the rain, tapping my belly. Her eyes grow in delight and she licks her lips. God damn, I could get lost in those eyes, and the new devious twinkle that she wears. Dropping to her knees, she looks up at me with hunger in her eyes, a playfully seductive grin pulling at her cherry lips. Starving, she slips my cock into her mouth, like a delicate lollipop.

"Aahh!" I gasp. All the way to the root she takes me into her warm, wet mouth, her jaw clamped down tightly around my pulsing root. Her other hand cups my balls, turning them around in her hand, tugging and kneading. Little explosions ring deep in my groin, bringing me to a boil. She pulls them down, away from my body and the weight is enough to send me over the edge. She pumps my flesh with her perfect mouth, her silky tongue running over my hard cock. A bead of cum gathers at the tip as she pulls it from her mouth. Grasping at my humming flesh she looks straight into my eyes, lowers her tongue and flicks the bead from my tip, taking it slowly into her mouth. Closing her eyes, she moans in delight, and the vibration rings deep in my boiling blood. Damn, she's good.

I haul her up from her knees, and demand that she wrap her tiny legs around me. She has got me so hot I don't care who is watching. The rain falls in a steady stream, coating us in slickness, we don't care, lost in each other, caught up in our own storm. This little shower is nothing compared to the slick, heady wetness that has spread between Sophie's soft, white thighs. She locks her legs around me and I spread her open with my hands, tugging her flesh until it is wide, and exposed. I rub her sopping wet slit across my cock twice before the sensation becomes too much. Pulling her down with all my strength I impale her on my begging rod. "Oh!" I clamp my hand over her mouth to stifle her scream and set a frantic pace. She meets every thrust, her thighs like vice grips around me, tensing and squeezing with every deep thrust. I am buried to the hilt, lost inside Sophie. This is rapidly becoming my favorite place to be, and it's almost over. I didn't think I could feel this way.

I wind my hand around the back of her neck and tug her hair, exposing her soft, white throat. I suckle and nip at her flesh as her walls begin to clamp and quiver around me. I still, stop her writhing, my hands heavy on her hips. Buried deep within her, I hold her, our eyes locked. I kiss her soft, sweet lips. Lifting her from my cock, she hovers with her folds resting at my tip, her lips parted against mine. I pull her down hard, thrusting into her at the same time and we collide, waves rippling through my belly. The force is savage and heavenly. She rebounds off and sets her own pace. Cum boils in my balls as she writhes against me, her juices matting in my curls, her clit hard and on display, sweet little cunt strangling me, sucking me deeper. I slide her off again and she pulls her bottom lip between her teeth, until white from the pressure. Her eyes bulge and beg for another. I thrust again, hard, slamming into her, my cock so deep I'd swear it was in her belly. She explodes around me in a flurry of pulsing muscles, a silent scream at her "O" shaped mouth. She rides me hard, her hands clamped to my shoulders, fingers digging into my flesh. Hair thrashing about her face, whipped into a fit. Her back pressed against the brick, I thrust into her again and again, each time claiming more of her for myself. Burying her face in my neck, she licks my throat up to my ear. The sensation rings in my balls and the force of the eruption rips a growl from deep in my chest.

"Your cock feels so good." Her breathy, staccato whisper pushes me over and I empty myself into her as she rides her orgasm, her pussy crushes me with long, hard spasms. Crushing me in a death grip, her legs pulse around my waist, her arms languidly draped over my shoulders, she hangs on me like a limp rag doll.

"Mmm." The smell of her hair is intoxicating, the scent of gardenias swirl around us in the heavy, rain filled air. I have to force myself to stop. I want to take her again, but not here. Out in the rain, exposed and on display. The thought makes me smile. She let me, not only that, but she dropped to her knees, right here on the pier.

"Never a dull moment," I mutter as my cock slides from her, still standing at half mast, ready to go again. I nudge her with my nose and kiss the corner of her mouth. Her eyes are closed but she smiles, like a child pretending to sleep. "Let's get out of here." I pull her legs from my waist and lower her to the ground, careful to support her. She is shaking and slightly off balance. I pat myself on the back for that and roll her skirt down to cover her up, running my hands about her supple, heated skin. Her cheeks are littered with dust and pebbles, no doubt from where her skin met the brick wall.

"Sophie," I whisper into her hair. It smells amazing, like rain and gardenias, and now us. Her skin glistens from the rain, or sweat, hard to tell which. She nuzzles against my neck and mutters under her breath before dragging her head back, her tired eyes meeting mine.

"We should get out of the rain." I zip up and straighten her dress while she watches me, her eyes so appreciative and warm. I take her hand in mine, reminded of how much smaller, more delicate she is, although she would never admit to being delicate. Her short, slender fingers lace with mine, I bring her hand to my mouth, placing a feather light kiss against the back of her hand.

"That was amazing." I stop and look down into her soft, satisfied eyes. "You are amazing."

She smiles a perfect little smile. The kind that raises her apple cheeks and crinkles her eyes, my favorite smile. She buries herself under my arm, and we walk to the car in languid silence. A week ago I didn't know her, now I can't get enough. And tomorrow I will let her go. A nagging voice in the back of my mind tells me it isn't going to be as easy as all that.

Chapter 20

I lay, rocked and exhausted in Rhys' strong arms, feeling his heart beat against my ear. I could lay this way for hours, basking in the slowly fading buzz of what he does to me, time and time again. Every time pushing me higher, farther, teasing me and testing me. My limits have been shattered by this man. I cannot believe that we had sex outside. I have never been so afraid and exhilarated. The thought of getting caught made me feel so naughty, and hot. His hunger for me is shocking and lovely. I am drained and renewed, all at once. He is quiet and his pulse is slow, controlled. Deep in thought, his soft fingers float over my skin, twist in my hair.

"She left." The silence broken, I turn in his arms to see the hard planes of his face shadowed.

"Who?" I ask, wondering what one sided conversation he has just let escape his mind.

"My mother, when I was five." His face twists into a sad scowl, but he is opening up.

"Oh." I wait, not wanting to push, but intrigued by his unprovoked confession.

"Just like that." He shakes his head, his eyes unfocused, lost. "She wanted more, whatever that means. Who does that?" I don't know what to say, what to think. I want to hug him fiercely, prod for more information. I want to cry for his loss. I want to slap his ice queen of a mother. But I wait. Wait for him to finish, guiding me. To tell me what he needs. Filling his chest with a deep breath, I ride the wave of his expanding lungs and watch his warm eyes dull. "She broke his heart."

"And yours, I would imagine."

"I have never forgiven her. His eyes were so hollow. Even as I boy I could see him breaking in front of me. For years his eyes were hollow. I will never forget that, never forget what he looked like, what it felt like to watch him live completely broken."

"I am so sorry, Rhys. I had no idea." I cannot imagine a mother doing such a horrific thing, laying such a burden on such a young child; leaving your own child, willingly. What kind of person, indeed. "At least you have a relationship now." Even though the thought of her now, standing at the bottom of the stairs provokes an entirely different response in my blood than it did this morning.

"No, it isn't what it looks like. She is a master of spin, my mother. She saunters in and out of my life when it suits her. I have just gotten used to it, that's all. Once I started making a name for myself, that is when she started coming around. She loves having me on her arm, something to show off, to brag about. As if she has anything to do with who I am, or what I have accomplished." The resonance in his voice is icy, a low simmering anger sitting just below the surface.

"You don't think her leaving like that has anything to do with who you are?"

"I don't know. I'm sorry I brought it up. I just….."

"I am glad you told me." I finish his heavy thought. It's clear she has a greater effect than even he can admit to. Of course her leaving has everything to do with who he is. But I won't be the one to tell him that. I just feel privileged that he has finally opened up about something, one small piece of the puzzle that is Rhys. And he revealed it to me. He shakes his head, as if to shake her out, closing his eyes with a deep breath. Wrapping a tendril of my hair around his finger his eyes warm and a grin pulls at his soft mouth.

"How do you do your hair like that?" he muses softly, twisting a rogue curl between his fingers, changing the subject.

"Rain, extreme humidity and a little brick dust," I tease.

"Well, I like it." He pulls me closer, burying his nose in my hair. Cupping my head, he tips my chin to look me in the eye. I could lose myself in him so easily, his skillful hands, wicked mouth. He makes me want to do things I thought I would never do. He said no romance, no emotion, and I agreed, and meant it. Why is it so hard to stay in the lines? We both caved so quickly, to the pull, the electricity between us. I know he feels it, too. We said the

274

words, but we didn't mean them. No emotion, no romance. He didn't mean it.

"You wouldn't rather it be longer, maybe blonde?"

"God, No! This hair. You. Are so fucking sexy. You have no idea. The way it whips around your face when you lose control. It's mesmerizing, addictive. It just makes me want to tip you over to watch it sway while I fuck you senseless, again," he growls against my ear. "It makes me want to lose control with you." His words grip me with force in the most dark and deep recesses of my body. To be wanted, appreciated in such a carnal, raw way is new. It makes me feel wild, sensual. Alive.

"You make me lose control. I have never felt that way before, never." He does something to my body that I think only he was meant to do. He knows it, reads it like a map.   "This is all rather new to me." We are so familiar, so intimate. More intimate than I have ever been, or ever expected to be. By this time there are parts of me that he is more familiar with than I am. He has made sure of it, given me so much attention I have never had. Loved me, or fucked me in ways I never dreamt of. And yet we are almost perfect strangers. And will be strangers again after tomorrow. I will be wiped away, never to be seen again.

Dark thoughts attempt to swallow my ecstasy, knowing that I will not see him again, unless by some happy accident. It's not as if he has to worry about ever running into me. We don't exactly run in the same circles. I roll around and press my lips to his chest, running my fingers across the light scattering of dark hair that makes him look so masculine, I love it. I run my hands up his chest and he shudders, before squeezing me, pressing his hips to mine. Up his throat, I scratch at the stubble that grows from days of neglect. I love the stubble, the vibrations rattle down my arms, sending a shiver down my spine. Placing my hands on his face, I look into those eyes and I am his, at least for tonight.

"Why is that?"

"What?" He props himself up on an elbow, ready to talk now that the focus is no longer on him.

"Well, you had a boyfriend. That much we know. And you were no virgin. So how is it that any of this can be new to you?"

My cheeks are on fire. Did I just burst into flames? Embarrassment roars through me and I want to hide. I don't want to have this conversation with him. I don't want to share my sexual history with anyone, much less Rhys. He is experienced, knows what he likes and wants, and clearly is used to being with women who are the same. I am not in his league, and now he wants to expose me. I roll onto my back and fling my arm over my eyes. Not wanting to look him in the eye when I confess. I take a deep breath and let it spread through me, willing my heart rate to slow, and keep a steady pace while I bare myself to Rhys.

"My ex was selfish." I peek at him to catch a sly grin rise on his lips. "He was my first and I learned from him. He never wanted me to move. He always acted like anything but missionary was kinky and sick." Rhys' face is impassive, his silence urges me to fill the quiet. "He was cold and mean. He never..." I pause at the thought. I don't know why, but I can hardly muster the words in my head, much less let them pass my lips.

"He never what, licked your pretty little pussy?" I choke on his words. They are hot, sexy and so dirty. He on the other hand, seems to take pleasure in such talk. I would be lying to say it wasn't growing on me.

"Yes, he never did that. Always said it was gross. So, naturally I thought I was gross." I peek out from under my arm to find Rhys staring right at me. He lifts my arm from my face, and rises onto his forearm, commanding my attention. Looking into his eyes, I cannot be embarrassed. He strips me bare, rakes me over and appreciates every inch of me. Over and over Rhys has showed me that He was wrong.

"I am happy for it. His loss is my gain," Rhys says, intensity shining in his eyes. "I like that I am the only man to do that to you. I licked it, it's mine.

277

You are a beautiful woman, Sophie. He sounds like an idiot." I roll onto my side, pull him to me and kiss him with all the force I can muster. Dirtier words have never sounded so pretty. I nip at his bottom lip until his tongue darts out to swipe and dance with mine. I am hungry, suddenly wild with lust. We are both starving, devouring one another's flesh with fervor, kissing and biting, consuming. I cannot get close enough to him, he is crushed against me and it is not close enough. I am here now. Right here, right now. And I need him like air. I will suffocate if he doesn't love me right now, my body dying for his brand of breath, his life force. He alone can make me feel more alive than I ever knew and I want it now more than anything, to connect with him in the most intense way, the most heavenly, devious way. A masochistic addict hopelessly hooked on Rhys. Like a moth to a flame, I know I will get burned, but I just need a little more heat, a little more light. One more hit.

***

I wander through the dark house alone. It is too big and empty, the life from the wedding an ephemeral memory, leaving behind two lonely hearts and a big empty house. Sitting at the beautiful baby grand piano in the solarium, I mindlessly tap the keys. I have prepared myself for the end, this affair with Rhys. I go back to the "real world" and he goes back to his world, the simple, clean end of an affair. Sorrow seeps from my fingertips as they float across the ivory keys. I turn my full attention to the piano and let both hands quietly lament, sorrowful strokes soothing my anxious heart. I close my eyes and surrender to my hands. The piano cries softly, but my fingers are heavy. Every note is one step closer to the end, I slow the tempo, wanting to drag it out, to make it last. But the end is inevitable, and my fingers glide across the keys as whispered sadness falls away and the only sound in the room is my ragged breath and a slowly breaking heart. I take my hands off the keys and run my fingers across my lips, provoking memories. Fresh memories of Rhys' warm mouth, his needy kisses, and the immediate absence of the way he makes me feel, happy, horny, frustrated, angry, and safe. Wanted. He makes me feel wanted in a way I never thought possible. When he kisses me it is hot with need, urgent and singular, like he has never kissed anyone that way before or since. I want to believe that is true, that this is just as new for him. The heat and familiarity, our bodies connected, like long lost souls, reunited. I turn from the piano to see him standing silently in the doorway, hiding in the shadows.

"Do you always linger in the dark?" I tease as he steps towards me wearing nothing but a smile.

Though his smile is dazzling it couldn't possibly detract from the beautiful form before me, bathed in moonlight. His broad shoulders accentuating the narrow waist and powerful legs that do this girl's body good. He clears his throat in protest as my eyes wander to the prize, already at half-mast and rising.

"Up here please, I am not an object to be ogled." His face is young and carefree, but his eyes are hungry as he stalks slowly towards me. "That sounded morose. Are you sad, Beautiful?" Careful not to reveal to him the deep ache that is crushing me at the thought of leaving, I smile.

"Just a little tired. It has been a long few days."

"Not long enough. I did not like waking up without you." He pulls me from the piano bench and hauls me into a deep, wet kiss. His lips soft and knowing against mine, perfect. He tugs at my backside, pulling me closer, humming in delight before he swats me playfully and pulls my hand.

"I am famished. Let's get a snack," he says, pulling me into the large kitchen.

"I don't know that I can concentrate on food with you looking like that." I wave my hand about his striking form and hard cock. "It is very distracting." I open the French doors to the oversized fridge and start searching for goodies as Rhys sidles up behind me. I turn around to catch him pulling at the hem of my shirt, the shirt I pulled from his drawer.

"Perhaps if we were on equal footing, it wouldn't be so distracting." He pulls the shirt over my head, leaving me heaving in the dull light of the refrigerator, wearing nothing but a pair of lacy boy shorts. I cover myself coyly, leaning into the cold air of the refrigerator. My nipples tighten as the cool air wafts around me.

"No, that doesn't help at all. Now I'm distracted." He grabs me around the waist and sets me on the counter, his eyes hungry. "Lay back, Beautiful. I know what I'm hungry for." He places his hand on my belly and slowly pushes me down onto the cool marble counter. I lay back and watch the stars in my eyes as he slides my panties to the side, teasing and pleasing me in ways I will never forget. Long fingers stroke my rapidly pulsing slit and his tongue rolls in circles around my clit, waking her up, igniting a deep sensitivity. His fingers slide in and out of me, a luscious deep stroking, while he blows ribbons of hot air over my pink folds. His mouth closes over me and I am lost. All that exists is his heavenly tongue and the soft light of the open refrigerator.

Chapter 21

Sunlight fills the room, but I wake with a shadow hanging over me. Wiping the sleep from my eyes, I nestle into the pile of white down in the center of the bed, breathing in the essence of the last two days, the smell of Rhys and sex. Mind blowing, life affirming, all-knowing sex. And now I go. After the most perfect seventy two hours of my sexual life, I must return to my reality. Three hours until my flight.

I carefully pack my bag, pulling on the linen dress I wore the first day he brought me here, lingering in his room. I don't want to leave anything, but I don't want to leave empty handed. I pull open one of his dresser drawers and pull out a freshly laundered tee. Worn heather green, with St. Andrews Rugby emblazoned across the chest. I bring it to my nose and devour the scent, fresh laundry, salty Miami air and Rhys. I toss the shirt into my bag and head to the bathroom, where I brush my teeth and hair before packing up my toiletries. In the mirror there is a new woman staring back at me, strong, sexual and confident, a quick study under Rhys' careful guidance. He showed me things about my body I could never have imagined, did things to me that I would never dreamed of. Things I liked, things I needed. He burned me to my core every chance he got, branded my sex like a cowboy. He has left an indelible mark upon my womanhood. I take his favorite bottle of cologne from the medicine cabinet and spray it into my bag before zipping it up.

Endings are inevitable by nature. Every moment we are hurtling towards an ending, nothing in this life is meant to last. This was not meant to last. We both know that. So why does it feel so sad? I would not delude myself into thinking that something could come of this. I have no desire for the fairy tale or the "red bottoms." I have seen enough of life to know how this would end, messy, with me, shattered, a desperate hanger-on, begging for scraps of his attention. No. It is best to cut the rope and go. The rope, my body quivers at the thought. I could easily melt into a sad puddle right where I stand. He has so thoroughly rocked me. Go with your dignity. Go while you are still wanted.

I drop my bags by the front door and watch Charlie fuss over the black Town Car in the driveway. He looks up and waves before returning to his obsessive polishing. I head into Rhys' office and find him tapping frantically on his keyboard, scowling at the screen. He is immersed in his work. He has neglected everything but me for the last three days, and now he must dig himself out. His beard is a little fuller, his curls a little longer, looping over his collar. I am sure that he is generally far more polished than he has been the last few days, locked up in this fabulous Mediterranean style den of iniquity. He has a dapper navy waistcoat on over his crisp white shirt. The cuffs hang open across his forearms, revealing his heavy, large faced Omega, reminding me of my limited time. A navy and green striped bow tie and a silk pocket square complete his working man's attire. The sight of him bowls me over. Every old fashioned, gentlemanly inch is perfect. Everything about the way he looks screams business and class. Something about that bow tie makes me weak, and horny as hell. My eyes dart about the room, coming to rest on a conspicuously empty spot on the shelf high above Rhys' desk. The picture of Nadja has been replaced by a scuffed, dingy white rugby ball. The whole scene converges on my senses and I am already damp, and needy. I am sorry to see him so busy, but not sorry to be the cause of his distraction. I walk around the back of his chair, careful not to disturb his train of thought. Running my hands over his fine linen shirt, down his chest, under his waistcoat, I rest my chin upon his shoulder and watch him type, a spreadsheet teeming with addresses and dollar signs.

I turn my attention to his neck, something I have come to know very well. I kiss his throat, then his jaw. There it is that smell, the scent of heaven that will linger in my nostrils for the rest of my days. His skin is soft and clean, his beard is soft, begging me to bury my fingertips in it. I scratch his face while I kiss him, pulling my fingers against the rugged hairs on his jaw. Dropping his fingers from the keys he turns his chair and pulls me into his lap. I fold easily into the space that was made for me, and look into his face. I am lost. Burying my hands in his silky hair, I pull him to me with the ferocity of a starving animal, and kiss him until everything falls away. Our lips tangle and dance before he takes my face in his powerful hands and guides me in the way he likes. He consumes my mouth with such passion. A lump in my throat forms, but I push through, kissing him harder. My lips are crushed to his, needy I nip at his bottom lip. I grind my backside into the fine fabric of his trousers, relishing the evidence of what I do to him. Wanting to pour everything I have into this kiss. To leave an indelible mark before we say goodbye. His length grows and twitches against his fly. I make him as crazy as he makes me. We are both panting, starving for breath when we finally come up for air. He holds my face in his hands, searching for something.

"That felt like Goodbye." He brushes the hair from my face, the pad of his thumb soft against my cheek, then forceful as he pulls at my bottom lip. I smile as well as I can, when Charlie steps around the door just as I open my mouth. He clears his throat to call Rhys' attention. We spin around in his heavy leather chair. Rhys lifts me easily and adjusts me in his lap, pressing his hardening member between my thighs. He gently rocks forward, pressing his suit, casually, as if I'm not sitting on a raging hard on. He continues to make tiny circles with his hips, torturing me silently while he talks with Charlie.

"Your mother summoned you," he grins, his freckled cheeks aflame. Their private joke, not lost on me. In one encounter I could see that she is a woman not to be crossed. "Drinks at the Ritz before dinner." Rhys just nods and reflects Charlie's crooked grin. "I have loaded your bags, Sophie. The car is ready to go when you are. Although traffic on the causeway is heavy so we shouldn't wait much longer."

"Thank you, Charlie." I smile widely at him. I like him. He is sweet, and loyal. He shares Rhys' crooked grin and wicked sense.

"We will be out shortly. Please close the door behind you," Rhys commands, and turns our back to a retreating Charlie.

"You have already packed your bags? Are you so eager to leave?" He asks, rolling his hips before he bucks me in his lap. Everything deep in me clenches and I shudder from the close contact. "I want you to stay." He pulls the fabric of my dress up and makes circles on my skin, kneading my backside, pulling me apart. He pulls my panties to the side and slides a finger across my cleft. I am sticky and wet for him already, just like he likes me. "I don't think you really want to go." Slowly his finger runs up and down my heated slit until he presses his way in and finds my throbbing clit. She practically calls out to him, '*Here I am*! *Please hurry*!' He presses and circles slowly, watching me come undone.

I open my mouth to answer, but only a low moan escapes.

"There's my girl," he purrs in my ear. "You don't really want to go. You want to stay and play." He plunges his finger into me and I gasp in pleasure. He adds a second finger and slowly circles my opening, stretching me. Pumping slowly at first, in and out, then faster and harder until I am resting in his palm, he grinds against me while he invades my body.

"I don't want you to forget me. What we have done, where I have been." His words are heavy, becoming a tidal wave that washes over me and I come, violently into his hand. My body shakes and I stifle a scream by biting into the arm he has wrapped around my shoulders. The feeling is so intense I feel like I am falling. Rhys continues his onslaught, until I cannot take another moment. I pull up from his lap, trying to escape his fingers, but he just holds me down and flicks my clit so hard that I come again. And it's like a train that I cannot stop, my body is stuck on repeat.

The eruptions roll through me, one meeting up to the other until they become one long note of heavenly white noise. I vaguely hear the slide of Rhys' zipper before he turns me around and spears me on his waiting erection. The fullness is shocking and perfect. He lets out a low deep breath as he pushes me down to the root. His head rolls back, and he reclines in the dark leather chair, tilting his hips. He rests his hands upon my hips, they are heavy, holding me in place. I watch his eyes change, they are hungry and ferocious. He rocks his hips against me before violently thrusting his cock deep. I bite back a scream as he settles into a torturous rhythm of deep thrusts and retreat. Each time he pulls me farther and farther off of his cock until it just rests against my swollen, sensitive folds. Then he dips back in and pulls me down.

"God, you feel so good, Sophie." The repetition is hypnotic and I find myself doing the work for him, raising myself up, teasing his head with my slick sex and then swallowing him whole. I feel a tremor flow through him and he stills me. Wrapping his arms around my core, he pulls me to his chest, an embrace rife with emotion. My chest opens and my heart threatens to leap and run willingly into his arms. He slowly rocks into me and begins to make slow love to me with his face buried in my neck.

The change in the mood of his passion is

palpable. There is suddenly something so desperate, so final about the way his hands clutch me, his fingers tearing into me, holding on for dear life. My center clenches as the next ripple of relief rolls through me.

"This doesn't have to be goodbye." His lips tremble against my throat. The words wash over me and I know I am lost. He picks up the pace as my muscles begin to tighten around him, milking him, pulling him deeper. His pace is frantic. He quickens, before emptying himself into me in long, drawn out thrusts. He collapses against my chest and I take his head against my breasts. I try to calm my breathing as he rests his head on my heart. My center clenches and throbs, the residual rhythm of his confession ringing in my ear, echoing in my loins. I hold him close to my heart for a long, painful moment before he slips from me and zips himself back up.

He picks me up and places me back in his chair before disappearing into his private washroom. Returning with a damp cloth, he drops to his knees in front of me and pushes my legs apart. The action is so intimate, so personal. His dark eyes cloud over as he gently cleans me up before resting his head, heavy in my lap. I stroke his silky hair and wait for him to speak, confused by his reaction and the sudden change in his demeanor. I don't want to think too hard on it for fear that I may convince myself that something bigger is happening. I need to remember exactly where I stand. I glance at his computer screen and see that my time is up.

"I have to go," I whisper, gently running my fingers up the back of his neck.

"Would you like me to accompany you to the airport?" he laments while drawing tiny circles on my thigh.

"Rhys." He looks up into my face and I see the turmoil in his eyes. Struggle hiding behind his beautiful features. His face is engrained in my mind. I know I can see that crooked smile whenever I like, but I would love to see it now. Instead, he is serious and stone faced.

"You have work to do, and you have to meet your mother." His face falls and I am stunned. *What is happening here?* "You wouldn't want me to get the wrong idea," I prod, trying to lighten his mood, but to no avail. He shakes his head while he listens, but doesn't retort. Rising before me and all six feet two inches of his frame looms large, dominating the room and my personal space. He is rigid and controlled, but frustration rolls off of him in waves. He pinches the bridge of his nose and lets out a heavy sigh. When his eyes open they have softened slightly, but his steely determination is clear.

"Right." He straightens his bow tie and waits, his beautiful mouth set in a harsh line.

I am stunned by his quick relent, but what did I

expect? My pulse races and my heart jumps into my throat. I don't want to say goodbye. But I cannot let him see that. I know this cannot go anywhere. Our lives are too different, too far apart. I am many things, a realist being one. I know enough about this man's past, and propensity for new, shiny objects that even a little infatuation could ebb in a moment. I know that nothing about this weekend was real. I know that if his past is any indication of my future, I have to say goodbye, and let it go.

"It was a pleasure having you, Ms. Noelle." His mouth rises in that panty busting crooked grin and he hauls me into his arms, melting me with a soft kiss. His firm lips tender against mine, urgent, like a starving man dying for the last drop of water. We dance and linger longer than we should, our hands and lips unwilling to let go, before he finally walks me to the car, and relinquishes his hold on me. He doesn't wait for us to pull away, turning his back and quickly retreating back into the house as soon as the car door shuts. The pleasure was surely all mine.

Chapter 22

I couldn't say just how I managed to get on the plane. I was numb as I walked through the airport. A welcome effect, airports are always so sad, people leaving something or someone. I hate them almost as much as I hate hospitals. As we take off and the cabin is gently lifted into the air I am pulled from the numbness I have been struggling against since he shut the door and turned his back. He walked away without a second glance. I wrap myself in the too small airplane blanket and curl up in the roomy first class seat Rhys has so generously provided, only after I vehemently refused to set foot on his private jet. I have already allowed myself to deviate so far from who I am and how I live. It would be too easy to be swallowed up in his life, consumed by all of the perks of being Rhys Slate. I had to stand my ground, even though a part of me is kicking myself for the lost opportunity.

The too-perky flight attendant pulls me from my reverie with the offer of champagne and I accept readily, anything to help me sleep. Before I know it, I am woken by the jolt of the plane coming down on the runway. I make my way through the airport the same way, numb, floating on residual pleasure, and physical exhaustion. The cold air is a pleasant shock when I step outside. The wind is gentle, and the moon is bright and full. I take a deep breath, filling my lungs with home. Fresh air assaulting my dull senses, waking me from my pleasure filled vacation. I glance down the curb towards the taxi lane when I see my name emblazoned across a white board; Ms. Sophie Noelle. I make eye contact with the man holding the sign and he quickly makes his way towards me. Scooping up my bags and tipping his hat before I can think.

"Ms. Noelle, I trust your flight was pleasant. My name is Frank, and I will be driving you home." He opens the back door of a sleek black Town Car and I almost expect Rhys to be sitting in the back. He isn't and I am relieved as I slide in.

"Um, yes. Thank you."

This has Rhys' signature all over it. His way of seeing me safely home, since I no longer have a phone. My phone. I can't believe I allowed myself to be out of touch for so long. My mind snaps back to real life almost immediately as Frank pulls out into traffic. Everything that I left behind, my Grandmother, the only family I have left, wasting away in a hospice, the ex who invaded my home while I was away. I long for Miami as it all comes rushing back. Everything I was trying to escape, still waiting for me when I return. What am I walking into when I get home? Will he be there? Please, don't let him be there.

We wind through city traffic before Frank pulls off the interstate, cruising through open space and sleepy bedroom towns before he pulls onto my street. He pulls around the front of my building and quickly opens the door for me before retrieving my bags from the trunk. He ushers me away from the car, and it is clear that he has been instructed to walk me to the door.

He produces a set of keys from his pocket. Two newly cut brass keys, hanging from a silver Tiffany key chain, and proceeds to open my front door. I look to him in question. Baffled and unsure as to why or how this man got a set of keys to my home.

"Where did those keys come from?" I ask, befuddled.

"They were waiting for me. I have been instructed to see you safely inside." The pity in his face is evident, as is his embarrassment. I don't have the energy to fight so I step behind him as he walks through the door and flips on the light. He places my bags by the front door and proceeds to sweep my apartment like a cop, every room, every closet, before he is convinced that we are alone and I am safe. He places my keys on the dining table along with a business card, UBER, Frank Rich.

"Please call me, Ms. Noelle, when you need a car, if you ever need anything. I am at your beck and call, at a moment's notice." I can't help but grin at his offer, it is so far out of my scope of living.

"I am not of the means to retain a driver, for any reason, but thank you, Frank."

"You are on account, Ms. Noelle. All of your charges will be covered." Of course they have.

"Please, call me Sophie. Thank you, Frank."

"Is there anything else I can do for you this evening, Ms. Sophie?"

"No, that's it. Thank you. Oh, and Frank," I catch his arm as he heads out the door, "please tell your boss that I am grateful."

He tips his cap at me and bids a Goodnight before I close the door and turn to my sad, small, empty apartment. Everything looks in order. In fact the tidiness of the space is strangely conspicuous. It doesn't appear that Collin has taken anything with him, or broken anything, his habit when he gets frustrated. I notice his keys on the counter, the familiar over-used bottle opener in the shape of a shark. Did he really relent so easily? That is not his way. I am overcome with relief and exhaustion. I don't want to think about anything. I make my way down the hallway, switching off every light that Frank turned on. I drop my clothes as I make my way through my room. Every step is heavier, weighted down with the realities I will face in the morning. A quick shower and I slip into bed without another thought, drifting on memories of Rhys, his hands, his mouth, and his inexplicable refusal to say goodbye.

A pounding at my door tears me from the most restful sleep I have had in days. The room is bright, but chilly. A moment passes before my body accepts that we are no longer in Miami. But there is something so comforting about your own bed after a few days away. Regardless of how wonderful those days may have been. My muscles are stiff, I have been twisted in ways I could never have imagined, and loved every minute of it. I stretch and grab my cotton robe before dashing to the door to stop the incessant racket. I glance at the clock and it is 8:15. What an unholy hour for someone to pound so loudly. I yank the door open on a startled young woman.

"I have a package for Sophie Noelle?" she asks, meek as a mouse. Where is the powerhouse that was banging on the door a moment ago?

"That's me." She hands me a small black cardboard box. It has no emblem, no shipping label, nothing.

She smiles a quick smile before turning on her heel and disappearing around the hedges that line the sidewalks. I look down at the box, set it on the kitchen table next to the inexplicable keys, and I know who is behind it all. Rhys. I open the box to find a brand new phone and turn it on. It is already charged and loaded with all of my old contacts, and one new one. On the home screen, staring back at me is a cocky grinning Rhys. I tap on the picture and an entire library of information pops up. His cell number, phone numbers for his office in Miami and New York, cell and office numbers for an assistant named Nina, business email and personal, addresses in New York and Miami. Every possible way to get a hold of him listed in one handy place. I ponder the bevy of society women and wannabes that would kill for just a fraction of this information. I scroll down the page to where he has listed special skills and laugh out loud.

Special Skills:
Knots, games, making Sophie lose control

I immediately type him a message.

Thank you for the new phone. Frank gave me a good ride last night. Thanks for that.
PS. How did he get my house keys?

The phone chimes back almost immediately.

I'm glad you made it home OK. You are welcome for the phone, I figured it was the least I could do, seeing as I confiscated and dismantled your last one. Frank is a lucky man.
PS. I had your locks changed.

My head is barely treading the surface of his casual declaration. He invaded my home and privacy, or better yet, he had someone else do it. I am upset. I think I am upset. I should be upset, why would he do that? How would he do that? And then I remember the last time I had my old phone. The day Collin called. Rhys must have overheard. But, changing my locks? Changing the locks of a woman you barely know, that's a little creepy, right? I stare down at my phone for a long minute, contemplating what to say, if anything.

Don't be angry, I was just trying to help.

I don't need your help!
Well, you have it whether you like it or not. He invaded your home when you were not there. What kind of gentleman would I be if I did not see you safely home? How did you sleep?

Don't change the subject.

I have a meeting, Beautiful, a lot of work to catch up on. Enjoy your new phone.

I pass the day cleaning my apartment, looking for clues of Collin being here, but I find nothing. The locks are new, just as Rhys said they were. But other than that it all seems to be just as I had left it. I unpack and shower, needing to get back into my routine, and get my mind ready for real life. My mind too easily slips away, musing on how wonderful it would be to live a life of luxury, with Rhys. To hold up in that mansion on Key Biscayne and just let the rest of the world fall away. The thought is a trap, distracting me from the very real task of jumping back into real life, my real life.

There is radio silence all day, until five thirty. My phone chimes with a message just as there is a knock at the door. I have to admit I'm feeling a bit skittish, afraid, or perhaps hoping that Rhys will appear. Or worse still, the specter of boyfriends past.

I can still smell you...

A beautiful bouquet of sweet peas, and big, white, double gardenias arranged artfully in a crystal vase sits on my stoop. The scent is heavenly, swirling in my nostrils, taking me back to Miami, to Rhys. I close my eyes and breathe deeply, pulling the floral essence deep into my lungs. It is hypnotizing, all consuming, and just like Rhys. I check the card.

I still smell you in my bed.

Wow, for someone who claims not to do

romance, he sure knows how to lay it on. I tap his picture on my phone and send him a message.

Gardenias are my favorite, did you know?

I smelled them today and thought of you. Now I cannot stop. Did you think of me?

Maybe…

I thought about kissing your neck. What did you think about?

As I read it a shiver rolls down my spine, my memory flashing to his warm mouth on my skin.

My private thoughts are my own, Sir.

You are being coy, Beautiful. Keep playing with me and see what happens….

I haven't begun to play with you, Mr. Slate…

I am aware, Ms. Noelle.
Now, I have an engagement.
Goodnight and sweet dreams, Sophie.

My mouth hurts from the permanent smile

plastered across my face. I lay down on my sad empty bed, holding my phone close. He has invaded every facet of my mind. I cannot seem to move away from him. He is everywhere. I am covered by him in every way, covered by his soft kisses, by his scent and his gentle touch, covered by his searing gaze and his rock hard body. I cannot escape him. His every touch is emblazoned on my memory, tattooed on my skin. He is there when I close my eyes, he is everywhere. But he is not here.

Chapter 23

Day two, post Miami. I visited first thing with my grandma, took her a Starbucks Venti Cappuccino. Candy, her overly sweet, Nazi nurse doesn't allow her to have caffeine, says it makes her too feisty. So I sneak her a cup every other week when I take her to get her hair and nails done. It makes her so happy, I can't resist. We went grocery shopping and I picked up the bare essentials for myself. Now, I work, to dig myself out from under the last five days of doing nothing. Well, not *nothing*. I have to immerse myself in work, editing my latest submissions, desperately going over my notes for my next proposal. I am fortunate enough to write whenever and wherever I like, but if I don't keep the pieces coming, I don't eat.

I do the final spell check on my latest piece about the newest food trucks in the area and send it off to Mary, my editor and friend. It is five thirty. I have been sitting at my computer for four straight hours. I get up to stretch my poor legs, and search for my sadly silent phone. I haven't heard from Rhys all day. Yesterday must have been a fluke, I suppose, the first day apart after such an intense exchange. I'm sure he is cooling off. The thought leaves me feeling bereft when my phone chimes. Think of the devil, and he shall present.

I can still taste you.

A faint knock at the door and my heart skips a beat. Anxious and blushing so deeply I feel it in my toes, my mouth goes as dry as the Sahara desert, suddenly parched. I pull the door open and am handed a bottle of my favorite white wine, Sophia, Blanc de Blanc, wrapped in pink cellophane, tied with a gray silk bow with a card attached, nestled in a small gift basket. The delivery guy doesn't ask my name or wait for a tip, he just thrusts the basket into my hands and turns on his heel. I grab my favorite glass, a small green jelly jar that my dad always drank from. I unwrap the cellophane and open the bottle. I run my finger tentatively over the edge of the card, anticipating what he has written. He is playing with me, building me up to something. I am intrigued. I run my finger under the seam and pull the card out of the envelope, plain white cardstock with shiny black scroll.

I wish I was there to lick your lips.

I read the card over and over, driving the message deeper into my belly, pressing my thighs together, my entire lower half throbbing, responding wantonly to his carefully chosen words. I close my eyes and picture him, kneeling before me, his hands pushing my knees apart, his mouth teasing and nipping at my most sacred parts. He is in my head. I grab my phone.

Sophia is my favorite. Do you have a cheat sheet?

Lucky guess. How was your day, Beautiful?

Better now.

Glad I could be of service. Anything else I can do?

Not from way over there...

Perhaps I could walk you through it.

Not a chance.

You would let me if I was there.

If you were here, you could do it for me.

Touché.

Thank you for the wine.

You are most welcome. I have a flight to catch. Sleep tight.

Good night, Sir. ;)

Elated and energized by our exchange I sip my crisp white wine and scroll through my phone. I want to go out. I need to go out. Excess energy courses through me and my body is humming for a release. I scroll down to Mary and check the clock before calling.

***

An hour later and I am strolling down Main Street, headed to the local bar to meet Mary for a drink and gossip session. Main Street is buzzing with families coming out for the first warm night of the season. Summer is hanging in the air, trees are starting to fill out, and the window boxes overflow with petunias in a rainbow of colors. Ice cream trucks and food trucks line the street, while people visit and children play. I duck into the dingy door of Pasquales and search for Mary. The bar is dark, even though the sun still sits high outside. The walls are covered with graffiti that could be as much as thirty years old. It has been the neighborhood bar here for decades. Worn and tattered stools line the heavily marred bar, while pleather booths run along the back wall. It is comfortable, lived in. The kind of place only a local could love.

"Tell me all about Miami? I want to hear every dirty detail." Eyes alight with anticipation, it is hard to resist Mary when she is in the mood to gossip. I swirl the scotch around, watching the amber liquid lick the sides of my glass, wrapping its legs around the fine crystal in a liquid dance, the smell of peat and Rhys slowly wafting from the rim, engulfing me in memory. I take a slow sip, letting the warmth spread through me like molten honey, and he is there, behind my eyes, his lips, his hands, his voice. As raw and silky smooth as if he were right here. I have developed a taste for scotch, a taste for Rhys.

"Since when do you drink scotch?" Turning her nose up, she takes a long swig of her Bud Light. Her dirty blonde hair sweeps across her shoulders as she throws her head back, draining the bottle. The faded jean jacket and well-worn Keds speak to her generation. Anxiously waiting for some details, she fiddles with the charms that hang at her neck. A gift from her children, three small silver discs, with differing birth stones that hang from a delicate silver chain.

I have developed a taste for many new things. I cannot suppress the grin that rises from my lips. A fire burns in my cheeks and I know I am beet red, blushing at the thought of the things I have developed a taste for. Knowing she is fishing for a distraction, I launch into the play by play of the trip. Mary and I have always shared everything. For four years now she has been my only close friend. And for two years she has been my editor and boss. She is like a big sister, mentor and best friend all rolled into one. She married fresh out of high school and promptly filled her home with children. Now, ten years later she is the editor in chief of the local paper, member of the PTA, wife, mother and friend. And the unfortunate receptacle into which she allows me to dump all my sadness and baggage. It will be nice to share some good news with her for a change. A nice juicy story to get her blood flowing.

She tips her empty bottle to the bartender, who just happens to be her little brother, Paul. He pops another bud light and slides it across the bar, all the while her attention is glued on the details. The hotel, the partying, the estate on Biscayne, I spilled it all, accept any mention of Rhys. I don't know why I held back, why I didn't mention him first. He is the first and only thing on my mind these days. So, why keep it hidden? Why wasn't I willing to share with Mary? Maybe I am afraid that if I say it out loud, it will sound ludacris. If I share what I have with Rhys will that make it less real? We share everything, Mary and I. I know she would want me to share this. I know things about her husband that I can never unknow, never. I knock back the last drops of scotch, licking the rim of the glass wanting to store the scent, the flavor, the feel of it. Mary is out of patience, glaring over her bottle of Bud.

"Who's the guy?" She demands, plunking the bottle to the bar.

"I don't know what you mean?"

"The guy? It's clear there was a guy. Look at you," she says, waving her hand about in the air between us. "You are glowing, you are drinking scotch? Hello, who drinks scotch? Rich men and drunks, that's who, so which is he?" She crosses her fingers "God, I hope he's rich!" The glimmer in her eyes tells me she is teasing, but a tiny pang tears at my heart from her sentiment. It didn't even matter who he was to some people, he was rich. That's what he is, who he is. Well, he isn't that to me. His money is not what I think of when I think of Rhys. No, I think of all the delicious things he did to me, the ropes, his mouth, just being with him. But who am I kidding? We were in a mansion, surrounded by luxury. He treated me to everything. His money had everything to do with what happened between us. The thought leaves a sour taste in my mouth and a knot in my throat. Was I really so shallow? Did I really care about Rhys or was I just swept away by all that he has to offer? I don't want the answer. I push all the doubt to the back of my mind.

"He was amazing! It was amazing. One of Matthew's friends, the best man actually." She rolls her eyes at the cliché of it all, and I concur. "He took me out for coffee to this little Cuban place and then to his family's house on Key Biscayne, which is where the wedding was. Oh, Mary, you should have seen it! I have never seen anything like the way these people live. The house was amazing, the wedding was flawless. He even lent his father's yacht to Olivia and Matthew for their honeymoon. They are cruising around the Mediterranean as we speak, on a private yacht, can you believe that shit? I felt so out of place, so poor!"

"Honey, everyone is poor compared to people like that. We just have to remember to be thankful for what we have. Now, back to the boy. Did you sleep with him? Are you going to see him again? Tell me please, I am an old married woman, you owe me this."

"He asked me to stay with him after the wedding. We holed up in his mansion and fucked like rabbits. It was amazing!" I bounce a little on my stool, the last sounds coming out in an excited squeal.

"Was he good to you?" Skepticism and concern are all over her face.

"Oh yes, Mary, so different from what I am used to, so different. He was so good." I drag out the word, wanting to emphasize how very good it all was! I cannot hold back the smile that threatens to tear my face in two. The thought of how good he

309

actually was could set me on fire and reduce me to a blathering idiot.

"Well, I am glad you finally had a good experience. I was worried that Collin had ruined you forever. I mean the ideas he planted in your head. Just thinking about it makes me want to slap him. I am happy for you, honey." She pushes a strand of hair behind my ear, a motherly smile upon her face. "You deserve it. Now tell me, what's his name, this mystery lover, will you see him again?"

"His name is Rhys." I bite down hard on my bottom lip to stifle the pleasure that jolts through me at his name crossing my lips. "Rhys Slate." I watch Mary's eyes grow into the size of melons, bulging from her head. Shock and awe seep from every pore as she chokes on her beer, slamming it to the bar. She sputters and slaps her chest, making a scene.

"Rhys Slate?" she demands.

"Do you know him?" I ask, shocked and worried by her reaction.

"Of course I do. He is like, an international billionaire playboy. He is covered in all the gossip columns. You really need to get out more, Sophie. I cannot believe you don't know who he is!"

"Well, I know now."

"Wow! Rhys Slate. When you move on you do it well, I will say that for you, Sophie. We will have to run a story about him now, maybe a little blurb about your time in Miami." She muses to herself tapping notes on her phone. "Oh golly, look at the time. I am about to turn back into a pumpkin, sweetie. It's a school night." She sings, picking up her purse and flushing out her keys. "I am so glad you had a nice time. Glad you got a good roll." She winks and the fine lines around her eyes crinkle, her blue eyes shining in the dull light of the bar. "I will see you tomorrow, we'll have lunch and you can finish telling me all about your new, rich boyfriend!"

"Mary! He is not my boyfriend. I'll probably never see him again." The thought hurts and I reflexively rub my chest, wishing it didn't twist into a knot at the thought of never seeing Rhys again.

"All the more reason to spill the beans. Love you." She taps the bar with her keys nodding at her brother as she rushes out the door.

"I will see you in the morning." I sit back on my stool, swirl the melting ice and think about not seeing Rhys again. I left Miami knowing that we had no reason to see each other. But that was before, before he insisted on staying in touch. Reaching out into my daily life by way of a quick, disarming text, but is that really enough to think that our ending hasn't come and gone? We were over the moment he put me in the car, we were over when we fucked in his chair. I could feel it then, I must remember it now. Suddenly I want nothing more than to be home, wrapped in his tee shirt. I leave a twenty on the bar, say goodbye to Paul and slink home, left raw by Mary's truth, and my inevitable denial.

Once I get home, I check my phone again, but nothing. No messages. He did say he had to catch a plane. I pull the shirt that I snagged from Rhys' drawer out of my dresser and pull it on. The feeling is immediate, warm and safe. The shirt smells like his room, like him, a heady cocktail of cologne, sea air, and his sweat. I scroll through my new phone to find a music app. A playlist springs to life, Breaking All the Rules. He makes his presence known at the most perfect time. Just when I want to feel him, he is there. I smile to myself and hug the phone before starting the music.

La Vie en Rose plays softly in the background, while I slide all the windows open to coax a cross breeze and lie down. The air is stagnant and hot. So dry that it rattles in my lungs, like sand. The darkness and heat conspire to put me right to sleep. A restless, dream filled sleep. I toss and turn, seeking relief from the heat. The heat from the early summer sun, and the heat between my legs. I ache for Rhys, wishing he were lying next to me, running his fingers over my hot, sticky skin. The thought helps me to drift, deeper.

I feel him slide in behind me, his arm curling around me, pulling me close, his chest softer than I remember. I surrender to the dream, curling into him, humming my delight. His hands move over my hips, pulling me closer. His fingers are a little too strong, digging deeply into my flesh. I writhe in my sleep, rolling against him. He whispers, hot against my ear, "*You missed me.*" Pressing his hips into me, grinding against me, he is rough. I smell juniper, and the sweet, metallic twang of gin. My eyes fly open and I try to roll away, but he crushes me to his chest. He is drunk, and his hands are all over me.

Chapter 24

"Get off of me!" I struggle against his vice grip, trying to get away, but he just pulls me in tighter. I kick and flail until I can land a blow hard enough to make him release me. I kick him, hard, in the shin over and over with my heel until his hands soften just enough. Biting into his arm, he shrieks and shoves me off the bed. I fall to the ground in a heap, tangled in sheets and pillows. He crawls to the end of the bed as I struggle to my feet. Grabbing a fistful of my hair and pulls me to him, trapping me between the bed and his body, hovering above me, wavering slightly.

"Who did you think I was, you slut?" He pulls my hair tighter, forcing me to be nose to nose, the stench of Tanqueray and Swisher Sweets assaulting my senses. He crushes his dry lips to mine, scratching and burning my mouth. He is sloppy and angry. He bites my lip, drawing blood, and then licks it away. He pulls my head back, anger raging in his droopy, drunken eyes.

"You had some fucking stranger come here and throw me out of my own house? You bitch!" He throws me to the ground, and falls back on the bed. I hit the floor hard, and struggle to get up and get away from him as quickly as possible. What the hell is he talking about? He sits on the edge of the bed, his head in his hands, mumbling to himself about keys and red-headed bastards. I back away, trying not to draw his attention. He shakes his head violently and focuses all of his rage on me. It flares in his eyes like a wildfire, out of control, unpredictable. He stands and stalks towards me, emitting toxic fumes and anger with every drunken step. I leap to my feet and turn to run, but he winds his stubby fingers tightly around my arm and yanks me back. It feels like he is trying to rip it off, he pulls with so much force.

"Are you fucking someone new? Is that who you had toss me out? I knew you were a whore. That's why I moved out in the first place." He slurs and spits into my face as he talks.

"You didn't move out! I kicked you out, you cheating son of a bitch! Twice, and I will gladly kick you out again. Now let go of me!" I try to pull my arm, but he squeezes it so hard and twists until I am backed up against him. My wrist is going to break if he doesn't let go. He tries to kiss my neck and my stomach lurches into my throat, it makes me sick. I swing around and slap him with my other hand. My palm burns and a loud crack echoes through the hall, he releases me to quell the sting. I break towards the door. I need to get outside. I have to get outside. Panic wells up inside of me, threatening to choke me, slowly robbing me of precious breath. My legs have turned to rubber, I feel like I am moving in slow motion. Every step takes an eternity, my feet heavy like stone. I reach the door and throw it open, running at a dead sprint into the courtyard. I turn back to see if he has followed me out. He is ten steps behind me when I run headlong into something hard as a rock, and fall back on my ass. I look up into the cool, impassive face of Charlie. Holy Hell, Thank God! He offers me a hand, pulling me to my feet just as Collin catches up to me. Charlie swings me behind his back, taking a defensive stance against Collin.

"Are we going to do this again?" Charlie taunts Collin. Again? They know each other. Flash of Charlie in Rhys' office that first day. The keys, the red-headed bastard.

"*Sophie?*" I hear him call my name before I see him get out of the car. Shining like a dark knight in a navy suit, he rushes to me as he sees Collin swing at Charlie.

"Is this the guy?" Collin pushes against Charlie, trying to stare down Rhys. "A fucking Town Car? What does a slut have to do to land a wallet like you?" Collin spits bile-filled insults, but I squeeze a Rhys' hand, silently begging him not to engage. "He looks like a pussy licker. How did you like the taste of my cock?" Rhys' eyes go black, cold and dead. He looks through Collin, rage marring his carefully crafted façade. "You know what man, she is all yours." Collin throws his hands

316

up, swaying back a step.

Anger seeps from every pore and Rhys snaps, he drops my hand, shoves Charlie out of the way and drives his fist straight into Collin's face, crushing across his left cheek. He falls back for a split second before landing another blow square in his gut. Charlie falls back and watches, shielding me from the melee. Why doesn't he stop this? Collin doubles over and Rhys drives his fists into him repeatedly, rapid fire, rage rolling off of him in violent waves, his fist pounding broken flesh, over and over. The dull sound of cracking ribs and angry growls fill the air. A slight whimper escapes from the bundle of clothing and flailing limbs that is Collin before Rhys winds up for one last blow. His eyes are vacant, his fist is bloody, and he is singular in purpose, unreachable. Fury mingles with the blood that oozes from his broken knuckles and he sinks Collin to the ground with a crushing blow to the side of his head.

He turns and grabs my hand dragging me towards the waiting car, Charlie following two steps behind us. I try to pull away, but he tightens his grip, his fingers digging into my flesh, pulling at my heart.

"Rhys, please. You are hurting me." I try to stop, to drag him back, but he lifts me from my feet so easily, and hands me over to Charlie, a perfunctory exchange between two bullies.

"Get her into the car," he commands, flexing his bloody hand, examining the damage. He is icy cold and deliberate as he slips from his jacket, rolls up his sleeves and removes his watch, slipping it into the pocket of his designer slacks.

"Rhys, please don't!"

Charlie casually strolls to the car with me trapped against his chest, his arms wrapped around my waist, my feet dangling like a child. "Charlie, put me down!" I command, pushing against his stone chest. His family mask is firmly in place, and I am no match for his brute strength. But I cannot let Rhys hurt Collin. I cannot let him risk anything for me. I kick and flail, trying to free myself from the vice grip of Charlie's arms, landing a kick square to his shin. He flinches before swinging my legs up over his arms, cradling me like a helpless baby.

"None of that," he admonishes in the Slate family tongue. He opens the car door and gently tosses me onto the seat, before shutting me in. I hear the clicking of the door locks and the privacy shield goes up, robbing me of my only view of the scene outside. Blood pulses in my head, shock creeping over me. I am worried about Rhys. I am worried for Collin. Rhys is a fighter. That much is clear. What is he doing here? How did all of this happen? My head swims through the sludge of recent events and I am overcome. Alone in the dark, trapped in the

318

back of Rhys' rented Town Car, I cry. Warm tears softly spill over the edge, leaving tracks down my cheek, while I silently weep. It is purifying and soothing, so I surrender to the deluge. I don't wipe away the tears or try and hide. I let them fall, gathering at my chin slowly raining salt and sadness upon my bruised and battered knees. I look down to see blood mingling with tears. I wipe the tears to reveal a large gash across my knee, from where Collin threw me to the ground, asshole.

Rhys slides into the back seat and I have no idea how much time has passed. My eyes are dry, but my cheeks are wet. Rivers of tears have stained them with a pale flush, my eyes are glossed over and heavy. And he looks amazing, here, in front of me now. Angry devils dance behind his eyes, they are dark and filled with anger. His body is rigid, having regained his focus and control. Blood covered knuckles flex in his lap, and he closes his eyes. I watch him for a long minute, the hard planes of his face, and the soft curve of his lips. Lips that are set in such a hard line, his jaw is tense and pulsing. I can't find my tongue, so I just watch and wait. I don't know how Collin got in my apartment. I don't know how I got out. I have no idea how Rhys got here, but I am so grateful that he is here. Everything is a tangled mess. The silence is deafening, sending a shiver rattling down my spine. I can't stave off the tremor that follows and the movement catches his attention and he turns his dark eyes on me. I sink back into the seat, putting more distance between us, unsure of his current state.

He slowly slides off the seat and onto his knees. Kneeling before me, his face is hidden by the darkness, but the glint across his eyes tells me I am safe.

"Are you hurt?" His voice is raw. I just nod in response, afraid of my own voice. His hands flow over my face, down my neck, across my collar and down both arms. He checks with his fingers for signs of hurt or struggle. I am thankful that there are no marks to be seen other than my knee. I fear his reaction. The fury that he fights is stifling. It is all around us, stealing the air. His hands travel down over my hips and stop, resting heavily on my thighs.

"That fucker!" he growls, moving between my legs. Brushing his thumb gently over the slowly bleeding gash, he murmurs incoherent thoughts to himself, laced with profanities and vitriol. His eyes are filled with such intensity, such concern, you could light a thousand torches with the slowly dying fire dancing in his shadows. He is struggling, livid and wired, and my blood fuels him. He leans close, gently blowing on my knee, small drops of blood still rising to the surface. He places his full lips to my broken flesh and flicks the blood away with his tongue. I watch in shock as his mouth closes over my knee and he kisses my flesh, lapping away all traces of blood. All traces of struggle. When he looks up at me, his eyes are full of something else entirely. Lust, anger, reverence and concern all merge into a steamy gaze that cuts me to the quick. Lurching from his knees, he takes my face in his hands, cupping me gently. He kisses me, parting my lips anxiously with his tongue, the metallic ring of my blood echoes from his tongue, filling my mouth, assaulting my senses. And then I melt into him. We are merged in every way, his mouth with mine, his hands on my flesh, my hands in his hair. We are becoming tangled, just as we once were, as we should be. As I want to be. As we need to be.

"What are you doing here?" The slightest crack in my voice betrays me.

"Are you not happy to see me?" he asks. All I can muster is half a smile. "You took something that belongs to me. I came to reclaim it. But I find, even in your state, it looks better on you." I blush from embarrassment at being caught. "So, you are a kleptomaniac? I would have never guessed."

"No!" I splutter, "I just wanted something to remember you."

"Was I at risk of being forgotten?" Rhys is many things, most of which, I can admit are still a mystery to me, but forgettable? No, there is nothing forgettable about Rhys.

"No, I just didn't count on you not forgetting

me the instant I left you."

"Humph. Well, I didn't count on any of this, on you." He shakes his head, trapped in a thought he refuses to share. "I just wanted to see you again."

"I am so sorry." I am overcome with regret. Unearned this time, but still sorry none the less.

"About what?" he pleads.

"Everything." The flood gates burst and I begin to ramble. "I'm sorry for taking your shirt. I am sorry that Collin was here. I am sorry about your hand."

Rhys stops me with a finger to my lips. "Stop. Surely you have nothing to be sorry for. I am flattered and rather humbled that you would take my shirt. It's cute. I like the thought of you in my shirt. I like the look of it. I am glad that I got to break my hand on that asshole's face." Pausing, he ponders the thought and flexes his hand. "You will never know how good that felt. What was he doing here anyway?" Oh, I could imagine, and have on several occasions. The thought of the sweet crack of my palm across his face calls a devious little grin to my lips. My palm itches for that slap.

"I don't know, I swear." I struggle to come up with an explanation. And it dawns on me, the windows, he must have climbed in. They were wide open. How could I not have heard him? The thought scares me and I turn back to Rhys' waiting face, panic creeping up my throat. "I think he climbed in the window," I whisper, barely able to say it aloud.

"Well, you can't stay here tonight. You really shouldn't stay here at all," he declares before backing down as my eyes rage. "We can talk about that later," he relents, taking the seat next to me, pulling me into his side. "Tonight you will stay with me." I look up into his warm green eyes and have no dispute. I want to stay with him, to wipe the night away. I know he can do that for me, make me forget.

"I just need a few things."

"Charlie will go back in for you." He is no mood to negotiate. "What do you need?"

"Um, a pair of jeans, panties and a bra, socks and sneakers, my purse and phone."

"Charlie, did you hear that?" I realize that Charlie had been sitting in the driver's seat this whole time. Oh, my god, he will be going through my drawers? I look back at Rhys, stunned and panicked at the idea of Charlie going through my delicates.

"Don't worry, he won't go through your things." As if he could read my mind, he rapidly put it as ease, pulling me into his lap as Charlie exits the car.

"So, how did you get here?"

"I am on my way to the west coast. I wanted to see you, so I arranged for a layover." The glimmer in his eyes and the lip trapped between his teeth tell his joke. "I have an early flight to San Francisco. Come with me."

"I can't. I have work." He pulls me closer and holds me tightly. Charlie returns with a packed duffle, sliding into the driver's seat. We ride in uneasy silence. Once we get to his hotel, he insists that I have a shower while he makes a few calls. I don't argue, knowing that I need a moment to myself, to collect my thoughts and wrap my head around all that has happened. I need the scalding hot water to wash away Collin's angry hand prints. Like invisible chains wrapped around my body, I have to wash them away, be clean of him.

Chapter 25

I am slow and methodical in the shower, careful to scrub every inch of my battered body. Soap runs over the deep gash on my knee and stings, but I welcome the pain. I wash my hair and face and just stand under the water, frozen, unsure of what will come next. The water cleanses me, pounding my flesh with a welcome, hypnotic rhythm that soothes my mind. I am able to shut it all out and surrender to the scalding deluge. Sinking to the bottom of the large walk-in shower, I sit under the falling water until it runs cool. Despair, shame, relief and self-pity mingle and dance with the water, swirling around the drain. My mind runs wild at everything that has happened in the last hour, Collin's arrival, my body and mind fooling me so thoroughly, even if just for a moment. And Rhys, he showed up and saved me.

Skipping the fluffy hotel robe for a large white towel, I dry my hair and then my body, wrapping it gingerly around me and step out of the bathroom. I want Rhys to make me forget. I am sure that is why he has brought me here, why he showed up in the first place. His hands can surely wash away everything that the soap missed. He hangs up the phone as I step out of the bathroom, watching me, his eyes wide and filled with worry. Grinning, I drop the towel and stand before him the way he likes, but immediately regret it. His horrified expression makes me wish I could disappear.

"Sophie, no!" He picks up the towel and rapidly wraps it back around me. The sting of his rejection is more vicious than any slap. I shrink out of his arms and back away, humiliated and pushed beyond my limits. I fight back tears and try to hide the hurt. How could I have misread this situation? How could I have been so wrong? He steps closer to me, slowly with his hands in the air, as if to pose no threat. I just stand, frozen to the spot, watching him, but unsure. Resting his hands on my shoulders, a small smile curves his lips and he kisses my temple. I look into his bright green eyes and lose my filter.

"I thought this is what you wanted." The strangled whisper barely escapes my throat.

"Oh Sophie, it is. It was. But now, I think we shouldn't." Great, even after he has his ass beaten, Collin still gets to interfere. He doesn't want me now because of what has happened, because of what I got him involved in. I am tired of being jerked around, tired of these men telling me what I need, what is good for me. Anger trickles slowly through my veins, mingling with my heated blood and I glare at him. "Sophie," his voice is quiet, pensive. "Believe me, I want to, but, after what has happened, I think you just need someone to hold you. I just want to hold you." I thaw a little, letting his words wash over me. Maybe it would feel good, just to feel safe. No pressure. I manage a small smile and he walks me to the bed. "Let's just be tonight, OK? You can lie in my arms. Just let me hold you."

Pulling back the comforter, he pats the mattress for me to sit. I slide under the covers, tossing the towel to the floor. I revel in the softness of the sheets on his heavenly bed, and watch him disrobe. He is slow to move, careful not to startle this frightened doe. One by one he unbuttons his dress shirt, then moves to his cuff links. He lays the shirt across the chair next to the bed and undoes his belt. Sitting with his back to me he pulls off his shoes and socks before he stands, pulling off his trousers. They lie on top of his shirt, so methodical and organized. He stands before me in nothing but his boxer briefs, shining like a white knight, the planes of his chest so familiar, the ripple of his abs calling to me. I want to touch him. I want him to touch me. But I lay still, and watch him slide under the covers. He pulls a pillow into his arms and we lie on our fronts just looking at one another for the longest time. A tense but comfortable silence that he breaks.

"I want to ask you something and I want you to be honest." Unsure, but wanting the silence to end, I agree. "Has he ever done this before? Put his hands on you?" I don't know what I was expecting, but it wasn't that. He struggles to keep his expression light, but his eyes are dark. A giant lump rises in my

327

throat and I look away, at the pillow, at my hands, over his shoulder, anywhere other than into his eyes. I do not want to admit it has happened before. That's when he used to get drunk, which became more and more often, he became increasingly more volatile. I don't want Rhys to know what he used to do to me, the things he used to make me do. I don't want anyone to know.

"I think I have my answer," he says quietly, reaching out and covering my hand with his. He squeezes my hand and that small, simple touch pushes me over the edge and slow, soft tears fill in my eyes. "Why Sophie? Why didn't you say something?"

My voice cracks, "He only did it a couple of times."

"Once is too many," he insists, not letting go of my hand. "God," he turns his eyes down. "When I think of how rough I have been with you. The ropes! You said you were scared, but I didn't listen. Why did you let me do that?" His thought hangs there between us while his pulse picks up and a fire rages in his eyes when they meet mine. "I wish that you could have told me."

"Rhys, you never hurt me. I like how you are, how we were." I squeeze his hand in return, pleading with him not to go there. Wishing I could wipe it all away. I don't want him to be angry or feel pain because of me, because of my mistakes, my weakness. "You don't understand."

"Help me understand."

"When my parents died, he was right there, ready to pick up the pieces. He was all I had. He was there for me when no one else was. I just got caught up, and things got out of hand. I didn't want to be alone."

"Oh Sophie," he sighs, like a heavy weight is being slowly lifted from his chest. "You deserve so much better. I am sorry."

"It's not your fault. It's mine. I never said anything to anyone, not even Olivia. I didn't want people to know. I don't like what it says about me." He pulls me into his arms, wrapping his protective wall around me. I tuck my head beneath his chin and listen to his heartbeat, a distraction from the strangling pain in my chest, the pain of the truth being spoken for the first time. I feel safe here.

"It doesn't say anything about you. It says everything about him. I want to kill him," he whispers into my hair.

"He isn't worth your time. Please, let's not allow him another moment of our thoughts." Exhaling a deep breath, he smoothes my hair and we lay wrapped around each other. "I just want to be here, with you. This feels good." His anger and frustration barely held at bay, his arms tighten around me, squeezing me possessively. I press my cheek to his chest, surrounding myself with his heady scent, listening to his slowing heartbeat, until I fall into an exhausted sleep.

I wake to find Rhys half a mile away, on the other side of the bed. Lying peacefully on his back, nestled in amongst the sheets, his arm slung over his head, softly breathing, he is so peaceful, otherworldly. Moments from last night creep into my conscious mind. The smell of Collin, gin-laced sweat and cheap cigars, the feel of his rough hands on me and his hot breath slithering across my skin make me shudder.

Stealthily, Rhys wraps his arm around me and pulls me to him. I twist and curl to fit his mold. He is cradled to me, pressed between my thighs. His warm lips on my neck send shock waves rolling across my skin. I close my eyes and listen. The sound of his lips on my skin, his breath against my ear and the pounding in my chest conspire to overtake me. A slow searing heat inches its way across my body, gaining momentum as he moves his lips across my shoulder. I roll my head, begging him to kiss my neck again. He runs the tip of his tongue up behind my ear and begins a slow torture with peppered kisses across my aching skin as his hips circle slowly. A slight flex of his arm and he pulls me deeper into his curve. Throbbing against my back, his touch is gentle and achingly slow.

"Is this ok?" he whispers. "I never want to hurt you, Sophie."

"I know you won't." The words barely pass my lips before his hips move.

"Close your eyes, feel me," he gasps into my ear and slowly slides into me. I hold my breath as he pushes himself to the root, filling me exquisitely. I stretch and twist around him, settling perfectly in his lap. His fingers lace with mine and he wraps our arms around me. With my hand in his he runs his fingers across my breasts. He grabs me and twists my nipple ferociously, pinching it tightly until all the blood is gone before ripping his fingers away. As the blood rushes back, the sensation rings in my head, but the silence is erotic and heavy, I bite back a cry as he does it again. His hips circle and twist behind me and his breathing picks up. Tightening his arms around me, I am immobilized by the cage his arms have made. Securely trapped against him, he bucks and rolls, sending a pulsing fire to every corner of my body. Swimming in the silence, hearing nothing but his increasing breath and strong heart beat is like being underwater. I am weightless, focused so minutely on what he does to me.

He growls in my ear and breaks the spell. Suddenly the room is full of sounds. Skin slapping skin, Rhys' labored growl as he tries to hold back, and my body screaming for a long overdue crescendo. He wraps his arm beneath my legs and cradles me as he slides deeper. Changing speeds, he sets a brutally slow pace of deep thrusts and slow retreat. A raging inferno threatens to consume me, he burns me from within. I will be a pillar of smoke and ash in his arms as my ears burn and my limbs turn to putty.

"Are you ready?" He thrusts so deeply I feel him in my chest. A slow, but powerful orgasm climbs my body, leaving tremors in its wake as Rhys slams into me. His body echoes in mine, bouncing from every surface, filling every last inch. His arms tighten against my legs and as he wrenches me down, sliding me to the hilt of his massive cock, he explodes. I am merely an extension of his body as moves me with ease. Violently thrusting into me over and over, he fills me up until he has emptied himself of all strength. Letting out a deep, cathartic breath, he loosens his grip on my legs, but doesn't release me. Pulling me closer to him, he nuzzles into my hair. His breathing evens and his heart slows while he remains within my walls. He throbs throughout my lower body and I relish the feeling of still being connected, still as one. Rolling onto his back, he takes me with him. Astride him with my back to him, he bucks his hips and I feel him harden like steel beneath me.

"Turn around," he demands in a husky voice. His cock is so big I can easily lift my leg over him and spin around to face him without letting him go. I smile to myself as I spin on his cock, like it's a carnival ride. A dirty fun ride. And I want to ride again.

"Take control, Sophie," he commands, spurring me on. I rest my hands on his chest and rock slowly, back and forth, grinding my clit against him. Our eyes are locked in a death grip as I ride him. Moving slowly up and down, pulling him deep and rising off of him. He puts his hands on my hips and guides me, pushing me back and forth. He fills me so exquisitely, pressing into me, pulling back. Stroking me just right. He takes my hands into his and I steady myself against his strength. Up and down I move, reveling in every moment, but not convinced for one second that I am in control. Heat rises from my toes and the fire spreads to my limbs, up my neck and across my chest. The detonation starts slow, like a chain reaction, tiny explosions rack my body. Rhys sits up, his eyes meeting mine and suddenly he grazes that deep rough spot, that G-spot that he helped me to find. His hands are splayed across my back, holding me tight as he rams into me, his orgasm building to a frenzy. His eyes are frantic as he pulls me across his lap and we both implode. I throw my head back and scream his name as he sinks his teeth into my collar bone, stifling his own cry. I ride him until we are both spent and breathless and then we sit. Connected so intimately, so thoroughly. I don't know how much time passed as we sat there, wrapped in each other, connected by breath and body. It could have been hours or mere minutes. How ever long, it wasn't long enough. When we finally pull apart his face is soft with concern.

"Are you ok? I didn't hurt you?"

"Rhys, you could never hurt me. That was...." I have to search for the words, there are no words. "Amazing. You are amazing. Thank you." He pulls me close and squeezes me before releasing a deep breath he had been holding, his shoulders finally relaxing.

***

"When can I see you?" I watch him pull his tie through his collar. His eyes rise to mine in the mirror, waiting for an answer.

"I guess when you have another 'layover'." I hop from the bed and make quick work of his collar before taking the tie from his fingers. I am not prepared for this conversation, wherever it may be going. After being tossed around last night and being overwhelmed this morning, my mind and heart need a break. I just want to bask in the temporary bliss. Absorb all of his attention. I don't want to rip the focus from that. He gazes down on me with those warm, sincere eyes.

"Seriously, Sophie, I want to see you again."

"I don't see how that is possible without me *getting the wrong idea*." He reaches up and grabs my wrists.

"You are feisty this morning. But I am in no mood to play, so let's cut the shit." His eyes burn through me and I feel like an errant child. "We are way past the point of no return here, Sophie. The wrong idea has come and gone. This is new territory. I flew across the country for you. I have been with girls that I wouldn't travel uptown for."

"You really know how to sweet talk a girl, Mr. Slate." I finish tying his tie, straighten it and stand back for him to see his reflection. But it is me who is suddenly struck by what I see reflected back. Rhys stands elegantly wrapped in his three piece suit, looking every bit the dashing, debonair playboy that he is. And next to him stands me cloaked in an old T-shirt, looking sorely out of place. I find it all a little hard to reconcile, even as he stands before me and declares that he must see me again. I feel like I am missing the punch line. Like it is all going over my head while I stand blissfully unaware of some inevitable truth that will reveal itself only to rip my heart from my chest and stomp it into the pavement. Thankfully, Rhys pulls me from my ever sinking pit of imagined despair with his strong hands. Pulling me to his lap, he wraps his arms around me and tips my chin so that I can look nowhere but into his deep green eyes.

"You have done something to me. I was not prepared for you. I thought I could walk away, but I

335

cannot. And last night just showed me that you need someone. You need me." I shake my head and try to tame my tongue before I lash out, tired of being told of what I need. "Stop." With a finger to my lips, he halts my train of thought. "I have never wanted to be needed. I don't like it anymore than you do, but there you go." His fingers trace the curve of my back and come to rest on my hip. His fingers flex into my flesh, urgency flowing from his fingertips.

"I don't know what you expect from me, Rhys. I care about you, more than I ever expected. But we live two different lives. I live here, you live there. What are we supposed to do?"

"We are supposed to try and make this work, Sophie. Do you want to see me again?"

"Yes," I reply without a second thought.

"Well then, we will make this work. I just cannot imagine not seeing you. In such a short time you have become something of a necessity to me. I just want to be near you, to talk to you, to hold you. We will make this work. I promise." And I believe him.

"I don't want you going back to your apartment. Do you have somewhere else you can stay?"

"I will figure it out. Don't worry about it, Rhys."

"I will worry about it, Sophie. Your ex broke into your home last night and tried to assault you.

You cannot go back there. Promise me." He is adamant, holding my hands tightly in his as we weave through early morning traffic.

"I promise." His eyes light up and he crushes his lips to mine, igniting another fire that I know will smolder all day. We say a painful goodbye in the back of his Town Car before he has Charlie drop me off at work, and they head to the airport.

***

"Sophie, I found a picture of your Mr. Slate." Rounding the faux corner, Mary purrs his name as if to mock me, still unaware that I spent the night in his arms and the morning under his spell. I will fill her in at lunch. "I want you to use this picture in a little blurb about Miami. Society, charity, rich playboys…. You get my drift." Teasing me she drops a photo onto what passes for my desk.

It's more my corner of a long table that I share with a copy editor and the only other staff writer. The operation is small, and doesn't try to fool anyone. The paper inhabits the third floor of the old Elks Lodge, basically a large banquet room with four long tables surrounded by a weaving temporary wall. An ancient industrial size copier sits by the window along with our other rudimentary office supplies. Mary's desk sits at the head of the room, surrounded by a virtual forest of indoor plants and

337

flanked by two temporary walls that are littered with her kid's coloring pages and random story ideas jotted hastily on colored sticky notes. My desk is less conspicuous. No plants, I tend to kill anything green, and no personal photos, just random stacks of paper that mean nothing to anyone but me. Every once in a while, Mary will bring a framed pic and sneak it onto my desk, but I just slip them into a chest of rolling drawers I have stashed under my desk.

"There." I look down on a picture of a red carpet. It looks like any other paparazzi photo that I have seen. A picture of Rhys on the red carpet should not be any different from any other. It shouldn't be a shock to see him there, he was in the public eye, a public figure. What did I care about yet another red carpet photo? Until the whole of the picture jumped off the page and punched me in the gut.

A perfectly posed red carpet picture of Rhys and Nadja, he is dressed in a simple Armani tux, minus the bow tie. It could be a fashion spread in Vogue. He shines like perfection under the scrutinizing lights of the photographers. A double gardenia blossom, pinned to his lapel. A double gardenia. His collar is open, casual. And next to him stands Nadja. In all her exotic, statuesque glory, she shines in a nude, strapless, body-hugging gown, with a sparkling, delicate diamond belt accentuating her tiny waist. The dress looks as if it were poured over her slight frame, fine ruffles of feather light chiffon float down from her hips. His arm is wound around her narrow waist, his hand resting possessively on her hip. A lump rises in my throat, but I push it back, wishing, hoping the photo is from before we met. Wishing away what I can clearly see and am unable to deny. The date on the picture is May 12. Thursday, the day after I left Miami, I feel sick, but ever the masochist, and morbidly curious, I look down to the write-up that accompanies the picture.

I am sick. Suddenly everything aches and I am totally alert. Every sense assaulted by the photo and its contents. My stomach lurches into my throat. What was I thinking? I have been walking around in a state of dream, locked away in my own lie. I feel so stupid! I let myself get swept away by him. By his hands, his mouth, his words. I was a pawn. And there he stands, with his arm around her. White noise fills my ears and I swear I can hear my heart, slowly fracturing into a million tiny shards. Barely holding it together, I wrap my arms around myself, knowing that the slightest breeze could blow me to pieces, a pile of glittering dust on the cheap carpeted floor. I am broken and I must hide it. How did I get back here so quickly?

The night was surely considered a rousing

success in the wake of raising well over 4 million dollars for charity. Helping Children is an organization that fights childhood disease and hunger. Operating in 32 countries they work to provide clean water, food and healthcare to vulnerable populations. The guest list was a veritable Who's Who of the entertainment and sports industries. Guests dined on Haute Mediterranean Cuisine, prepared by Celebrity Chef Tony Santorino. A silent auction followed. The lots up for auction were diverse, ranging from a set of box seats to a Miami Heat game, to a Private Island Getaway. Surely the success of the evening is due in no small part to the Charming Mr. Rhys Slate and his very lucky companion, model Nadja Vladova. These two society fixtures Co-Chair the foundation they founded together in 2001. They are both very active in several other charities and foundations, but this annual gala has garnered accolades for both that are not soon subsiding. Partners in charity, one has to wonder if they have reunited in love as well. It seems this on again, off again couple is very much on. There has been no confirmation from either's publicist, but pictures abound of the couple sharing a private laugh, dancing and enjoying the evening's festivities together. Could there be possible wedding bells in the future for this powerhouse couple? Surely a wedding between Mr. Slate and Ms. Vladova would be the social event of the year.

Rhys and Sophie's story continues in
Speak
Book 2
The Voice Trilogy.